A COUNTRY KISS

Ramsdell moved toward her in three purposeful strides. He caught her at the back of her waist with his right arm and drew her roughly against him. "I can't do this properly, my fair Constance, not with one arm in a sling, but I vow I have been longing to kiss you from the moment I awoke to find you asleep in my bedchamber. I know I shouldn't, but I'm going to anyway."

She could have protested. She certainly could have easily fended him off; instead her right arm snaked tightly about his neck and she leaned against his right side, careful not to put pressure on his injured arm. "Oh, Ramsdell," she breathed against his lips.

Then he kissed her, a warm, searing kiss that sent ripples of pleasure cascading in wave after wave down her neck and side clear to her toes. She fit perfectly against him, just as she knew she would and she wanted the kiss, the embrace, to go on forever.

A breeze dipped down into the center of the maze, catching at the hem of her amethyst silk gown and tugging at her ankles. The sun was warm on her shoulders and back. Ramsdell's arm and hand were restless over her waist. He held her in a tight grip as though he feared she would run away if he released her. He drew back and kissed her eyes, her cheeks, her face. "I shouldn't be doing this."

Her voice caught on a light gasp. "No, you should not. But I am not a schoolroom chit, Ramsdell. I understand that you are giving no promises. So, kiss me again, if you please. . . ."

Books by Valerie King

A DARING WAGER
A ROGUE'S MASQUERADE
RELUCTANT BRIDE
THE FANCIFUL HEIRESS
THE WILLFUL WIDOW
LOVE MATCH
CUPID'S TOUCH
A LADY'S GAMBIT
CAPTIVATED HEARTS
MY LADY VIXEN
THE ELUSIVE BRIDE
MERRY, MERRY MISCHIEF
VANQUISHED
BEWITCHING HEARTS
A SUMMER COURTSHIP
VIGNETTE
A POET'S KISS
A POET'S TOUCH
A COUNTRY FLIRTATION

Published by Zebra Books

A COUNTRY FLIRTATION

VALERIE KING

Zebra Books
Kensington Publishing Corp.
http://www.zebrabooks.com

ZEBRA BOOKS are published by

Kensington Publishing Corp.
850 Third Avenue
New York, NY 10022

First Printing: November, 1998
10 9 8 7 6 5 4 3 2 1

Printed in the United States of America

"For when I see you even for a moment, then power to speak another word fails me; instead my tongue freezes into silence, and at once a gentle fire has caught throughout my flesh."

—Sappho c. 612 B.C.

ONE

The sound of splintering wood and screaming horses penetrated the serenity of Constance Pamberley's sleep one early July morning. She opened her eyes, uncertain, precisely, of what had awakened her. She listened, but heard nothing untoward.

Perhaps she had imagined the sounds. She hoped so, for if she was not greatly mistaken, the same sounds had attended the numerous coaching accidents that had beset Lady Brook Cottage for the past several years.

She lay in the bed of her childhood, content, at ease with the world, and, as always, letting the excitement of the day begin to build within her before settling her bare feet on the cold wood of her bedchamber floor. She extended her arms over her head and indulged in a catlike stretch.

Somehow, amid the difficulties of her existence—which were numerous—she had learned to take great pleasure in each day, knowing that the sun wouldn't set without presenting at least one surprise to enliven even the dullest of homey chores. For Constance, life was an adventure to be lived out in the unexpected twists and turns of fate, of things spiritual, things temporal, of things known and things unlooked for. Of course, what made every manner of ill endurable was that she was the present owner of Lady Brook Cottage and would be until the day she died. Of additional succor was the fact that no genteel country house within a twenty-mile radius of Lady Brook could boast so fine a cook as the old brick mansion possessed.

She smiled and mused that perhaps without Cook, life wouldn't be such a fine adventure, that perhaps a delectable apricot tartlet or a flaky pigeon pie was the true source of every present happiness.

She chuckled to herself. Such were the ridiculous ramblings by which laughter made her life bountiful.

If she had any wish at all, though, she found she occasionally longed for someone, *for a man,* with whom she could share her ridiculous musings, ruminations, and thoughts. Were she to have some such person with whom she could share her sense of the absurd, she truly believed she would want for nothing.

She was the eldest of five beautiful sisters who were woven into the fabric of a dozen surrounding neighborhoods as intricately as a medieval tapestry. The Pamberley ladies of Lady Brook Cottage were essential to their small part of Berkshire. There was not a lack in the countryside that the ladies failed to put right—posies for the infirmed widows who lived above the candle shop, pots of honey for an old sailor dying of consumption, delicate watercress to tempt the appetite of a waiflike girl in nearby Wraythorne, the only surviving child of the blacksmith, whose family had been decimated by scarlet fever two winters past.

A distressed whinny caught her ear. Her bedchamber overlooked the front drive of the ancient house, and so it was when she heard the horse's cry, she knew she had not imagined the crashing sounds that had awakened her.

She threw back her bedcovers and slipped from her bed in order to determine which carriage and driver had come to mischief on her property. The bend in the road that led to the front drive of Lady Brook was very sharp, and if a traveler did not pay heed to the handmade wood sign which her gardener, Finch, had made only last fall to give warning to potential danger, an accident could easily ensue.

She crossed her bedchamber and pushed back the somewhat threadbare draperies of a faded chintz that had hung in symmetrical diligence over her windows throughout her nine and twenty years. Drawing back the shutters, she saw at once that her darkest suspicions were correct. She shook her head in dismay but not surprise at the sight of the cut and limping horses struggling in harness, the low wooden fence torn from its nailed posts, and the still form of a man lying facedown at the exact point where her beautiful purple petunias met a neatly scythed lawn.

She shook her head. "Not again," she murmured.

Over the past several months five such accidents had disturbed the peace of Lady Brook, bringing an equal number of young gentlemen to the portals of the mansion. More than once she had wondered if the spirit of Lady Brook, resonating in every mellowed, rosy brick of the rambling house, had been for years beckoning, from all parts of the kingdom, beaus for her comely yet somewhat isolated sisters. Another absurdity? Perhaps. Probably. Undoubtedly.

She heard the sounds of her sisters scurrying about in the hallway, calling to one another about the man lying prone among the petunias. She knew that the poor fellow would be quickly attended to by a number of capable feminine hands. Her own duty, therefore, was turned away from the gardens and toward the less noble occupations of sending for the head groom. Stively would know precisely how to tend to the injured horses, while his stable boy—a lad of fifteen by the name of Jack Smith—would be sent to fetch Dr. Deane from the next town of Four-Mile-Cross.

However, she would not, under any circumstances, perform these tasks in her nightgown.

She restored the shutters and quickly stripped off her nightclothes to don a patched linen shift, a serviceable gown of faded peach jonquil—which, during her London Season ten years earlier had been a very fetching walking dress— silk stockings tied up with embroidered garters, and half-boots of polished kid that bore a number of ugly scars but which had also been quite à la mode the year of her come-out ball. She quickly brushed out her long, light brown hair, tied it into a loose knot atop her head, surveyed and approved of her appearance, and went immediately to the kitchens, where she informed the butler of the accident.

"What, again?" he queried, a pinch between his brows. He finished sipping his tea, clattered the cup on its saucer, and scratched at his balding pate. "I told Finch not to put up that fence. Better for the horses to crash through the shrubbery, I said, than a fence. I told him so again and again."

Constance smiled. "Yes, Morris, you gave him sage advice. But he was more interested in protecting my petunias, I'm 'fraid, than in considering the fate of an overeager whipster who ignored his elaborate sign."

Morris, who had been with the family from the time her father, now deceased, was a boy, set aside his copy of *The Times* and prepared to take up his duties. He instructed one of his two underlings to come with him to attend to the stranger and informed the other to prepare a surgery for the doctor in the buttery. "And, Thomas, bring along the slats and canvas. We'll be needing to cart him in here, I 'spect."

Constance, satisfied that suitable arrangements were under way, left the house by way of the kitchen door. She skirted a wide, neat vegetable garden in which Cook was busily admonishing a hardworking kitchen maid to get every weed that might choke the roots of her prize broccoli plants, and hurried to the gate that led to the stables. She caught Stively and stable boy Jack just as they were leaving the carriage house to determine for themselves which horses of their neighbors had found themselves in mischief.

"No, no. Nothing so simple," she cried. "I'm 'fraid there's been another accident."

"What, again?" Stively queried.

Constance nodded. "I think once we get this unfortunate fellow tended to, if he's not broken his neck, we ought to consider hiring Mr. Bellows to widen the curve and straighten out the lane a bit. If the truth be known, we should have done so years ago."

Stively's countenance stiffened. His face grew alarmingly red. "You can do so if you wish, Miss Pamberley, but you'd as lief hire the schoolmaster or . . . or the beekeeper to do the job as well or as timely." Stively had no patience with Mr. Bellows, who, in his opinion, had more hair than wit and was an obnoxious bagpipe. That Mr. Stively and Mr. Bellows were leading scorers on opposing cricket teams may have added to the head groom's poor opinion of his adversary, but Constance was not inclined to make this observation. Mr. Stively would never be moved from his opinion of Mr. Bellows, and that was that.

She let the subject drop and addressed the stable boy.

"Jack," she called to the young man, who had quickly stripped his cap from his head at her presence.

"Yes, miss?"

"Pray saddle Old Nobs and ride to Four-Mile-Cross—no, stay a moment. You had best take Lord-a-Mercy. He is quicker off the mark than Nobs, and the fact is, you'll have to press him the entire way to Four-Mile-Cross. We'll be needing the doctor as quick as the cat can lick her ear."

Jack's face began to glow, and his eyes lit with the wonder of angels. "Lord-a-Mercy! Yes, Miss Pamberley. Oh, indeed, yes!"

She adjured him, "Be careful—no cramming him at fences or the like. Stay to the lanes, and when you've come back, Morris will reimburse you for the tolls. Have you enough for the tolls?"

Jack colored a trifle, then lifted his chin. "That I 'ave, miss."

She had regretted her words the moment they left the tip of her tongue. She knew Jack had ambitions and that he was careful with every tuppence. The truth was, from the time he had arrived to serve on her estate some five years past, he had put her strongly in mind of another stable boy, Jaspar Vernham, who had gone on to make his fortune in India since leaving Lady Brook. Jack showed every likelihood of following in Jaspar's footsteps. However, she could hardly retrieve her thoughtless query, and merely nodded for him to go. She then wheeled around and left Jack to the supreme enjoyment of riding the best of her horses all the way to Four-Mile-Cross. No doubt he would be the envy of his friends for weeks to come.

She followed in Stively's wake, heading down the avenue that led to the front of the mansion. She walked briskly, her long stride eating up the distance rapidly. She was the tallest of her siblings, a fact that had perhaps been the prime reason she had not as yet found a suitable mate. She was a Long Meg, something that had troubled her no small degree when she was still in the schoolroom and about to enjoy her first London Season.

As the years had worn on, however, her height had lost its dread and had become a source of great pleasure for her. For one thing, she was immensely gratified at being able to look Marianne's lovesick and usually frantic beaus directly in the eye when she needed to warn them away from her sister's wretched flirtations. For another, she delighted in plucking apples from the upper branches of the orchard trees which Celeste—a year younger than Marianne—could not reach.

She loved that she sat taller in the saddle than even Katherine, who was the finest horsewoman in three counties, and nothing pleased her so much as being able to reach books on shelves that her youngest and most studious sister, Augusta, found impossible to procure without a footstool or ladder. She had come to be proud of her height. She carried herself with dignity, and secretly adored the fact that some of the villagers had taken to calling her The Gentleman.

She was also proud of having received no fewer than eight

offers of marriage since having left the schoolroom so many years before, and only one from a man shorter than herself.

Eight, and all eligible *partis*.

Eight, and not a one that had remotely touched her heart.

She sighed at the reminiscence, unable to comprehend fully why her heart was so stubborn. As she marched toward the front of the house, she recalled vividly to mind how her fifth suitor, an elegant man who had also crashed his light racing whisky in the front yard of Lady Brook, had suggested to her that her loyalties to her mother, to her sisters, and to her home would never allow her to properly love a man. She wondered now if this much was true.

What was the truth, after all?

Only one of her eight suitors had been unworthy of her hand in marriage. Lord Upton had been at the time, and was even yet by all accounts, a libertine of remarkable proportions. His marriage proposals had only followed her refusal of his offer of a carte blanche! What a dreadful creature *he* had been!

But the others had been, one and all, good men, worthy men, devoted men. Still, she had rejected them because her heart would be fastidious. Or was her heart merely too full of her duties to family and property that she couldn't love?

Regardless, at nine and twenty, though hardly an antidote, Miss Constance Pamberley was, most regrettably, a confirmed ape-leader.

She did not repine at her single state. Not by half. She lived fully and experienced great joy in managing her estate, in caring for her widowed mother, who was also infirmed, and in providing a home for her four younger sisters as well. Indeed, should she never leave Lady Brook Cottage, she would die content. She wanted for nothing except an income to make a hundred much-needed improvements in the house, in the surrounding gardens, in the outbuildings, in the home wood, and in the several fields attached to the estate. Money was all that the Pamberley ladies needed. That, and a serious realignment of the treacherous corner that had caused yet another accident near the petunia border.

When she rounded the row of rangy rhododendrons, lush from their recent spring growth, the scene before her appeared so familiar as to seem unreal. Pieces of the low white fence, constructed to give way in case of just such an accident, lay scattered about the lawn and the flower bed. All of her sisters were in their robes and mobcaps. Augusta, the youngest, peered into a book. She was probably consulting an apothecary's volume for the treatment of unconscious victims. Katherine was examining one of the horses' fetlocks along with Stively. Marianne was kneeling on the grass, supporting the poor young man's head on her lap, and bearing a most beatific expression on her pretty face, while Celeste was adjuring Finch and Morris not to cut the boots off the young gentleman if they could possibly help it.

"Though they are dusty," Celeste was saying as she peered closely at them, "they are clearly of the finest quality."

Augusta joined in the present controversy. "You should check each leg and ankle for swelling." She turned a page. "But do not tug on the boots until you are certain the leg is uninjured."

Morris looked up at her and rolled his eyes. He had had more years' experience than could ever be put into a book. He began a careful exploration of the man's legs as Constance joined the circle surrounding him. She watched his careful hands, then turned slightly at the sound of pounding hoofbeats. Jack, astride Lord-a-Mercy, sailed past the row of statuesque elms, waving his hat to her just before he turned into the lane. The injured horses lifted noble heads and shivered as Jack guided the fine bay north toward Four-Mile-Cross. The hoofbeats died quickly away.

Constance returned her attention to the stranger, only this time her gaze landed squarely on his face and she gasped. "Good heavens!" she cried. "I have never seen a more beautiful countenance! If he were not dressed in a coat and breeches, I would have supposed him not of this earth!" The young man had a delicate appearance, an alabaster skin, fine features, and loose, blond curls brushed *à la cherubim,* a style wholly befitting a man whose face brought images of Michelangelo's works strongly to mind.

Marianne lifted glowing green eyes to meet her gaze. "Is he not magnificent? I do hope he is injured sufficiently to require his staying in our home for at least a fortnight." Her thoughtless words brought every eye upon her. She had the grace to blush. "I—I mean. Oh, dash-it-all, what a stupid thing to say! I do beg pardon, Constance! I wasn't thinking!"

"No, dearest, you weren't," she responded with a chuckle and a smile. She turned to Morris. "What do you think? Has he broken—anything?" She dreaded the thought that he might have tumbled from his curricle and shattered his spine.

Augusta drew close and snapped her book shut. "Yes, Morris, what do you say?" Augusta, though frequently lost in the library for hours on end, and who relied more than she ought on the knowledge from books, enjoyed a tender heart.

Morris leaned back on his heels and frowned. "He has movement in all his limbs—"

"Thank God," Constance breathed in unison with Augusta.

Morris continued. "However, he has quite a lump at the back of his head."

"I see," Constance said, her heart lightening. "Well then, let's move him to the buttery—"

"Not the buttery, Constance!" Marianne exclaimed, petting the young man's head as she might a cat. "Take him to one of the spare chambers that he might enjoy a comfortable bed." She looked down at him with a sigh. "He is clearly a gentleman and would be used to a good bed and properly aired sheets."

Constance frowned at her next-oldest sister, who was gazing on the young man's face with a familiar expression that bespoke a sudden infatuation. For that reason alone she would rather the young man be taken by cart to Four-Mile-Cross and placed in the care of the good doctor and his wife than that he should remain at Lady Brook. Marianne was given to bouts of violent affection. She could not therefore like the sudden appearance of so beautiful and yet clearly so reckless a young gentleman on her lawn, especially when he bore no signs of wealth. By evidence of the cut of his ill-fitting and rather worn clothes, albeit at odds with the quality of his boots, as Celeste had noted, he could not be a man of means. The curricle, too, showed signs of neglect. The horses, which Stively and Katherine were leading away to the stables, were hardly of the finest blood.

Of what use, therefore, would it be to encourage even the smallest *tendre,* when her undowered sisters must wed gentlemen of fortune? No use at all!

Regardless of her practical misgivings of the present situation, especially Marianne's tendency to fall in love at the drop of a hat, she could hardly send the young man away merely because he was so handsome and so poor. The lump at the back of his head might be of imminent danger to his health.

She again considered Marianne's suggestion that he be taken to a bedchamber instead of to the buttery. In this she concurred. Dr. Deane might not be able to attend to him right away because of his present duties, and until the young man regained his senses, she would not know how ill he actually was.

She nodded to Morris, who had risen from his knees and who was now awaiting her orders. "The bedroom in the south wing," she said at last, "next to the nursery."

"The nursery!" Marianne exclaimed, shocked. "But that is all the way on the other side of the——" She broke off, realizing her sister's intent. Anger vied on her pretty face with embarrassment, both of which brought a rosy glow to her cheeks.

"Precisely," Constance stated, meeting Marianne's gaze.

Marianne pursed her lips, but Celeste quickly interjected, "I believe that will make it easier as well for the maids to tend to him. The servants' stairs are quite close to the nursery."

Marianne glared at her eldest sister. "He will need far more attention than what our overworked servants can possibly provide for him."

"Since I have every intention of placing him in the excellent care of Dr. Deane as soon as he may be fetched from Four-Mile-Cross," Constance said repressively, "we needn't concern ourselves with the difficulty of his care." She could see the militant light in Marianne's eye and immediately nodded for Morris and the footman to cart the gentleman to the appropriate chamber.

Marianne's lips were clamped tightly together in strong disapproval as she rose to her feet. She walked beside the litter, holding the young man's hand and bearing her part with all the appearance of martyrdom. Augusta and Celeste followed, leaving Constance alone to stare at the wreckage behind her.

She heard Celeste say to Morris, "If you will have the undermaid launder his shirt immediately, I'm certain I can stitch up this tear with no one the wiser." Celeste was an accomplished needlewoman.

What Morris said to her was lost in the increasing distance as the processional moved toward the house.

Constance surveyed the damage. The curricle, sitting lopsided in the bed of petunias had lost a now-splintered wheel, and Stively had had to cut the traces in order to free the horses. The pole was also shattered. The body of the light vehicle looked alarmingly tweaked. She believed its days as a useful conveyance were at an end.

She began picking up pieces of the fence and wondering what ought to be done next. She stepped through the breach and into the lane beyond, walking along the macadamized road to the dangerous turn that had set her household at sixes and sevens so many times over the years. She shook her head. A dense silver fir forest and a deep ditch had prevented the repairs for the past decade since her father's demise. The cost of effecting the much-needed repair had always been beyond her means.

Now, however, she felt compelled to see the job done regardless of the expense. She would have to borrow a portion of the required amount, of that she was sure. As for the rest, she had been setting aside a quarterly sum in hopes of one day purchasing the abandoned field that marched along the boundaries of Lady Brook. Only the previous day she had been able to add another fifty pounds to her fund. She understood now the field would have to remain fallow for several more years. The money must be spent correcting the lane, or one day an unlucky traveler would not survive an accident.

She glanced up at Finch's beautiful sign, warning all drivers to take the bend slowly. She realized his efforts may have achieved the exact opposite effect than what he had hoped. After all, what aspiring nonesuch, with a pair of lively steppers in his possession, a well-sprung conveyance, and the exuberance of masculine youth, would ever see such a sign as anything but a direct challenge of ability?

She picked up a rock and with several careful, sharp blows separated the sign from its post. Tucking it under her arm, she headed back to the breach in the fence. Finch, who had returned to begin repairing the damage to the front landscape, saw the sign and gasped in horror. Constance lifted a hand and gently silenced him. She explained her reasoning, and though he shook his head in dismay, he couldn't help but agree with her since the last three accidents had occurred within a two-month period from almost the day following the erecting of his well-meant sign.

Constance handed Finch's creation back to him and watched him amble in the general direction of the stables behind which his gardening sheds and succession houses were located. Once again she was left alone at the location of the accident.

A brisk wind suddenly picked up, whipping at her faded peach skirts and blowing wisps of hair about her face. A strange excitement coursed through her, a sure indication that fate was stirring up her life again. After all, who was the extraordinarily beautiful young gentleman who had just been delivered to her front door? Even during her London Season so many years earlier she had not seen so handsome a countenance. What were the odds, then, that circumstance alone had delivered him to Lady Brook? Surely some larger scheme was at work.

But what foolishness was this? What air dreams? What vague musings and stupid ruminations?

Nothing to signify, she thought with an amused sigh, only the secret wishes and longings of a responsible young woman who *always* set aside romantical notions for the duties of the day.

But just once, how very nice it would be if Lady Brook would take her interests to heart, her desire for a friend who could share in her thoughts, her daily employments, and in her sense of humor.

Just once.

"Thank you, Simbers, but I have already been informed of Mr. Kidmarsh's absence." Lord Ramsdell used his most repressive tone. He touched a linen serviette to his lips. He took his morning cup of coffee leisurely in hand and sipped with what he knew was maddening nonchalance. He steadfastly ignored his servant's concerned eye.

Simbers, the butler of many years and his father's butler before him, cleared his throat and danced on his feet. He moved the dishes around, clattering and clinking spoons, forks, and china together, hoping to gain the attention he sought. Clearly, he felt his master was not showing a proper concern for the boy. Ramsdell continued to ignore him.

When the aged retainer, spry and energetic for a man of two and seventy summers, had twitched the tablecloth three times and cleared his throat twice as many, Ramsdell could no longer pretend he did not exist. He settled his cup with an irritated clink on its companion saucer, sat back in his chair, and glared at the old man. He refused to speak. Any of his London servants would have known better than to address him when he evinced such unwelcoming signals, but his country retainers, who had known him as a boy, were rarely intimidated.

Simbers opened his mouth and stirred up his vocal cords. "But, m'lord—and I do beg your pardon for pressing you in this manner—the poor lad has not been seen or heard from since one o'clock yesterday. Langley waited up for him all night, continually climbing and descending the stairs to his master's bedchamber with pails and pails of hot water hoping, believing, that at any moment good Mr. Kidmarsh would return home."

Lord Ramsdell lifted a brow. "And apparently Langley thought he would be in need of a bath?"

Simbers appeared offended, his thin lips gripped together in a straight, disapproving line. "Whenever the boy is chilled, Langley puts him straight into a hot bath!"

"Ah," Ramsdell responded, his lips twitching.

"Just so," Simbers retorted. "I—we—your staff cannot help but feel that some mischief is afoot." Here he shuddered dramatically. "Cook has had certain *visions* this morning that indicate that Mr. Kidmarsh has *suffered an accident.*"

Ramsdell considered this. Cook was prone to *visions* whenever they served her. He chuckled inwardly. His staff was hopeless in their attentions to his cousin and ward who had lived with him from the time he was birthed. His uncle, within a week of Charles Kidmarsh's entrance into the world, had died of a fit of the ague. He had left his son heir to one of the largest properties in England, but unfortunately his death had also left Charles bereft of a balancing force in his life. Mrs. Kidmarsh was overprotective in the extreme.

Charles's mother had come to live with her sister—his own mother—an arrangement that had always been a trifle queer except that the sisters were deeply attached to one another. Mrs. Kidmarsh had despised the notion of roaming the expansive halls of Kingsholt Manor with no one to keep her company.

Both ladies were presently touring Europe, a venture that had been forced on Mrs. Kidmarsh by Lady Ramsdell in hopes that Charles might be given a chance to grow up a little. At seven and twenty he was hopelessly unprepared to take on the ordinary duties of life, having been wrapped in wool linen most of his life. The absence of his parent, therefore, was perhaps the uppermost reason Charles had availed himself of the opportunity to escape Aston Hall yet again. With the protective forces seriously diminished, undoubtedly he believed he would enjoy a longer holiday than usual. Ramsdell's servants might be vigilant in their watch over him, but Mrs. Kidmarsh was nothing short of a lioness.

Poor Charles. He was little more than a schoolboy in mind and heart. Ramsdell knew the boy had growing up to do, especially since much of his own life, from the time Charles had enjoyed his first London Season six years earlier, had been spent extricating the halfling from a dozen scrapes. Four of the unfortunate occurrences had involved elopements with completely unsuitable females—two undermaids, one opera dancer, and the fourth with an impoverished young woman who, as it turned out, was the Duke of Moulford's current mistress. When the elopement was discovered, His Grace had demanded satisfaction from Charles, who was no more suited to confront the offended peer across twenty paces than he was to marry the stupid female in the first place.

So it was not with a complete lack of understanding that Simbers was expressing his concern. Charles Kidmarsh was not yet fit to take up a manly place in the world. Overprotected, he lacked true judgment and fell from one scrape to another. Just how Ramsdell should counter the inept attentions of mother, aunt, and staff, he had never quite known. He was himself concerned that Charles had "disappeared" again, but what his cousin did not need was one more doting relative or servant bent on rescuing him again.

What to do?

He addressed his butler. "The young master," he said with unruffled calm, "has had three such disappearances in the past year. Each time, he has merely escaped my house to be away from what I have always considered to be an inordinate amount of coddling and physicking."

"M'lord!" Simbers cried, aghast. "You forget yourself! Master Charles was always of a sickly disposition and only by the careful ministrations of your aunt, your mother, and— if you don't mind my saying so—*your devoted staff,* is he alive today!"

Ramsdell drew in a deep breath. "To my recollection, the only time I have ever seen Charles Kidmarsh near to sticking his spoon in the wall was the time the surgeon leeched him to the point of death."

Simbers grew very stiff and disapproving. "He was suffering a humor of the blood!"

"Fustian! But I won't argue the matter further. I have long since understood that I am the only person in my house who holds to this opinion. I beg you will believe me, however, that Charles will not come to harm with a few days ruralizing."

"Even if this much is true, that his health is sufficiently vigorous to withstand an inflammation of the lungs or even the ague," the old man said with a shake of his head and deep furrowing of his brow, "I daresay you are forgetting *that other matter.*"

"That other matter?" he queried.

"That *other matter,*" Simbers reiterated solemnly.

"Oh," Ramsdell murmured. His butler was right, of course. Charles would likely come back betrothed from another venture into the world, left unchecked. "The devil take it!" he cried, rising swiftly from his chair and throwing his napkin on the table. "Don't look so deuced triumphant! If I find him, *when* I find him, I might just decide to take him on a three-year voyage—around the world!—and maybe, just maybe, he would come home a man!"

Simbers bore these harsh words bravely. "He wouldn't survive a fortnight at sea, m'lord."

Ramsdell rolled his eyes and headed to his rooms. He shouted for his valet who was, oddly enough, close at hand, as were half the servants of his household, including the long-suffering Langley, who had been Charles's personal servant from the time he was a young lad. His own man, Marchand, informed him that his carriage had already been ordered around, his portmanteaus had been packed these three hours and more, and proper traveling clothes were laid out on his bed, waiting only for the appearance of his lordship.

He went to his bedchamber, vexed almost beyond bearing. He grumbled his way through his valet's ministrations. Trotting down the stairs, he ignored the expressed hopes of his staff that poor Master Charles would be found alive, and finally took up his place in his traveling chariot as one who had been persecuted for years.

He ignored the wafting kerchiefs that waved from the windows and from the front steps of Aston Hall. He ignored them all!

If—*when*—he found Charles, he thought maliciously as the coach bowled down the avenue, he would wring his neck and put an end to the dastardly business once and for all!

TWO

Five days later, Constance wore an elegant dove-gray morning gown of twilled bombazine charmingly detailed with puffed sleeves for the strict purpose of charming Dr. Kent. She was hoping, by gentle persuasions, to convince him at last to move the stranger still inhabiting the nursery bedchamber to Dr. Deane's house at Four-Mile-Cross.

The gown was one of her best. A month ago, Celeste had stolen the dress from her wardrobe and secretly embroidered an adorable chain of minuscule white roses at the high neckline and added a quarter-inch strand of white lace to the top of the band collar. The effect was subtle, pleasing, and feminine. Constance had appreciated the beauty of it but adjured her sister that her time would have been better spent hemming a frayed tablecloth or reweaving one of the sheets. Celeste ignored her, as all her sisters tended to do when she argued for practical concerns over a more pleasing aesthetic approach to their labors. The truth was, Constance took great delight in Celeste's roses and lace and wore the gown quite often.

Dr. Deane, upon examining the young man, had initially insisted on consulting a colleague on the case. It would seem that the blow to the head the poor fellow had suffered during the accident had caused a breach in his memory. When he had regained consciousness, the young man—who the ladies had taken to calling Mr. Albion—could not recall his identity.

Dr. Deane knew very well how to deliver babies, treat rheumatic symptoms, and ease the pain of those afflicted with consumption, but he was in no way prepared to prescribe treatment for a man who was experiencing a lapse of the brain.

Dr. Kent was a famous London physician who frequently consulted with the royal doctors on the progress of King George III's incomprehensible madness. So advanced was the king's disease that he had been forced to forfeit the throne in favor of the Prince of Wales, who now reigned as regent. Dr. Kent's reputation at court was renowned and Constance had found him knowledgeable, sensible, and highly skilled. She respected his abilities greatly and had the utmost confidence in him. Unfortunately, his opinion was at odds with her own regarding Mr. Albion's fate, and the good doctor was proving nearly as stubborn as she.

"How long do you suspect his amnesia will beset him?" Constance asked for probably the twentieth time.

The physician stamped his cane on the wood floor. "I have told you, Miss Pamberley," he responded forcefully, "cases of this nature have been known to resolve in a day, others not for years. There is no way of knowing. How am I to convince you of my beliefs?"

She ignored this. "But you have said there is nothing physically wrong with him, so could he not be moved without harm?"

"Without *physical* harm. But he is so well settled within your walls, and gives every appearance of thriving under the care of"—he pointed his cane toward the door—"your sisters, that I am convinced he ought to remain right where he is. I fear that to move him to a place where he will be surrounded by a new passel of strangers would cause permanent damage. But this I have said before. *Several times.*"

"You add no confidence to my fears, sir," she retorted, pacing the library, also for perhaps the twentieth time. "I am convinced his family is nigh on sick with worry at his absence. We do a great disservice keeping him here. He has been in our house five days now and not one inquiry!"

"So you have said," he responded wearily. "More than once!"

She heard a thump against the door and then Katherine's hushed voice crying out, "Do stop shoving at me, Celeste! Marianne, what did the doctor say?"

All four of her sisters were clustered on the other side of the richly grained mahogany door, waiting the outcome of the interview. She had already told them—as well as the young gentleman—that she felt obligated to place him in the care of Dr. Deane at Four-Mile-Cross. No one had as yet come to Lady Brook asking after Mr. Albion. Dr. Deane, with his large practice, would undoubtedly enjoy greater success in finding Mr. Albion's family.

The younger sisters had protested strongly against Mr. Albion's removal from the house, since his health was obviously so precarious. Actually all had protested except Augusta, who had listened to the quarrel with intense misery, especially when Constance firmly announced Mr. Albion must go. Then she had turned the shade of oyster pearls and fainted.

Once she had been revived through the help of Marianne's vinaigrette, the argument had been rejoined and each sister had pressed home her own particular point. Katherine insisted the poor gentleman was still not sufficiently recovered to be moved from the sickroom, Celeste stated emphatically that she had not yet completed stitching the rents in his coat sleeve to her satisfaction, and Marianne announced that she had fallen so violently in love with Mr. Albion that were he to leave Lady Brook she would fall into a decline and perish.

Augusta was still too dizzy from swooning to add her voice to the quarrel.

Constance, viewing Mr. Albion through a practical eye, felt these arguments were ridiculous beyond words. For one thing, Marianne frequently fell violently in love and prophesied her demise in the absence of her current favorite. For another, though Mr. Albion gave the appearance of bearing a delicate constitution, she was convinced that any young man bent on taking Lady Brook Bend at a neck-or-nothing pace could not be as helpless as he appeared. Finally, with regard to his apparel, Celeste was merely being overly fastidious, as well she knew.

Constance was convinced that he must go, and the sooner the better.

"So, Dr. Kent, are you telling me that in your opinion, he should stay?"

Dr. Kent nodded impatiently. "I have said nothing else for the past hour." He rose to his feet. "You are a stubborn young woman and in many ways persuasive, but your tenacity in holding me captive in your library all this time, and pelting me with the same questions again and again, will not move me to alter my opinions. And now, if you please, I must go. I have a patient awaiting my attention in Reading."

Constance felt a measure of panic rise in her chest. Dr. Deane would not take Mr. Albion without Dr. Kent's approval. She tried another tack. "But, sir, will you not at least stay to nuncheon? You must be feeling a trifle peckish since it is past noon."

Dr. Kent dipped his head and glared at her over his spectacles. "I wouldn't stay if you were serving a twelve-course meal such as is served at the Pavilion!"

His words, his demeanor, brought a reluctant smile to her lips. She surrendered. "Very well—if you *must* go."

He chuckled. He seemed to understand her quite well. "Thank you for the brandy—it was very good. I am sorry I can't be of service to you." His eye then took on a peculiar gleam as he looked at her steadfastly for a moment. He touched the tip of his finger to his chin. "Miss Pamberley, by any chance, are you in need of a husband?"

Constance was entirely taken aback by this odd turn of

conversation. "No, as it happens, I am not," she stated, wondering what he was about. She couldn't help but smile.

"Pity."

"Now, why is that?" she asked. "Do you have a nephew in need of a housekeeper disguised as a wife?" Dr. Kent knew she saw to the management of Lady Brook.

He gave a crack of laughter and his blue eyes sparkled. "I like your manner of funning very much, and your style, though a trifle managing, quite pleases me—arch, determined—you've no idea! But I must confess, I do not have a nephew, I was thinking of myself. I am a physician by choice, but I have a snug property in Wiltshire, four thousand a year, and a dislike of children." His gaze grew penetrating. He added, as though recollecting for a moment his initial impulse, "Besides, you are uncommonly pretty. You might even be beautiful were you to wear something other than what is by general account I am sure a quite fetching cap."

Constance was astonished. "Are you offering for me, Dr. Kent?" she asked, dumbfounded.

He nodded and smiled. He was probably fifty if a day, balding, and portly. He was also oddly attractive in a compelling way. She admired his strength. Not many professional men would have withstood her badgering as he had. She respected him for that.

Alas, however! He was assuming a great deal about her. But then, he couldn't know how much she longed for love, for a true love, for a husband and home to call her own, and . . . for children.

She extended her hand to him. "You do me a great honor," she said kindly and sincerely. "But I cannot accept of your offer."

"Are you sure? I have an uncanny sensation that we should deal extremely well together."

"You may be right. However, my answer must be no."

"Well," he said, showing a faint but amused disappointment, "I know better than to try to argue you into the arrangement."

She laughed with him. Then, for her sisters' benefit, she said in a loud voice, "I am sorry you must be leaving now. I shall have your coach brought round at once. Pray, let me escort you to the drawing room." She heard her siblings scurry down the hall in the general direction of the nursery, undoubtedly to relate their news to Mr. Albion.

She led Dr. Kent to the formal receiving room of an elegant azure blue and waited with him until his traveling chariot arrived. They chatted for some few minutes, and when the wheels of the conveyance were heard to crunch on the gravel of the drive, she began slowly walking him to the door, aware that she was reluctant to surrender his companionship entirely. She enjoyed the company of intelligent, strong-minded men. She had been her father's favorite, and his demise eleven years earlier had been a significant loss in her life. With some reluctance did she lead Dr. Kent to his carriage.

Lord Ramsdell had searched through Bedfordshire for five days, hunting his cousin, who had decided that on this particular adventure he would avoid the main highways completely in order to evade his pursuer. But this morning, having on a whim decided to venture into Berkshire, he found the news he had been seeking. At a village just to the south of a mansion known as Lady Brook Cottage, he had finally learned of Charles's whereabouts. Apparently, a young man fitting Charles's description, but suffering from some sort of memory loss, had crashed into the fence at Lady Brook and had been cared for by five spinsters of small means since.

Ramsdell received the information at first with relief, then with strong irritation that he had been forced to hunt for his cousin for days on end and now must rescue him from a household of impoverished females undoubtedly determined to keep him. The landlord at the Turtle Inn had opened his budget quite thoroughly on the precise nature of Pamberley sisters—their beauty, their penurious state, and the managing eldest sibling who would not permit any of the ladies to marry unless the husband was in possession of a fortune.

He was in no tender mood to deal with a set of country mushrooms. So it was that he found himself nearing the now-infamous Lady Brook Bend in the devil's own temper. Through the fine tall fir trees he could see the outlines in the distance of a mellowed brick house reputed to have some fifteen bedchambers and a fine prospect of the entire neighborhood positioned as it was on a lovely rise.

When the lane opened up into a long, inviting stretch of excellent highway, he slapped his spirited team across their backs with the reins and let them have their head.

One more turn, if he had judged the landscape properly, would bring him to Lady Brook.

The wind moved briskly over his face, and for the first time in his vigilant pursuit of a relative he intended to strangle when next he laid eyes on him, he felt better. He was an accomplished horseman and driver and had been a member of the Four-in-Hand Club since his first days in London. He was fully confident he could manage the turn which the landlord of the Turtle Inn indicated had been the bane of many a notable whip. Charles, apparently, had succumbed to the difficulty of the endeavor. For himself, he would be appropriately cautious, yet would hold nothing back.

The turn approached quickly. He could see the bend was sharp, yet the remainder of the lane was sufficiently wide for two coaches to pass each other. He eased his horses back a trifle and began rounding the bend with skill. He had succeeded at a dozen far more difficult than this, and he scoffed at his cousin's lack of skill. He was not prepared, however, for the deer that bounded some ten feet out of the forest directly in front of his horses, then darted back to safety just in time. His horses were not prepared either. They immediately bolted and swerved, and before Ramsdell knew what was happening, his team was racing through a breach in a white picket fence, crossing a border of some kind of purple flower and dashing headlong over a wide stretch of green lawn. In a matter of seconds the path would take them crashing directly into another coach and pair, beside which stood a tall woman and a portly gentleman, who were eyeing his approach with horrified eyes. He realized they would not have sufficient time to move.

He rose up like a gladiator, knowing such an effort was his only chance at saving the lives before him as well as his own. He let go of a dreadful oath and pulled with all his might on the reins.

Time had slowed to a standstill for Constance. A tall, broad-shouldered man careening across her lawn in a dashing curricle led by two panicked chestnuts was heading straight toward herself and the good doctor. She was frozen by the knowledge that she would soon be dead, as well as the physician, who took strong hold of her hand and cried, "By Jove! What a way to pay one's debt to nature!"

Constance had laughed a little hysterically, then the driver of the curricle had risen up like an ancient Celtic warrior commanding his chariot.

"Hell and damnation!" he had cried, cursing the air. He pulled hard on the reins. The horses swerved and drew to a painfully abrupt halt directly beside Dr. Kent's traveling chariot. The warrior, however, was sent flying through the air to strike the ground hard and tumble twice across the rough gravel to land facedown at her feet. His cheek was scraped and bleeding, he had lost his hat, and his left arm was bent at an unnatural angle. He didn't move at all, but his back rose and fell with reassuring regularity.

The very air grew remarkably quiet. Even the habitually noisy robins and larks had silenced their melodies for a brief moment. The only sound to be heard was the blowing of the chestnuts and the shuddering of their flanks as they stood frightened and paralyzed on the drive.

She heard the door behind her open. Constance turned, her eyes dry with shock, and watched Morris step out onto the shallow steps.

The butler surveyed the odd scene before him. His bushy gray brows rose in some surprise. "What, again?" he queried.

Constance nodded slowly.

Dr. Kent turned and stared at him for a stunned moment, then met Constance's shocked gaze as she slowly shifted back to the man lying at her feet. He queried, "Just how often does this happen?"

"This is the sixth, no, seventh, occurrence this year," she stated faintly. "Recently, when I was inquiring of the landlord at the Turtle about Mr. Albion's possible identity, I learned that Lady Brook Bend has gained a certain notoriety among the sporting set."

"Indeed! It seems he was right. I know this man. He is reputed a great Corinthian in London circles, a nonesuch, which makes it a wonder that he was unable to navigate the bend better than this."

"What is his name?"

"Ramsdell. Viscount Ramsdell. A rather hardened fellow by all accounts. Good God, will you look at that arm! Well, well, it appears I shall be staying with you for a little while longer after all." He then took command of the situation by ordering Stively to see to the horses and carriages and Morris to bring several pairs of hands to move what anyone could see was a large, well-built man of athletic physique and undoubtedly corresponding weight.

Constance added, "Prepare the buttery. He's broken his arm and perhaps more. Dr. Kent will need room to work."

* * *

Ramsdell awoke and didn't know where he was. His head ached like the devil, and other parts of him as well. His face burned in spots. His left arm was wrapped up tightly and strapped to his chest. He felt as weak as a kitten.

Good God, he'd taken the devil of a spill!

The accident came back to him—the deer, the fright of his horses, the mad dash across a lush lawn, the sight of a man and woman . . . Had he killed them?

He squeezed his eyes shut, trying to remember. He didn't think so, but his memory was hazy.

Where was he? How long had he been here? Where was here? He smelled herbs or something of the like.

He opened his eyes and stared up at a faded blue canopy. The walls to the right were painted a pale blue and a sampler stitched quite intricately and portraying an elegant peacock was the only adornment. The wall opposite the bed held a single chest of drawers on which three tapers glowed softly. Beside the chest was a closed door, leading, he supposed, to a hallway beyond.

With some difficulty, he turned his head to the left and saw that the fireplace was aglow—how odd for summer— and a heavy pot, hung on a bracket over the coals, sent aromatic steam into the air. Ah, a broth of some sort. With a harder twisting yet, a strange view came into sight of a tall woman, stretched out in what seemed to him a deuced uncomfortable half-reclining position, asleep on a daybed. She was dressed in nightclothes and a robe with some sort of cloth clutched in her hand.

She awoke suddenly with a start, seemed to recollect herself, relaxed, stretched, and yawned. Her long, light brown hair was draped about her shoulders and down the front of her robe. Though she looked very tired, he could not remember seeing such a beautiful face before—or maybe he was dreaming, or perhaps the firelight was confusing his eyesight. Still, she blinked several times, apparently trying to awaken herself.

He had a marvelous view of an oval face, sparkling light blue eyes, a straight nose, slightly bowed lips, and a chin with a dimple. He felt the strangest tug somewhere deep in his chest. He smiled faintly. He could fall in love with such a female.

Good God! He must be delirious to have had such a thought. He was long past his salad days and the foolishness of tumbling in love at first sight. For all he knew, she meant to compromise him by her presence in his bedchamber at what appeared to be an ungodly hour and demand he marry her.

He drew in a long, deep breath and felt very sad suddenly. When had he become so dashed cynical?

She glanced toward him. Had she read his thoughts? She sat up, her brows lifted in surprise. "Are you awake?" she asked softly.

"What a silly question," he said through strangely thickened lips. His mouth was wretchedly dry. "Of course I am."

The relief that flooded her face, however, did not add to his confidence one whit.

"You are awake," she stated. "Do you know where you are?"

He closed his eyes and concentrated very hard on the question. "Lady Brook," he said, "by my closest estimation." He opened his eyes and looked at her. "Am I right?"

"Yes, precisely." She rose from the chaise longue and took up a straight-backed chair next to his bed. She drew very close and took hold of his hand. He was immeasurably comforted by the touch of her soft, warm fingers and again his chest tightened and tugged. He swallowed.

She said, "Now, you must tell me exactly what you are feeling at this moment."

She was searching his eyes, and he was embarrassed by the question. Should he tell her of the sudden rush of affection that seemed to be pouring out of his heart toward her at this very moment? Was that what she meant for him to say?

She explained. "The doctor has left specific instructions to be administered once you awoke, so you must tell me, are you chilled, or hot? Hungry, thirsty?"

Oh, *those* kinds of feelings. "I feel as though I'm lying in a lake of water, and, yes, I feel cold."

She smiled faintly. "You've been perspiring for the past several hours. You may feel uncomfortable because of it, but I assure you, it gave us such hope."

Hope? "Why?"

She pinched her lips together quickly. He didn't like that. She meant to conceal something.

"No," he said sharply. "Tell me."

She drew in a deep breath as though to fortify her nerves. "You suffered a terrible fall and broke your left forearm in two places. The bone—" She broke off for a moment before continuing, her eyes searching his. "The bone pierced the skin. There was a great deal of blood and later infection, but you were fortunate to have been in the hands of a very fine surgeon at the time. Indeed, I have since considered the circumstances and timing of your arrival as extremely fortuitous."

"Dear God," he breathed, looking away from her and staring up at the faded blue canopy again. An accident would explain everything, of course—the sticky dampness of his clothes, his parched throat, the terrible weakness in his body. "May I have a little water?"

"Thirsty?" she asked.

"Terribly."

She rose, and from a pitcher close at hand poured him a glass, then held it to his lips. He struggled to lift his head, but she slid an arm under his neck to support him and with some skill positioned the glass just so. Before long he had finished it all.

"Much better," he murmured. "I thank you."

"Are you hungry?"

"No."

"You will forgive me if I force a little broth into you. Dr. Kent was very clear about this."

He smiled. "Kent, is it, eh? From London?"

"The very one. You have heard of him?"

"He probably doesn't recall, but my aunt consulted him once regarding her son. I thought he gave her quite sage advice, which she promptly ignored. I probably wouldn't even be in this scrape had she followed his recommendations. Therefore, I shall drink your broth, with gratitude."

He could see she seemed a little puzzled by what he had said, but her shoulders relaxed suddenly. "Good," she said. He hadn't realized how tense she had been until that moment.

She propped a pillow under his shoulders, again with great care. She overlaid his arm and chest with a large square of linen. From the fire, she withdrew a steaming pot and ladled out what was a weak vegetable and chicken broth into a bowl, which she let cool sufficiently before feeding him. She had an excellent technique as she spoon-fed him. He told her so.

"Thank you. I am an old hand at this, I will confess. Mother suffered a fit of apoplexy some few years past and never regained the use of her limbs. I and my sisters have cared for her since."

He nodded as she lifted another spoonful to his lips. He had told her he wasn't hungry, but every sip of the broth seemed to awaken him to his body's need, and he couldn't get enough of it. But the energy required in the simple act of swallowing soon overtook him, and he found himself ready to resume his slumbers.

"We must change your nightshirt and sheets first, though you won't like it a bit," she said sympathetically. "But Marchand is here. I would have awakened him sooner, for he has been in such a state, but I didn't want to disturb his sleep.

We have taken turns caring for you and he only recently drifted off. He's very devoted, you know."

He was surprised. How could his valet be here? "Marchand is here?" he asked. "But how, when?"

"I sent for him some time ago. He has been at Lady Brook for a sennight now."

"What?" he cried. "Good God! How long have I been— have I been unconscious all this time? And how much time would that be?"

"Ten days in all. You've been very ill. Surely you know that by now."

He considered just how weak he felt and how much he ached from head to foot. "Yes, I suppose I do."

"Let me send for your valet."

She left the room, and he had the devil of a time remaining awake until Marchand and two other men quite unfamiliar to him returned to help him. Their hands and movements were not nearly so gentle as the young woman's, whose name he realized he hadn't learned in their brief conversation. He longed to be back in her tender care, but the delicacy of the current occasion prohibited her presence. When fresh, dry sheets were surrounding him and a clean nightshirt cloaking his sore body, he asked Marchand if she had gone to bed.

"Miss Pamberley? No. She is waiting in the hall. Shall I fetch her, m'lord?"

"Yes, if you please." So, she was Miss Pamberley, one of the five sisters whom the landlord at the Turtle had referred to.

Marchand turned away, his face lined with care. His silence bespoke the serious nature of the situation. Only a brush with death could have stolen his valet's tongue as it had.

"Marchand," he called to him.

His valet turned back, and he saw that tears were brimming in his eyes.

"Yes, m' lord?"

"Thank you for coming."

Marchand made a strange swiping movement with his hand and uttered a choking sound as he quickly left the sickroom.

A moment later, Miss Pamberley returned and again took up her place beside the bed. "I am instructed to give you a dose of laudanum and water." Her shoulders tensed and she waited as she looked down at him.

"Kent's orders?"

She nodded.

"Very well." He was a trifle confused by what he could see was her apprehension. Again he watched her shoulders relax, and this time she smiled fully.

"What is it?" he asked, smiling with her. "I vow I am convinced you expected me to refuse the draft."

She chuckled. He heard her chuckle, a delightful sound that again drew a tug of affection from deep within his chest. How strange to feel that way when he didn't even know this woman.

She explained. "This is the first time you have agreed to anything that has been suggested to you over the past ten days.

He was aghast. "I must have been delirious."

"Very much so. You argued with me and fought everything until the fever sunk you into unconsciousness two days past. I was relieved for a time, but then you were far too ill and far too silent. After a few hours, I found I wanted you battling me more than anything." She chuckled again and he saw that tears shimmered in her eyes. "We were all so frightened, you see, and—"

She started to rise from her chair, but he leaned over and caught her arm with his right hand and prevented her from doing so. "Poor child," he said. "You're fagged to death."

She nodded and blinked away her tears. "I am."

"Thank you, Miss Pamberley."

As he released her hand, she rose from her chair and prepared the laudanum. Again she gently slid her arm behind his neck and supported him while he drank the bitter liquid. By then he was beyond exhaustion. When he was done, he looked at her, certain there was much he needed to say to her, much he ought to say, but his mind grew foggy with sleep and with the first curls of the strong opiate. "I'm sorry," he murmured, closing his eyes.

He wasn't sure, but as he drifted away, he was convinced he felt her lips pressed to his. Or perhaps the laudanum was giving him a very nice dream. . . .

THREE

Constance awoke late that afternoon, surprised that the first sensation she experienced was a strange fluttering in her stomach. She could not at first comprehend why such a pleasurable form of excitement was teasing her until her thoughts landed on Lord Ramsdell, and the sensation rose to a sharp peak.

"Oh, dear," she murmured, closing her eyes. She could not remember having felt this way in years—fourteen years to be exact, when she had developed a truly reprehensible *tendre* for Jaspar Vernham, her father's stable boy.

He had been nineteen at the time and she a tender fifteen. Tall and handsome, Jaspar had been a god walking among the horses and towering nearly half a head over her own height. She knew he had been much taken with her, and an easy familiarity had developed between them. His accent had been low, of course, but everything else about him was exceptional—he read voraciously and his everyday prose was remarkable, his conversation was intelligent, his manners unexceptionable, and though she knew he held tender feelings toward her, he never once crossed the pale. Except in birth, he was very much her equal.

She had, however, forced a kiss from him the night before he left for India and bade him promise to write to her often, a promise he had kept quite faithfully. A friendly correspondence had ensued, and she had been apprised of his every success in the land of elephants, heat, and torrential seasonal rains. She was expecting his return to England within the next twelvemonth, at which time he hoped to purchase a snug property, take a wife, and raise—in his terms—a passel of lively brats.

He had always called her a brat during her growing-up years, and even now referred to her in just such affectionate terms in his letters. She understood him, or at least thought she did—he wanted to keep their relationship in a comfortable place. For that she was grateful. She had long since forgotten the butterflies and the farewell kiss and knew Jaspar now as a dear, dear friend whose company she hoped to enjoy once he returned to England, but nothing more.

How strange to think, however, that in all these years, and some eight, no, *nine,* offers of marriage later, the only man to have come close to arousing those early compelling sensations within her heart was lying across the hall in one of her bedchambers, gaunt from his vigorous battle with a near-crippling infection, and that, after having nearly gotten himself killed on her property. Because he was a peer of the realm, her interest in him seemed ridiculous in the extreme. What? Would only a nobleman do for Miss Pamberley of Lady Brook Cottage?

As she glanced toward her windows, she noted that she had forgotten to close the shutters and the faded chintz drapes before sliding between the sheets. A warm afternoon light streamed into her bedchamber, casting the pink accents of her room into a rosy glow.

She rolled slightly onto her side, her gaze fixed to swirling sunbeams, and sighed with deep contentment. Ramsdell would live. She sighed and smiled. She could be at ease in her mind now, and she could recover from ten rigorous days of nursing. Knowing that Ramsdell was safe had caused her mind and body to sink into a stretch of slumber that had been as peaceful as it had been long. She felt rested and alive, even though a bone-weariness still clung to her.

From the onset of the recent raging fever, Dr. Kent had prepared her for the probability that Ramsdell would not survive the night. Yet, somehow, in the depths of his illness, his body and spirit had surprised them all—he had embraced life anew.

The entire experience had affected her deeply but not unexpectedly. She had cared for her father in just the same way when a terrible fever had taken hold of him. He had spoken incomprehensible things to her in a delirium, he had become a hollow, unspeaking shell in his unconsciousness, he had never awakened again. She and her mother had wept over his body, and together they had buried him.

Yet Ramsdell had lived.

She swiped at surprising tears. She was so grateful the ordeal was over. Only why had she placed a kiss on his lips just before she had quit his bedchamber?

In part because she was so relieved and in part because Ramsdell was in too many respects every woman's ideal. He was quite handsome, tall, and dark. His chin bore a noble line that spoke of medieval campaigns and wars waged on the Continent in more recent centuries. His lineage could be traced back to the Conqueror. Her closest friend, the parson's wife, had come to call during Ramsdell's illness, and had told her all she knew of the viscount, which was significant since she was an inveterate gossip and was acquainted with all the aristocratic lines crisscrossing England.

"You have Ramsdell in one of your bedchambers?" Sophia Spencer had exclaimed with a hand to her bosom. "But, Constance, you can have no idea! There are scarcely a handful of families who can claim to be descended from William's conquering nobility, and the Ramsdell family is one of them!"

Constance had been too worried at the moment to have been astonished by Sophia's exclamations. However, the danger to his life had passed and she could now be properly impressed. According to Sophia Spencer, he was worth at least seven, possibly eight thousand per annum, a sum that was staggering to Constance, given her need to maintain her household and lands on less than six hundred per year. How much good he must accomplish on his own estate!

Her mind drifted into a pleasant reverie. If she had such an income to lavish upon Lady Brook, what wouldn't she do to improve the property? She would drain some of the bottom lands to the south that were invariably sloppy during the early spring months, so much so that she had come to call them the marshlands. After draining them, she would plant an orchard of peach trees, which she would harvest and sell to the voracious London markets. She would buy up the acreage she had been coveting from the old priory lands that had not been inhabited for some thirty years and plant flax or possibly wheat. She would buy more land in the coming years and rent it to a tenanted farmer of superior intelligence who had studied Coke's progress over the years. She would restore Lady Brook to her former gentle magnificence. She would . . . She would . . . There was so much she would do.

But these were dreams in which she did not indulge frequently, for the thought of them, however pleasant for a time, generally tended to lower her spirits. She was not in possession of such funds, and undoubtedly would not be so in the near future. Besides, all her savings were now being spent on cutting a new lane through the fir forest.

A light scratching on the door disturbed her reverie. "Come," she called out over her shoulder. From the corner of her eye she saw that Celeste, her middle sister, had entered the room. She looked very fetching in a white gown some few years old that bore a new pale pink ruffle about the bodice. A small spray of rosebuds and ivy adorned her white-blond hair, which was arranged becomingly in curls atop her head.

"Good afternoon," Celeste called to her.

"And to you, dearest," Constance returned.

Celeste smiled, crossing the room to round the bed. "How are you feeling?" she asked, her smile softening into a faint expression of concern. "Are you greatly fatigued?"

Constance sighed and shifted to sit up in bed. "To own the truth, I find I am very much refreshed, though I must confess to a certain latent fatigue. But do tell me, how is Ramsdell? Has Dr. Kent been to see him?"

Her sister nodded. "Hours ago. He arrived shortly after nine o'clock, and when he left the viscount's chamber he was beaming. I told him you had left strict orders that when he arrived you were to be awakened, but he was adamant that you should rest. He said he did not want another patient on his hands and that you were to be coddled for a day or two just to be sure you did not fall ill." She settled herself on the side of the tall bed, both feet dangling toward the floor in a childlike manner.

"Of the moment, I am grateful he rescinded my orders," Constance said. "So tell me, how fares our other patient?"

Celeste's pretty face took on a glow. "Mr. Albion improves daily," she reported.

Constance watched her carefully. She was aware that during the past seventeen days, Mr. Albion had charmed all her sisters, for he was a handsome young man of considerable address. She had also learned his identity from Marchand. His name was Charles Kidmarsh and he was cousin and ward to Lord Ramsdell, a fact she had kept to herself, bidding Marchand to do the same. Time enough, once Ramsdell gained a little strength, to sort out precisely how the matter of his amnesia should be handled.

For the present, she was more concerned that any of her sisters should tumble in love with a man whose portion was unknown to her, but which she believed to be quite small. There had been nothing on his person at the time of the accident to indicate otherwise to her.

As for Celeste, her light blue eyes certainly gleamed when

she spoke of Mr. Albion, but beyond this Constance was unable to detect a deepening of her sentiments.

"Did Dr. Kent see him as well? Is there the smallest sign that he might be regaining his memory or at least some knowledge of his own identity?"

"As to that," she muttered, her face taking on a darkling aspect, "I wouldn't know. Marianne locked me in the nursery when Dr. Kent came to speak with him. I wanted very much to pound on the door and demand she release me, but how would that appear to Mr. Albion?" Her blue eyes were wide, as though the question would make perfect sense to Constance.

Constance, however, was alarmed. When Marianne took to such ridiculously childish stratagems in order to gain a stronghold in her pursuit of a suitor, she was also equally as likely to consent to a scandalous elopement.

Celeste then brightened and added. "But you cannot have heard the latest. Katherine and I have come to believe that Mr. Albion is acquainted with Lord Ramsdell in some manner. Of course we told Alby, Mr. Albion, of his arrival and of the accident but from the first, whenever Ramsdell's name was mentioned, Alby became quite agitated. I once pressed him about Ramsdell, but he vowed the name meant nothing to him."

She sighed before continuing, "He possesses the sweetest, most tenderest of hearts. He always inquires after Ramsdell, you know, wanting to be informed almost hourly of the precise state of his health. He had tears in his eyes when Marianne told him this morning that Lord Ramsdell would live. But then, we had all become such watering pots that it was no wonder Alby was so moved." Her face then grew mulish again. "It was shortly after that, when Alby had singled me out to read the next few stanzas of Byron's 'Corsair,' that Marianne lured me into the nursery as though she had some great secret to tell, then locked me in!"

"How did you get out?"

"I called to Finch from the nursery window, of course. He sent one of the maids with the key."

"Ah," Constance murmured.

By the end of Celeste's recital, Constance felt a little more at ease. Her middle sister seemed more interested in competing with Marianne than with actually engaging Mr. Albion in a serious flirtation. For this she was grateful. Of all her sisters, only Celeste was close to marrying.

For the past two years, she had been courted by a well-to-do baronet by the name of Sir Henry Crowthorne. Sir Henry, bless him, had formed a deep attachment to Celeste and had made his intentions clear by attending to her quite fastidiously at every social event the Pamberley sisters attended.

Celeste, however, had remained somewhat aloof to his careful attentions. She was in constant pursuit of whichever beau Marianne had at that moment claimed for her own. But Sir Henry was a tenacious suitor if not a gallant lover, and Constance hoped that in the end his perseverance would win the day.

She considered Sir Henry a proper match for Celeste. He had a tidy property some ten miles south of Lady Brook, an easy competence, and fine, gentle manners. She had encouraged him to walk in the shrubberies with Celeste as frequently as propriety would allow, trusting that the baronet, some eight years Celeste's senior, would know how to make use of the endorsed privacy without going beyond the pale.

His only flaw, which could not help but sway Celeste's heart away from the poor fellow, was that he had a common face. His dark brown eyes were nicely expressive, but this feature could not overcome a somewhat bulbous nose and thin lips. He was not in the least beautiful, like Mr. Albion, and Celeste, at two and twenty, was too young in mind and years to realize that a loving husband was far preferable to one who was handsome yet lacked steadiness of character, a kind nature, or plain common sense.

Celeste could not *love* Sir Henry, yet she confessed she

enjoyed his company and mild sense of humor more than any other gentleman of her acquaintance, so she was not averse to having him underfoot at Lady Brook. Herein lay Constance's hope that the courtship would one day end at the altar. Or, at least, that was her hope until Mr. Albion arrived. Even though she had spent the past ten days caring in turn for her sickly mother and Lord Ramsdell, her younger sisters had occasionally pelted her with numerous complaints about the conduct of one or the other of her siblings. She did not need to be exceedingly quick-witted to conclude that the source of the tense undercurrents among at least her next three sisters was Mr. Albion.

On the other hand, Augusta, the youngest, seemed somehow set apart from the competition for Mr. Albion's attentions, though she was frequently known to spend hours reading to the now nearly recuperated young gentleman. She would have to remember to praise her for her sensible conduct.

Celeste interrupted her reverie. "I nearly forgot. Mama wishes to speak with you. I had brought her a copy of *The Morning Post,* but she wouldn't cast her eyes on it. She seemed distressed, and when I asked if she wished to speak with you she blinked a yes."

Constance nodded. Her mother had suffered the apoplexy several years before and could neither speak nor move her limbs. Somehow, over time, however, she had learned to communicate through blinking. One for yes. Two for no.

The realization that her mother was distressed prompted Constance to immediately slip from bed and don a robe of fine linen which, though patched in three places, still appeared in excellent condition. Celeste, following her from the room, exclaimed, "You cannot even tell where I mended it!"

Constance turned to smile at her. "Of course not! You are the most accomplished needlewoman I have ever known."

Celeste smiled and blushed with rosy pleasure. Her dimples showed, and she looked to be about fourteen, except that everything else about her was far too womanly for *Alby* to set down to indeterminate youth.

Now that she knew Mr. Albion's identity, Constance wondered how soon she could send him back to Ramsdell's home in Bedfordshire. She decided she would broach the subject with the viscount as soon as he appeared to be gaining strength.

Constance held her mother's hand and smiled lovingly down at her. Mrs. Pamberley was little more than a frail image of her once-beautiful and strong self. Her eyes, however, seemed not to notice that her body was as useless as a limp rag, for they watched Constance even now with sparkling blue intensity, never drifting once from her eldest daughter's face.

"You cannot tell me, Mama, that you were worried about my health when you know I am never ill?"

Mrs. Pamberley blinked twice. No.

"So what is your concern?"

Mrs. Pamberley's eyelids fluttered, an ominous sign that she was indeed distressed. Constance knew to begin pelting her with questions. Her mother held her eyes wide until she mentioned Mr. Albion. She blinked once.

"Oh, that." Constance sighed.

Blink.

"Well, it was terribly unfortunate that Ramsdell should have arrived, suffering so dreadful an accident at the very moment I was hoping to move Mr. Albion out of the house. But there was nothing else I could do."

Blink. Flutter.

"If you are worried about Marianne and Celeste—"

Blink-blink.

"Katherine?"

Blink-blink.

"Not Augusta?"

A single steady blink.

"Augusta and Mr. Albion?" Constance queried, astonished.

Another steady blink.

"But how strange. Has Augusta mentioned him to you?" Her mother blinked once. "How curious! To think of Augusta, who is usually so unmoved by masculine beauty and charm, to have been taken in by Alby?"

A fluttering ensued. Constance laughed. "Have you not heard your daughters refer to Mr. Albion as *Alby?*" Two blinks. "Yes, it is quite true and excessively absurd." She hesitated for a moment, then added, "Don't fret, Mama, I shall take great care to see that Augusta does not lose her heart to Mr. Albion."

Her mother sighed, and she knew now her parent would be at ease. After tending to her needs, she promised to see for herself the precise state of Augusta's sentiments toward their impoverished guest and left to dress for dinner.

When she emerged from her bedchamber an hour later, she was gowned in soft cambric overlaid with a tunic of lavender silk. A matching silk cap covered her light brown curls, which she adjusted with a slight tug before leaving her room. Stepping into the hallway, however, she was greeted with a sight that not only stunned her but set her naturally suspicious mind on edge.

"Hello, Constance!" Katherine called to her. "Only do but look! Alby is walking!" She had one arm around Mr. Albion's back and was helping Marianne, along with Celeste and Augusta, to aid the young gentleman on what appeared to be a first excursion outside his bedchamber.

She was struck by many things. The young man's legs, though lean, appeared quite strong, his face was a perfectly rosy hue that had nothing to do with the exertion of making his way down the hall with the support of four able young women, and he was even more handsome than she had remembered.

Since Ramsdell's accident, she had ventured only twice into Mr. Albion's supposed sickroom, and she realized, each time, she had found Alby in a perfect bloom of health. Her suspicions deepened.

All the ladies were presently smiling and giggling and offering every manner of support as the young gentleman appeared to struggle with each step. Constance scrutinized his efforts. She could not help but feel he was shamming it, but to what purpose? To enjoy the attentions of some of Berkshire's prettiest maids? Perhaps. Her sisters presented as charming a country portrait as any bevy of youthful females could. Not a one was platter-faced. What man wouldn't want to be cosseted by so many willing and quite lovely ladies?

She met his gaze, lowering one of her clearest stares upon him, and did not miss the quick blush that added to the color of his cheeks. "How happy I am to see that you are finally abroad, Mr. Albion, but I am grievously concerned. Because of the way you struggle to walk, when even a simpleton can see that your legs are nearly as firm as iron, I have begun to wonder whether your mind was not more aversely affected than we have supposed. You know, I understand that Bethlehem Hospital is experimenting with electrical shock in the treatment of some of their patients. Perhaps Dr. Kent might know more on the subject."

A stunned light entered Mr. Albion's beautiful eye.

"I—I don't wonder if Dr. Kent is well acquainted with such a treatment, Miss Pamberley, but I assure you, I feel quite well and am remembering a great deal—just not my identity. Perhaps I have been relying too much on the kindness of your sisters, when I should be attempting to walk on my own."

"Perhaps," she agreed.

"Ladies," he said, glancing at each sister in turn, meeting

each gaze as though that particular female was his favorite. "Do you think I should try?"

The result was a unanimous no, followed by a variety of exclamations.

"You are still too weak!" Marianne cried.

"What if you should fall?" Celeste exclaimed, clasping a horrified hand to her mouth.

Katherine cast Constance a reproachful glance. "How can you suggest such a thing, when he is just now emerged from the sickroom? Have you no sensibility?"

But it was Augusta whom Constance watched. The quiet young woman clutched a book to her bosom and shuddered. Her face turned ominously pale. She appeared close to swooning—again.

Oh, dear, Constance thought. It would seem for the first time in her life that Augusta Pamberley had tumbled violently in love and with a man who by nature and by circumstance was not in any way suited to husband her.

Mr. Albion protested. "No! No! Your sister is very right. I must attempt to walk without your aid sometime, and it might as well be now."

Constance then watched a performance so pure as to make even the great Edmund Kean gnash his teeth with envy. Mr. Albion struggled forward several steps, his knees threatening to give way at any moment. He murmured to himself, appeared to battle his weakness with a supreme effort of the will, and walked, haltingly, limpingly, weaving from side to side, toward her.

All four sisters moved as one behind him, their arms outstretched as though to catch him the moment he fell.

Only he never fell, never tripped, never even stumbled. He merely struggled valiantly on, passing Constance in the hallway but refusing to meet her eye.

"Fustian," she murmured to him as he limped by. She watched him start for the barest second, then continue in his forward march as though he were bearing a heavy cross upon his shoulder.

Constance let them go. She had something of far greater moment to attend to than Mr. Albion's bamboozling conduct. She would deal with him later, but for the present she needed to see for herself that Lord Ramsdell was indeed recovered.

Ramsdell was irritated as he stared up at the blue canopy. He had never been one to bear even a hint of illness with a proper measure of equanimity. He was a man of sport, strong in body and determined in competition. He never refused a challenge, whether shooting pistols, fencing, riding a race over devilish country, or driving his curricle across England against the clock.

He was proud of his prowess, but more than that, he loved the sensations he experienced when he gave himself to the heat of the moment. He felt fully alive and something more—a spiritual connection to all the dynamic forces about him—the heat of the sun, the strength of a northern wind, the power of a lightning bolt.

But right now, staring up at the canopy, his soul was agitated beyond words. Never in his entire existence had he known a moment that he could not control—until then. He was so weak, he could hardly move his head, none the less his arms or legs. He felt as though he'd been struck by lightning and every ounce of energy drained from him in a single swoop. Marchand had to support him so that he could drink the vile potions Dr. Kent had prescribed for him. Marchand had to turn him over in bed to change his sheets. And worse, he knew quite well that Charles had somehow tricked a passel of silly females into believing he was not only ill but that he could not remember who he was, and there was not a thing he could do about it!

Damn and blast! he thought.

A scratching on the door interrupted his charming train of thought. "Come!" he barked through dry, cracked lips.

A lady entered the room. A tall lady, the woman from his tortured dreams. His heart turned over in his breast. He had thought he had made up the female, but it would seem he had not. She was striding toward him, her elegant shoulders well laid back, her breasts high and firm, her face as beautiful as he remembered. She could not be the woman Marchand said ruled the household with an iron fist? Impossible! The angel who had spoken softly to him in the midst of his delirium cannot have the raw will to manage the house and so many absurd females as well.

But if she was, what the devil was such a young and such a beautiful woman doing wearing a cap! He was irritated all over again as he watched her approach his bed.

"May I sit with you for a few minutes?" she asked politely. That voice! Something deep inside his chest began to ache at the pure feminine strains.

"Yes, of course," he said, swallowing with some difficulty. His throat burned and his chest ached.

"Would you like some water?" she asked, a slight frown marring her brow.

How very perceptive of her. He nodded, watching her carefully. She was the eldest daughter of Lady Brook, and from what Marchand had gleaned from the servants, she ran the household with an efficiency matched only by his own housekeeper at Aston Hall.

She poured a glass of water, and before he could even begin struggling to sit up, she slid an arm under him, cradling his shoulders with expert care and strength, somehow knowing precisely how much water he could manage at a time.

He drained the glass. He was grateful yet at the same time irritated that she had divined his need and so masterfully provided for him. He did not like being beholden to her, or to anyone. He grunted a thank-you.

"Cross as crabs this evening, I see," she said, her lips twitching slightly.

He sighed heavily. "I beg pardon for not concealing the truth of my sentiments more carefully, but I am not used to being abed."

"Never?"

"Never."

She nodded. "Neither am I, so you have my sympathies."

He grunted faintly. He might have been charmed by such an admission, but for the present he preferred to remain irascible, especially since the lady in front of him was so very pretty and he was, yes, susceptible to her.

"Marchand says that you attended me day and night for over a sennight. I am indebted to you and I thank you—very much."

She did not respond for a moment, but held his gaze firmly. Some emotion worked in her, but he could not comprehend it. She glanced at her lap and swallowed. Her hands were clasped tightly together. At last she lifted her gaze to meet his and began somberly, "I was never more grateful than when your fever turned last night. You see, I feel partly to blame for your accident. We—I should have had the lane straightened some time past. I have since hired workmen to cut a new lane through the forest. Only, pray assure me that you feel much more the thing this evening, for until I hear you say it, I shall not be convinced you truly are recovering."

He shifted his head slightly, better to see her. The light was on the wane and the chamber was filled with the warm glow of fading sunlight. He saw the self-blame in her eyes and felt a new irritation grate within him. He recalled the news Marchand had brought him about Lady Brook, how Simon Pamberley had died at an inauspicious moment, deeply burdened with debt, leaving his wife and children impoverished. In his opinion, Pamberley should have seen to the lane long before his demise.

He did not, however, voice any of these thoughts to the

woman before him. Instead, he answered her plea and related his present condition to her. "Except for a weakness I find appalling," he said, "I am in excellent health. I've little doubt I shall be fit to travel in a day or two."

"A day or two!" she cried. But a flush quickly suffused her cheeks. "That is, Lord Ramsdell, I don't mean to give offense, but I shall be astonished if you were ready to travel within a fortnight."

"I shall be ready," he reiterated coldly, "in two days time."

He glowered at her, narrowing his eyes and pinching his lips together. Any of his servants—well, any of his *London* servants—would have been quaking in their boots at such ominous signs.

Miss Pamberley, however, began to smile, a most unfortunate happenstance to be sure. The smile began as a tightening at the sides of her lips and then a slight chewing on the inside of her lower lip. Her cheeks stained and her eyes began to dance. She surrendered to her amusement and showed him a row of white, even teeth. Faith, but she was even prettier when she smiled.

"Now, what have I said to amuse you?" he asked coolly, hoping she did not see any evidence of the admiration he felt for her.

He watched her swallow and blink. "I have it on excellent authority that you are accounted something of an ogre, m'lord. I now believe it to be true."

"And are you always given to listening to gabblemongers?" he snapped, attempting a quelling tone to his voice.

But the lady was not quelled. Instead, she clucked her tongue. "Pray, do not come the crab with me, m'lord. I have been too used to having my own way to be dampened by a show of your fangs. Besides, I believe we both want the same thing, do we not?"

He searched his mind trying to determine what that might be. For the life of him, he could not believe that she was at all inclined to permit him to drag her into his arms that he might kiss her. Still, some strange flicker of hope rose oddly to the forefront of his mind and danced there with great enthusiasm.

"And what is it we both want?" he asked. His gaze fell to her lips, which were rosy and beautifully shaped.

"We both want Mr. Kidmarsh out of this house as quickly as possible."

FOUR

Constance knew she had given poor Lord Ramsdell a shock, but given his pricklish conduct, she thought it might benefit him to be stunned a little.

"So, Charles is here," he said, a quick frown splitting his brow.

"Yes," she stated, nodding. "Until your valet arrived, I did not know who he was, since during his accident he struck his head and awoke with a severe lapse of memory. Marchand, however, confirmed his identity a few days past. He also told me of your relationship to Mr. Kidmarsh, that you are his guardian, and that though he is long past his majority, he remains in your care."

If she wondered how a man could reach the age of seven and twenty and still require his guardian's vigilant watch, she kept her musings to herself. However, she felt some of the blame must be laid at Ramsdell's door, surely, but it was hardly her place to remonstrate.

"So he is here," he murmured. "And how is he? I mean, other than his amnesia?"

"He is uninjured, and from what I can apprehend, in excellent health."

He scrutinized the woman before him, wondering how much she actually knew of his ward. He assessed her prim posture and direct gaze. He now recalled the landlord at the

Turtle Inn and his gossip concerning Miss Pamberley, tha
she was pushing for advantageous marriages for her sister

Why, then, would she want Charles to leave, unless, o
course she didn't know about his wealth? "I don't reall
understand, Miss Pamberley, and I would appreciate bein
very clear about this. I have my own reasons for wantin
Charles back at Aston Hall, but why, exactly, do you wis
him to leave Lady Brook?"

A faint blush touched her cheeks. "I hope I am not bein
indelicate," she said, "but I have only one object where m
sisters are concerned, to see each of them properly settle
in acceptable marriages."

He lifted his brows. At least she was straightforward abou
her objectives.

She continued. "I am sure you know precisely how w
are situated, since I have never had the smallest reliance o
the discretion of our servants, or in a certain publican of th
Turtle Inn." She smiled. "I don't fault any of them, I assur
you. Such is the way of the world. But Mr. Kidmarsh's cir
cumstances cannot possibly be of any use to us—and her
I pray you will not be offended—but his poverty makes
match between any of my sisters and your ward an impos
sibility."

He wasn't certain how she had come to the conclusio
that Charles was impoverished, perhaps because Charles wa
his ward, but he saw no reason to enlighten her otherwise
He chose to address an entirely different aspect of the subjec
at hand. "You speak as though a match would be inevitable."

She chuckled and clucked her tongue. "Have you forgot
ten in your illness either how beautiful Mr. Kidmarsh is o
how charming?"

Ramsdell smiled. "Good God, I believe for a moment I
had. After all, he is merely *Charles* to me—my cousin, the
much-cosseted son of my overprotective aunt, the doting ob
ject of my entire staff."

"Well, I feel it my duty to advise you that Mr. Kidmarsh

s presently ensconced in the nursery bedchamber, where he
has been abed for over a fortnight without any evidence of
being in the least ill. He has since *charmed* all my sisters
into waiting on him hand and foot, day and night."

Ramsdell laughed outright. "That would be my cousin. I
only wonder that you did not send him about his business,
for you seem, and pray accept this as a compliment, a woman
of some ability."

"I might have done so," she responded promptly, "but at
the very moment I was beginning to suspect your cousin of
shamming it, your curricle came careening across my lawn.
I have since been remarkably busy."

She met his gaze, her own seemed locked with his in some
mysterious way she had never before experienced. The same
sensations to which she awoke earlier that afternoon assailed
her anew. Her stomach became riddled with waves of pleasure and excitement. Ramsdell, even with a pale complexion
and hollows beneath his eyes, was a dashingly handsome
man and in possession of a fierce spirit that appealed mightily to her.

He did not answer her right away, but seemed somehow
caught himself, a fact that caused the waves within her stomach to crash about wildly. She knew the strangest impulse
to kiss him again. Her lips parted, she even felt herself strain
toward him. His eyes, which she now realized were an exquisite gray, seemed filled with a light that defied description.

What was he thinking? she wondered. Would he even want
to kiss her were such an eventuality possible? But what absurdities were these? She was thinking like a schoolroom
chit and not a mature woman of nine and twenty.

Her common sense, therefore, rose up and pierced the
strange longings of her mind. She reminded herself that Lord
Ramsdell could never be seriously interested in a portionless
female who lived in the rural haunts of Berkshire and who

spent her days tending to her mother, her sisters, and Lad
Brook.

No, not by half. His future companion, by the basic rule
of their shared society, must be a great London hostess an
the daughter of a peer. She must be in possession of som
great property that would add to his own estates and increas
his consequence. She must know people of influence an
thereby increase his consequence.

In stark contrast, she was the daughter of a commone
who had inherited a tidy though impoverished estate, bu
who was without even a drop of noble blood and lacked eve
the pretense of a proper aristocratic connection. Even worse
her father's death had revealed a mountain of gaming debt
that had robbed her family of what little prosperity they ha
once enjoyed. She might be the owner of Lady Brook Mano
but the estate and her birth hardly befitted a viscountcy a
grand as Ramsdell of Bedfordshire.

She sat back in her seat and waited for him to continu
the conversation. He seemed slightly befuddled as h
watched her, and his gray eyes were still cloaked with som
heavy emotion she couldn't quite comprehend.

Finally, he cleared his throat. "So tell me of Charles's ac
cident."

Constance obliged him, keeping the history brief since sh
knew he was probably growing weary of company. However
when she had related the particulars to him, he commence
pelting her with every manner of question until she wonder
if what he had said about being fit to travel in a day or tw
might not be far from the truth after all. Though he wa
suffering from some weakness of body, he was certainly
ready to talk and to begin the process of solving the problems
created by his ward.

"Do not fret, Miss Pamberley," he said at last. "I shal
have my cousin out of your house as quickly as I can, then
you may be comfortable again. I only hope my—our—presence here has not been too taxing."

"Of course it hasn't," she responded politely. She then changed the subject slightly. "As to your cousin's identity, what would be your preference—do you wish him known to my family, to the staff? Because he could not recall his name, my sisters have been calling him Mr. Albion."

"Mr. Albion. How clever." He pondered her question and decided that the longer she remained in ignorance of his fortune, the better. Once his identity was common knowledge, surely someone would appear to disabuse her mind, and then she would feel quite differently about his cousin's presence in her home. "I think things ought to remain just as they are for the present, until I can leave my bed and converse with Charles myself. Whether or not he is feigning either the extent of his illness or his amnesia is not for me to say, but I shouldn't like to have the controversy of his identity further exacerbate his condition, supposed or otherwise."

"I believe you may be right. Besides, until you are prepared to put him into a carriage, there is no point stirring up a wasp's nest."

He smiled. "Precisely, for something tells me Charles will not want to be leaving Lady Brook anytime soon."

Constance couldn't agree more. She then expressed her gratitude to him and afterward left him to the ministrations of his valet, who had brought up a tray of food for his master.

As she left the chamber, she felt she should be quite satisfied with her conversation with Ramsdell. After all, she had succeeded in gaining his support with regard to Charles. However, the thought of this man leaving her life so abruptly—after he had required her attention day and night for such a long time—did not give her even the smallest measure of comfort.

Of course he would not be leaving immediately, and his own insistence he would be well enough to travel in two days' time was a complete absurdity. Therefore, what harm would it do to visit him once or twice—perhaps later this

evening, for instance—and gradually become accustomed t
his departure.

How very sensible her thinking could be at times!

Throughout the evening, which became interminably long
Constance fidgeted and fussed, looking at the clock an
wishing for once that time would hurry up. She was not use
to waiting with intense anticipation for a particular hour t
arrive, but after she had left Ramsdell in Marchand's car
late that afternoon, she had determined in her own mind tha
she would pay him a final call at eight in the evening, whicl
she felt to be quite reasonable and perhaps even a socia
requisite.

The trouble was, she could hardly wait for the hour t
arrive, a fact that was distressing her as much as precisel
how much she was anticipating seeing him again. She kep
telling herself she was merely eager to see that he was im
proving and to determine for herself that his fever was gon
for good. But when she had chosen to dispense with her caf
that evening, she realized that she had been fooling hersel
and that her true intent was for him to see her as something
other than just a spinster who cared for her sisters and he
ailing mother.

So much for her common sense gaining command of he
sensibilities.

Even Mr. Kidmarsh's disturbing and quite flirtatious presence in the drawing room that night, for the very first time
did not have the power to divert her attention from the lethargic ticks of the ormulu clock above the mantel.

She glanced at it again—*fifteen minutes until eight.*

She resumed reading the sonnets of Shakespeare and re-
pressed a deep sigh. She heard Celeste giggle and Marianne
laugh. Katherine cried out, "Oh, Alby, tell another London
anecdote. You cannot imagine how bereft we are of stories.

Do the ladies all dress to the nines when they drive out in Hyde Park?"

"Indeed, yes, for the truth is that the proper daily excursion is more an excuse for cutting a dash than for taking the air to benefit one's health."

Constance watched and listened, recalling her own Season so many years earlier, before her father's death. She had enjoyed every moment of it, dancing till the small hours of the morning nearly every night and sleeping a good part of the day. She couldn't recall having seen Ramsdell then, and Mr. Kidmarsh, two years her junior, would have been at Eton or perhaps Harrow at the time.

An odd sensation of loss struck her suddenly and quite forcibly. She remembered how very much she had been looking forward to the following year's jaunt to London. However, her father had died when the first frost was hard on the ground. The reality of his irresponsible gaming soon followed. Her portion and her sisters' were long since gone, gambled away.

Fortunately, the lands had been untouched and the rent rolls had sustained their property, though meagerly, all these years. But they had had little money for the fripperies so necessary to every lady's general contentment, and certainly not for the much-needed improvements about the manor house.

Her dreams as well as the hopes of her younger siblings had been buried with Simon Pamberley. She had not been to London, therefore, since her first Season, but Alby's anecdotes were bringing every memory of that marvelous spring back as though it was yesterday.

Surrounded as he was by such a doting audience, he launched into a description of Astley's Amphitheatre, which had Katherine's eyes lit in a glow. She felt sick at heart suddenly. Katherine would adore the astonishing horsemanship of the Astley riders. How much she wished just once Katherine could see the famous show.

Her gaze shifted to beautiful Marianne and to Celeste. How they would have taken the entire town by storm, perhaps making brilliant matches and outshining the daughters of dukes and earls. And Augusta! She could have gone to the British Museum or the Royal Academy, not to mention the Tower of London.

As she looked at Augusta, her thoughts cleared sufficiently to become aware that the youngest Pamberley sister was sitting on a footstool beside the chaise longue on which Alby was situated. She held her hand inside a copy of *Ivanhoe*, marking a place for Alby, who had just a few minutes earlier been reading to them. She was watching him with her heart in her eyes, her face aglow. Was it her imagination, or when Alby turned toward her did his expression become quite fond as well, or was that his charm, that he could simply reflect whatever his admirer was at that moment feeling?

She suddenly hoped very much that Ramsdell would become well enough in the next day or so to take Alby—Charles—back to Bedfordshire. Augusta was indeed badly smitten, and the longer Charles remained at Lady Brook, the harder for her poor heart to bid farewell to a man she would never see again. Besides, she was already quite miserable with remembering what her life, what their lives, were supposed to have been.

She glanced at the clock quite impatiently and was rather surprised to find that for the first time that evening—probably during her quite ridiculous reveries about London—the hour had advanced to ten past eight. She rose at once to quit the drawing room. She might have explained where she was going, but since Alby held the attention of her four sisters in rapt awe, she kept her peace.

She made her way slowly to Ramsdell's bedchamber. Her heart was beating quite traitorously in her chest in loud thumps. For the life of her, she could not bring her pulse to a normal tempo. She smoothed her skirts, and the wisps of hair at the nape of her neck a dozen times in her progress toward his room. She laughed at herself for being so silly, yet she would fidget and her heart would beat.

She reached his bedchamber and lifted her hand to knock. Her fingers trembled. She stamped her foot, shook her head, and rapped lightly three times. After a moment, Marchand opened the door to her. She inquired if his lordship was yet asleep and whether he needed anything.

She saw that he was about to suggest she inquire on the morrow, but Ramsdell's voice intruded. "Marchand, if that is Miss Pamberley, I would have a word with her."

Marchand seemed slightly distressed but acquiesced in his quiet, gracious manner. He accompanied her to the side of the bed, but the viscount glanced at him and said kindly, "Do go to the kitchens, Marchand, and enjoy a glass of brandy for me. Dr. Kent left strict orders I was not to have a drop of spirits until I was better recovered."

Marchand coughed faintly, intending to protest and glancing more than once at Constance, but Ramsdell added, "Please. It would gratify me to know that you had a respite. Besides, Miss Pamberley can tend to me if I need anything."

Marchand responded in a tight voice, "Yes, m'lord."

Constance had the distinct impression he was disapproving of her, or at least of her visit. She followed him with her gaze as he left the room. When the door was shut upon him, she turned to look at Ramsdell and found that he was smiling faintly as he watched her.

"You must forgive him, you know," he said. "He has been with me since I can remember and has very particular ideas about young ladies of quality visiting men in their chambers, especially so late at night."

The absurdity of the notion, since Ramsdell was so ill, quite fit Constance's sense of humor, and she couldn't help but chuckle. "I know very well just how devoted he is to you, but perhaps you ought to explain to him that you could hardly ravish anyone in your present condition."

Now, why had she said something so provocative to him?

He seemed a little surprised at first, and then his features softened into a smile and something else. He sighed and scanned her from head to foot. "More's the pity," he remarked.

How odd to think that something she normally would have found reprehensible, when spoken by Ramsdell seemed more a compliment than an insult. The ocean began to roll through her stomach, and she caught her breath. He was looking at her again in that way of his. She could feel the strength of his soul as he gazed at her and scrutinized each feature.

"Where is my quizzing glass," he stated at last. "I could look at you for hours. Faith, but you're uncommonly pretty. What a tale I shall be able to tell once I've returned to Aston Hall, of the lovely woman with the face of Aphrodite who nursed me back from death's door. I'm glad you left off your cap. You are far too young to be covering up your hair in such a fashion."

There were many things she could have said to such a comment, uppermost a depressive reminder that she was nearly thirty and of an age to wear caps and dark colors and all the other accoutrements of a confirmed ape-leader. Instead, she let the compliment swell her heart.

So he thought her uncommonly pretty. How nice. How very, very nice.

She had meant for this visit to entail one or two pertinent questions about his health, perhaps an expressed hope he was feeling better tomorrow, and a quickly spoken goodnight. Now, however, she found herself thanking him as she drew forward a chair and sat down next to the bed. She then added, "When Mama became ill some seven years ago, I felt compelled to take on a more austere demeanor, wearing caps and the like—especially since I was only two and twenty at the time. The merchants, seeing that I was woefully inexperienced, attempted time and again to humbug me with wretchedly inflated bills and the like. You've no idea."

He smiled. "Of course that is the way it would be. But

how clever of you to have dealt with them so masterfully." His tone became laughingly sardonic. "And I'm very sure that donning a cap at two and twenty would have made you look like an antidote."

She laughed, remembering the confusion of that first year. "I was so green," she remarked. "You would have been greatly amused. But I soon settled down to learn how to manage everything, and before the year was out I was being treated with great respect, even a certain fondness that has saved me many a tuppence since."

"I've little doubt of it," he said sincerely. He shifted to a slight angle on his side so that he could see her better. His left arm was still heavily bandaged and pinned to his chest so that he had only slight maneuverability. "Everything changes when the reins are passed, doesn't it? Moreso, I think, when the moment arrives unexpectedly."

She knew he was speaking as much of himself as he was of her. "When did you inherit Aston Hall?" she asked. "I apprehend the event was unlooked for."

"Yes," he agreed. "I was twenty-six at the time—which was, good God, eleven years ago."

She considered this, tilting her head slightly. "That would explain it, then."

"What?"

"Mr. Kidmarsh has been downstairs surrounded by my sisters for the past two hours, speaking of all his London experiences. I couldn't help but be reminded of my come-out Season. I recalled meeting a great many people and seeing numerous notables, but I couldn't remember having ever seen you. But, of course, then, you would have been in mourning, for that was eleven years past."

"A long time ago." He searched her face and her eyes. "I should like to have met you then. You are lovely now, but I would imagine in the first blush of youth you must have set the entire *ton* on its ear."

"Hardly. I am quite tall, you see, a regular Long Meg, and

though I may not have a mountain of experience, I do know that there is scarcely a gentleman around who enjoys being looked square in the eye by any female."

He laughed outright and continued chuckling for a moment. "You have the right of it. There can be no two opinions on that score." He then waggled his brows. "I'm a tall man. I'm sure you couldn't look me directly in the eye."

Her heart turned over. He was flirting again. She wondered just how much taller he was than she and what it would be like to really look up to a man in that way. She recalled the moment of his accident when he had risen up in his curricle, like a mythological god, and pulled his horses to a halt. He had seemed like a giant.

"You are blushing," he said, teasing her a little more. "Have I said something improper?"

"No," she responded promptly. "You've *said* nothing improper, you've only inferred it."

He grinned. "So I have."

But she was liking this conversation a deal too much.

He said, "I returned to London the next year. Did you not want a second Season?"

She sighed. "Papa died that fall and—" She hesitated telling him the truth, for it was still a painful subject.

"And?" he prompted.

Constance could think of no reason to refuse confiding in him. After all, he would be gone in a handful of days so what harm could it possibly do?

"And . . ." she began again, "all that I was used to taking for granted was gone—except our home. London might as well have been as far away as China." She paused, but when she saw the concerned light in his eye, she couldn't help but continue, "I don't repine, I promise you, especially since at least I had one Season. My sisters have had far fewer advantages."

"What happened? A loss on the 'change?"

She shook her head and chuckled a bit. "Papa—whom I

adored—had taken to gaming at the various East End establishments that spring and the Season prior, I think. His pockets were well to let when he passed on."

"My poor child," he murmured.

"Oh, no, pray! I will tolerate a great deal from anyone except pity. The Season was a thrilling event and something I shall never forget, but I'm convinced that over time the delights of Mayfair would have worn thin had I continued attending that riotous event annually. Tell me this is not true."

Ramsdell sighed. "Very much so," he said. His eye took on a faraway expression. "The faces become too familiar; the feminine artifices used to make the most brilliant match of the Season a trying affair, the sheer opulence and extravagance becomes mundane, if that is even possible. I've taken to refusing more invitations than I accept when I am in London. The world, the beau monde, becomes a stifling place indeed." His eye cleared a little. "Of course, that might be different were you there."

His smile showed he was teasing and flirting again.

"Are you always so wicked when you are ill?"

"You forget—I am never ill. I have never been ill except for this ridiculous accident. So I can't possibly answer your question."

"You amaze me. You don't even seem tired. Are you not fagged to death of the moment?"

He seemed pleased by her compliment. "I daresay it's the company," he responded generously. "Oh, you are blushing again. How delightful!"

The air seemed to crackle. He fell silent as he watched her, his gray eyes smiling. She could think of nothing to say. She didn't want to speak. She wanted to look into his eyes and drink from his soul.

"Did you kiss me?" he asked abruptly.

She felt her cheeks warm.

"Oh, glorious day, *you did!*" He was smiling hugely. "I

recalled your lips pressed to mine, but I was convinced until this moment that I had imagined it."

She felt even the edges of her ears begin to burn. She had hoped, trusted, that the laudanum would have tricked his memory. Apparently, she was wrong. She placed her cool hands on her cheeks. "I do beg your pardon, m'lord. The gesture was not meant to be flirtatious or offensive. You see—"

"You don't need to explain," he interjected. "How could I possibly have been offended when I fell into the sweetest slumber ever with the feel of your lips on mine. As for flirting, what a ridiculous notion to think you might have been flirting with a near corpse."

She felt compelled to say, "I cared for my father when he was ill in a like manner. I—" Tears danced on her lashes.

"No, pray don't cry. I never meant to overset you—"

"I didn't want you to die," she blurted out "All the sensations were too familiar. I wanted you so to live, and when you did, I said a prayer of thanksgiving and kissed you."

"You saved me," he whispered.

"No," she chuckled. "No. You had already chosen life, Ramsdell. I was just expressing my gratitude, that's all."

Fifth Viscount Lord Ramsdell looked at Miss Constance Pamberley and felt his heart lurch and strain toward her. From the moment she entered his bedchamber, he had felt lit with a fire he couldn't understand. When he had said that part of his strength was a result of her company, he had meant it. He was drawn to her, he was taken with her, and the rapport he felt conversing in this so-delightful manner was like nothing he had ever known before. He realized with a start that had he been even half recovered, he would have slid from bed and gathered this beauty up in his arms and kissed her quite thoroughly. But perhaps his weakened state was proving a blessing of sorts, because warning bells suddenly clanged sharply within that portion of his mind relegated to common sense.

Where could such a kiss end?

What was he doing, flirting hell-bent with a woman who was little more than an innocent for all her abilities and even her age?

Even so, he felt poised on a precipice above a clear blue sea, ready to dive in and enjoy a marvelous swim.

Yet again, he had to ask himself—to what end?

A country flirtation amid his set, in which the rules were straightforward and understood by all was one thing. But this—the camaraderie resulting from Miss Pamberley's nursing, coupled with his admiration of her person and her character, were not covered by the careful rules of his usual society. What if she tumbled in love with him? What if he tumbled in love with her, which, given the peculiarly powerful sensation that seemed to surround his heart in just speaking with her, he suspected was a possibility.

Yet the question would not go away—where could any of this end?

He had never been a man to follow his impulses—as Charles was. He laid out his course carefully, and with allowances for one or two happy accidents along the way, he stayed with his course and because of it enjoyed a comfortable life full of excellent friendships and an estate that was growing annually. He sat in the House of Lords and involved himself in the pressing social issues of the day. And he was waiting for exactly the right woman to marry—the daughter of a peer, endowed with a proper portion, and prepared to become a notable London hostess. A woman who was his equal in every way—intelligent, sensible, and, hopefully, loving.

Miss Pamberley was the latter but certainly not the former.

He watched her rise to her feet. "You are tired," she said graciously, a half-smile on her lips. "I'll leave you to your slumbers. Good night." The smile wavered for a moment on her lips, then disappeared. She turned away from him. He wasn't fooled. There was a certain tightness about her eyes.

She had understood his silence, and he had little doubt that the expression on his face had betrayed his thoughts.

So much the better. Flirting with her had been foolish in the extreme. Far better to end the possibilities now.

"Miss Pamberley," he said as she moved away from the bed.

"Yes?" she turned back toward him, her expression guarded.

He extended his right hand toward her. She looked at it for a moment, then came forward and laid her hand in his. "Thank you for everything," he said softly. "Had our circumstances been different . . ." He looked at her. He willed her to understand.

She smiled down at him. "Yes, but if only you had not been such a very tall man."

He chuckled and released her hand. She left with her head high. She was dignified to the last.

He should have been utterly gratified by the exchange, but with the passing of a bare handful of minutes after the door closed behind her, something inside him began to hurt.

FIVE

Constance did not visit Lord Ramsdell again over the next several days. Instead, she questioned Marchand at the beginning and ending of each day regarding his master's progress. His recitals were succinct and quite tactful, but she gained an increasing sense that Ramsdell was proving to be a difficult patient, something she could easily understand.

By the fifth day, Marchand's eyes and lips had grown pinched with extreme forbearance, and she could see that he was nearly worn to the bone waiting on his fractious master. She desired very much to give him a much-needed respite, but she knew instinctively that Ramsdell would not allow it.

The viscount was a man of sense and discipline, just as she was a woman with similar qualities, and she knew very well he would not be gentle in his dismissal of her next time. Therefore, she stayed the impulse to offer her assistance, which, she believed, would have been refused anyway.

Still, she was troubled by Marchand's suffering and hoped that some circumstance might arise that would allow her to offer her help regardless of Ramsdell's wishes.

As she went about her business on the fifth day, she recalled to mind the conversation she had shared with him that first evening of his recovery. In all her nine and twenty years she had never enjoyed such an easy, exciting rapport with a gentleman. She had felt in those brief minutes that she had met a soul so similar to her own, she wondered whether it

was possible she had known him or met him before, perhap
even in another life, which was silly, of course, but the ser
sation was so profound, she couldn't help but wonder.

Yet, he was a peer of the realm, and she a spinster daughte
of a country gentleman whose death had revealed the scan
dalous nature of his gaming habits. A connection betwee
her family and his, even in friendship, was unthinkable.

Besides, friendship was not in the least what had bee
ebbing and flowing between them that night, not when sh
had spoken so scandalously of ravishment and he had con
fronted her about the kiss she had placed on his lips the nigl
his fever turned.

She had even shed some tears after leaving his room tha
night, so unlike her, tears of regret that her future must b
endured entirely without him.

Then she had awakened the next day, set her shoulders t
the work in front of her, and ignored the occasional flutterin
of her stomach when Ramsdell's name was mentioned b
her sisters or Alby. She had turned her interests elsewher
and had directed her attention instead to Mr. Kidmarsh, wh
was still pretending not to know his name or his residence
or his family, yet, so surprisingly, could recall every othe
detail of his life—every trip to London, every fox hunt, ever
ball he had ever attended, the vile taste of the waters at Batl
the color of the draperies in the music room at the Brighto
Pavilion, all the cities he had visited in Europe three year
before—including a lengthy recounting of the battlefield a
Waterloo—the brilliance of Turner's paintings, the odd whit
flecks in John Constable's extraordinary work, his first meet
ing with Lord Byron—*all this,* and yet he just could nc
seem to recall his own name.

Constance still felt it was not her place to confront hin
about his identity. Because his guardian was under her rool
she felt the obligation belonged to him, and when he wa
fully recovered, the viscount could address the matter witl
Alby himself. However, her sympathy for Alby's "delicat

constitution" ended the second day of her self-induced banishment from Ramsdell's rooms. She had risen early that morning, before her sisters had awakened from their slumbers, and happened to observe Alby racing Lord-a-Mercy across the east lane in a neck-or-nothing fashion that would have astonished her had she not long since suspected his duplicity.

Later, she had caught him entering the door of the morning room, which opened onto a sweeping terrace, his face flushed and his brow beaded with perspiration. He had appeared so guilty that she could have laughed had she not feared he would misunderstand her amusement, for he was in so many ways an ungovernable child. She withheld her laughter, therefore, and merely leveled a stern stare at him, offering her hope that his damp brow was not the first sufferings of a brain fever.

Poor Alby! He had fallen all over himself assuring her that it was no such thing, he was perfectly well, she needn't have any fear on that score! He then nearly let the cat out of the bag by begging her, "Pray do not send Marchand to me."

She eyed him curiously, a faint smile on her lips. "Why ever would I do that, Alby?" she had asked with a great pretense to innocence.

His blush deepened. "I—that is, yesterday he came to see me and . . . and spoke to me as though he knew who I was. He began twitching at the sheets and touching my forehead and begging to know if I was well. I *can't bear* to be cosseted in that manner, you've no idea!"

His story had been almost convincing, except that he had stammered a deal too much to be entirely credible and his cheeks were a fiery red. Regardless, she suspected his complaints of Marchand might be true. Even Ramsdell had hinted that his staff *doted* on the poor boy.

She had let him go after that, assuring him that Marchand was fully occupied tending to Ramsdell and that he had nothing to fear from her.

He had been fulsome in his gratitude and had left her o
a hasty stride. Afterward, he had become wary of her, ye
even more respectful than before, which was a good thing
since a direct result had been that he had begun to tempe
some of his flirtations with her sisters.

She had since that time started observing Charles Kid
marsh with fond detachment. Though his presence was
threat to the hearts of her sisters, especially to Augusta'
otherwise he was in every way a quite harmless creature. H
never crossed the line and seemed inordinately content t
amuse them all, a propensity that kept her house full c
laughter, and that made the evenings a joy.

But today, nearly three weeks since Alby's arrival at Lad
Brook, she decided that the household must begin resumin
its more normal workings and occupations. Many of th
household tasks were not being attended to properly wit
two patients in the house to occupy the staff and all the Pam
berley ladies.

She wasn't certain when the notion had bit her, perhap
when she heard Alby complain bitterly to Augusta that muc
of his life had been lived in the sickroom, but it came to he
that a mite of labor would not be a bad thing for Alby.

Therefore, she presented him with a choice—he could s
idle with no one to keep him company since all the sister
had numerous chores to perform, or he could offer his as
sistance in helping the ladies perform their tasks. In additio
to sustaining the usual ladylike occupations of practicing th
pianoforte and vocalizing, reading for the strict purpose o
increasing their knowledge, and painting with watercolors
the Pamberley sisters were constantly employed in repairin
their clothes as well as the household linens, enhancing thei
gowns with embroidery and other frippery, sewing baby an
children's clothes for the poor, gathering honey for both Lad
Brook as well as to distribute to the needy, berrying in sea
son, collecting fruit from the orchards for preserves for th
winter, delivering bread to the parson to be passed amon

those in need, and visiting the sick and infirmed among several surrounding villages and hamlets.

Alby was stunned when she read him the list of the ladies' duties and watched as he blanched. "I had no idea," he said, looking much struck. "Have I—have I been keeping them from all this?"

Constance was surprised at his display of conscience. She decided he ought to hear the truth. "Yes, you have, but I'm not certain the holiday they have enjoyed was an unfortunate occurrence. My sisters have not laughed so much in years, and for that I am grateful to you."

His face grew pinched and his gaze dropped to the carpet. What his thoughts were she could not guess, but she was pleased that when he met her gaze once more there was a determined light in his eye. "I shall be happy to offer my assistance to whatever tasks will require the most effort. I have been so appreciative of my time in your home, Miss Pamberley."

"I can see that you have," she responded sincerely. She considered him for a moment and realized that there might be one singular purpose to which his talents could be put to noble use. She said, "I was wondering how you might feel about reading to my mother, especially since you excel at it as you do. Augusta told me she introduced you to her the other day. I realize that her infirmity might be unsettling, so if you feel disinclined to take up such a role as I am suggesting, I will understand." She smiled. "Though I don't hesitate to tell you she particularly favors the novels by the author of *Waverly.*"

His eyes brightened. "As do I," he responded. Some strong emotion began working across his face. After a long pause he continued. "I would be happy to read to your mother. I have spent much of my life within the confines of a sickroom, so much so I'm fairly certain I know precisely how she is feeling of the moment." Again she heard an edge of bitterness to his voice.

"Excellent," she added.

All that remained now was to which of her sisters ough she assign the role of helping Alby learn better how to communicate with her mother. The best qualified was Augusta who had a dozen times more patience than any of the others Yet, she already understood the state of her youngest sister's heart, and for that reason felt ill at ease about giving the task to her. On the other hand, Augusta would make the entire experience for both Mrs. Pamberley and Charles a pleasant one.

In the end, she chose to send Augusta, which brought a rush of pleasure to the young woman whose complexion immediately began to glow.

Constance shook her head as she watched the pair amble toward the stairs. What would be the end of this *tendre?* she wondered. At least she could count on Augusta's sensible nature. Unlike Marianne, Augusta would never consent to an elopement.

She gathered her remaining three sisters together and discussed how best to tackle all the work that had piled up since Alby's arrival three weeks earlier. None of her siblings showed much enthusiasm until she mentioned that she had persuaded Alby to assist them in their chores. A rainbow might as well have suddenly appeared over the table of the morning room in which they were situated, since each expression changed as though a cloudburst had just been followed by brilliant sunshine.

A general excitement ensued along with a lively discussion regarding which tasks Alby should help complete. Settling this complex problem, since there was so much work to be done, required arguing the matter out for a full forty-five minutes, something Constance was content to allow her sisters to do.

In the end, a list was drawn up so that when Alby returned to the morning room, rather subdued by his visit to Mrs.

Pamberley's sickroom, Marianne happily showed him his assignments.

Constance bit her lip as Alby stared at the list and paled. She wondered if perchance he was beginning to regret that he had agreed to offer his help. Perhaps once he had tasted of the rigorous regimen of manor life, his memory would return in full force and he would be more than content to resume his identity as Charles Kidmarsh, impoverished ward of Lord Ramsdell.

Well, only time would tell.

She couldn't help but chuckle as her sisters swept him in a brotherly manner out of the morning room and toward the door to the terrace. Collecting honey was the first object of the day, and though Alby was obviously trepidatious, she was proud that he squared his shoulders and accepted his fate in a manly fashion.

Perhaps there was hope for him yet!

He stepped onto the terrace with all the ladies clustered about him supportively. They were busily instructing him on how to behave around the several beehives in the northeast field of clover, then the door shut firmly on Constance. She finally let go of a trill of laughter that had been trapped in her throat.

Poor Alby!

That evening Alby was quiet as the ladies sang their duets. He seemed very tired, and when Augusta quietly inquired whether he was feeling well, he smiled faintly and said, "Very much so. I've never known one could ache in so many odd places. Even my feet hurt."

"Well, we did walk all the way to Hartfield, which was a full five miles—and back again."

He chuckled faintly. "I thought we would never get there and the return! Good God, how do you do it every day?"

Augusta patted his shoulder. "We don't. Sometimes we go to Farnbury, which is seven miles distant."

Alby groaned and shook his head. "Not tomorrow, I hope."

Augusta smiled sweetly. "No, not tomorrow." She then blushed a trifle as she added, "You were very kind to those children, Alby. Most gentlemen would not have taken the time to play blindman's buff and tell them conundrums."

Constance watched his face as he grew thoughtful. "I like children, to own the truth. I was an only child and I really didn't get to play as other children did growing up, so today felt as though I were putting my childhood right."

"How sad for you," she blurted out sympathetically. "I've never known a moment without the company of my sisters. I don't think I should have liked growing up alone."

His face grew rather hard. "No one should have to. The expectations are really wearing on the—but what am I saying? I must be boring you to tears."

Augusta was quite ready to protest, but Alby shook off his fatigue. "No, no! Do not argue with me. I refuse to dwell on any of my supposed miseries and instead intend to see you and your sisters entertained." He immediately gained his feet, and turned to Marianne, who was at the pianoforte. "Will you play us a country dance, Miss Marianne?"

Marianne agreed readily because dancing quickly followed and the result was a lively half hour that set a perfect end to a long day.

The next morning, Constance fully expected Alby to announce to the world he had miraculously regained his memory in the middle of the night. From what she knew of his upbringing, she would have supposed he would rather resume his identity as the much cosseted Charles Kidmarsh than wear himself to the bone aiding her sisters in their numerous chores.

But in this she was happily disappointed, for the first thing Alby said to her upon arriving at the morning room for breakfast was that he desired very much to read again to Mrs.

Pamberley before engaging in the chores of the day, if that would suit her.

Constance was stunned by his noble attitude. "Mr. Kid—I mean, Alby, how very thoughtful of you. When I spoke with her yesterday afternoon, I asked how she enjoyed your reading ability and she fluttered her eyelashes. Her eyes were glowing with pleasure. You really do know how to make each of the characters so distinctive, so alive. I am indebted to you and"—here she hesitated, for she did not want to embarrass him, but decided to speak her mind anyway—"and I'm very proud of you for entering the spirit of our household with such a willingness to work."

He seemed stunned at first, then a strange, almost sad expression came over his face. "I didn't think a home could be like this. All of you help one another at every turn, and each has a share in the labors."

"Yes, but only because we are as poor as church mice," she responded almost gaily, for she didn't want him to think more of her home than was seemly. "Had matters been different, I daresay we would have had servants a-plenty and lived lives of lavish self-indulgence."

His expressive face twisted with scorn. "Indulgence is not necessarily all that one would believe it to be. Yesterday"—and here he straightened his shoulders—"was one of the happiest days of my life."

He then dumbfounded her by asking if he could take Mrs. Pamberley's breakfast to her.

Constance wasn't certain just what to say. "I—I suppose so, but you must understand the care with which she must be fed."

"I have had much experience having a spoon shoved down my throat," he stated almost to himself, "but I believe I could do a better job than most . . . and I want to, if you would but let me try."

"Come with me, then," she said. "We'll ask Mama."

Mrs. Pamberley was clearly astonished and did not blink

at first. But after a moment of gazing into Alby's direct, un-flinching stare, she acquiesced with a single, confident blink and a crooked smile. Constance stayed with him in order to make certain he could manage the awkward task. He fumbled a bit at first, but eventually found by supporting her properly with pillows and sliding his arm beneath her shoulders he could feed her with ease. After five minutes, he was in full command and performed the task with surprising gentleness, as though he had been doing it all his life.

Constance observed him, aware that more lay beneath the surface of this childlike man than she had at first supposed, and decided that fate, indeed, must have brought him to her door. His profession of having enjoyed the preceding day, along with his desire to be of service to her mother, spoke of an awakening spirit and a growing maturity. Lady Brook, indeed, might just make a man of him.

When she returned to the morning room, she found that her sisters were nearly finished with breakfast. She told them of Alby's kindnesses toward their mother, and a brilliant silence filled the room.

Augusta spoke for them all. "He is an angel."

"I am beginning to think so," Constance said.

Celeste added her thoughts. "Even Sir Henry, who has a good heart, never offered to read to Mama or to . . . to feed her."

Marianne said, "Alby is a strange man, isn't he, Constance? I mean, he's not like other men at all. I've begun to think there's something wrong with him."

These words brought Augusta to her feet. "How can you say such a disloyal, ungenerous thing, when he has kept you laughing and dancing for days on end?"

Marianne had the grace to blush. "I didn't mean to disparage his character—" But she could not continue. So long as Alby appealed to her sense of what a gentleman ought to be, he was acceptable to her. But a man in a sickroom was apparently not her idea of manliness.

Constance said, "I think you are forgetting, Marianne, that from all that Alby has told us of his youth, he was frequently in the sickroom himself, as a patient. I think I understand his wish to help, because he knows how trying it is to be cared for by rough hands, overly loud voices, and clumsy fingers."

Marianne blushed a little more. "He is being compassionate then."

"Yes," Augusta said softly. "He is defined by his compassion. For instance, I think he knew what we needed in our home more than anything was dancing and laughter. Don't you remember, that after speaking of London and all the balls he attended, when you expressed your great longings to dance and have a great many beaus, he immediately suggested we dance? Why do you think he did so?"

Marianne stared at Augusta and blinked several times. "I see what you mean now. It was almost as though he had read my mind and set out to please me."

The ladies then described a dozen ways in which Alby responded instantly to their wishes and longings, whether with the suggestion of a stroll about the rose garden, or an anecdote about London, or Bath or Brighton, or getting up a country dance.

It was therefore not surprising that when Alby returned to the morning room, he was greeted with at least a half dozen requests to know in what ways the young ladies could tend to him. The effect was extraordinary. Alby stared at them as though they had just come from the moon. "I—I don't know what to say in the face of such kindness, except that truly nothing would please me more than to join you in your tasks today."

As they set about reorganizing the day's events, Constance left them to see to her mother.

Mrs. Pamberley expressed her deep gratitude for Alby's presence in her room by blinking no to such comments as awkward, frightening, or barely endurable. She settled only for *pleasurable.*

Did she want him back on the morrow? A long, single blink.

She left her mother, to begin her own day's activities, which involved conferring with Cook about the week's menus, and with Stively about the needs of the stable and the status of the wheat fields.

She did not get far, however. She nearly collided with Marchand, who left Ramsdell's rooms in a state of extreme agitation. "What is it?" she cried at once upon seeing his distress.

"I—I—" He could not get past this single word.

She nodded, trying to encourage him, but he couldn't speak. "Come to the library," she said at last, believing she understood the problems pressing the overwrought servant. "We'll discuss the matter in private."

After several minutes of plying him with questions, the truth came out. Ramsdell was insistent on leaving his bed, but Marchand feared for the weakness of his legs. "And I am not strong enough to support him," he cried. "If he falls, he could reinjure his arm, and what if the wound tore and became infected again—he is so stubborn!"

Constance saw the panic in his eyes and turned the matter over in her mind several times. "I would like to see him," she announced at last.

"I shall wait here," he stated, surprising even Constance. Marchand had previously been entirely disapproving of her presence in the sickroom once Ramsdell regained consciousness.

She made her way slowly to Ramsdell's bedchamber, wondering just what she hoped to achieve by seeing the viscount. Six days had passed since her last encounter with him, and she knew very little of the nature of his progress except for the brief words exchanged with Marchand. Perhaps more than anything, however, she wanted to judge for herself the precise state of his health as well as his mind so that she would know better how to advise Marchand.

She scratched lightly on the door and heard a sharp, "Come!" barked from the other side. She was a little startled, but when she opened the door she saw the reason for Ramsdell's irritation.

"Oh," she murmured, then swiftly crossed the chamber to his bed. He was sitting on the side, his brow damp with perspiration. He was wearing breeches and stockings, which apparently he had put on by himself, but his shirt was hanging half off his back. His complexion was chalky from the effort of dressing himself.

"Good God, why are you here?" he snapped. "Where the devil is Marchand?"

"As to that," she responded softly, drawing his shirt from behind his shoulder and draping it over his bandaged arm, "your valet is sitting quietly in the library, worrying himself to the point of illness over your health."

He grunted. "It is time I left this room," he stated belligerently.

Constance leaped back and looked him in the eye. "I couldn't agree more," she said firmly. She did not mistake the look of surprise that flashed across his face.

"Well, if that is so," he said, "I wish you might tell my valet. He nearly swooned when I made known to him my intentions and then he refused to dress me."

She smiled. "Do you believe I have the power to sway his opinions?"

Ramsdell scowled at her but did not answer her question.

"Do stop playing the ogre," she coaxed, "and try for a little reason, if you would."

"A little reason!" he exclaimed. "How can I be reasonable, when I have been tied to this bed for weeks—"

"Less than a sennight since you regained consciousness," she interjected.

He scowled a little more. "He is driving me to distraction

with his constant fussing and tugging at the counterpane and asking me every quarter hour whether I am feeling too warm, or too cold, or in need of laudanum, or tea, or a pastille."

Constance held the shirt-sleeve up and looked at it for a moment. At this last remark, however, she caught his eye, "He did not suggest burning pastilles, did he?" she queried.

"Yes, he did, not an hour past."

Constance chuckled and reverted to studying the garment and his arm carefully.

He continued. "I couldn't bear it a moment longer, the cosseting and fidgeting. I begin to understand even better why Charles keeps running away from my house. The only wonder is that he did not do so *years* ago. I vow had I been him, I would have long since signed aboard a twenty-gun sloop, as . . . as a cook or something, than to have endured—"

"Do you know how to cook?" she asked, glancing at him, then turning away to search for a pair of scissors. She found what she needed in the top drawer of the chest of drawers. She was a great believer in having a dozen pair scattered about the house for convenience's sake. She returned to his side and to the dangling sleeve.

"No, I don't cook," he responded irritably. "That is not the point."

"I realize that," she retorted, "but I couldn't help but be amused by the thought of you cooking for thirty or forty men in the confines of a warship—or would it be closer to a hundred? How many men are aboard a twenty-gun sloop?" She carefully began cutting the sleeve of his shirt along what would be the inside of his arm and separating the side seam as well.

"Whoa!" he cried, catching her arm and preventing her from cutting farther. "What the devil—I mean, just what do you think you're doing? Weston would be astonished to see that you had ruined one of his finely crafted shirts."

She shook off his hand. "If you please, I'll demonstrate for you." She arranged the left front of his shirt over his chest and, buttoning it, lifted his heavily bandaged arm just a trifle. Her fingers brushed against the thick layer of hair covering his chest. She positively refused to feel anything but a detached interest in getting him dressed. Still, her fingers would tremble and her heart hammered away loudly.

"Weston?" she queried. "Yes, your London tailor. Well, I daresay he will not mind once he learns we had to accommodate your broken arm somehow and at the same time help you to present a proper appearance before the world." Once the cut was completed, she laid the fabric over his bandaged arm, slid the cuff about his wrist, and fastened the buttons. She gently tucked the fabric around his arm. "Celeste will be able to fashion plackets on the inside with buttons or hooks as fasteners to give a better fit for you, that is, if you wish for it. She is an accomplished needlewoman. Your coat you might want to wear slung over your shoulder for the time being, until you heal a little more. Eventually you will be able to slide your arm into your coatsleeves. But first, your waistcoat."

She lifted it off the back of the chair and carefully guided his broken arm through the wide armholes. When she completed buttoning the vest, she asked, "Do you wish me to fetch your coat?"

She glanced at him and saw that he was staring at her in wonder.

"Yes, if you please." His tone was almost pleasant.

She walked to the wardrobe and saw that Marchand had brought four coats with him. "Which one?" she inquired.

"The blue superfine will do."

She took the finely made coat from the hanger and returned to him. She helped him slide on the right sleeve and carefully pulled the coat across his back, settling the left sleeve over his shoulder.

"Now then," she said, stepping back from him. "You look very pale, and Marchand's greatest concern was that you would be too weak to support yourself once you stood. Do you think you can stand?"

"Stuff and nonsense."

She took his measure. "Perhaps so, but I believe Marchand is a trifle exhausted from worrying about your health and isn't thinking clearly. Why don't you walk about the chamber with me, for I'm very strong, you know, and I haven't the least fear that you will fall."

She smiled down at him.

"How do you do it?" he asked.

"Do what?"

"Manage me with such deftness as though you've been doing so for years?"

She met his gaze and felt her stomach squeeze up into a tight knot. "I have been used to dealing with my sisters, I suppose, and early on I learned that nearly every conflict has a basis in something practical—not enough buttons, or dolls, or ribbons. In this case, not enough nurses for you. Come. Stand up, then. Let's see this prowess of which you boast."

He planted his feet more than a foot apart and slowly rose up before her. He gained his height and the first thing that struck her was that he was several inches taller than she. He was right, she could look up at him. Her heart shattered into a thousand pieces.

Oh, dear. He was just the right height.

"How do you feel?" she asked, trying for an indifferent tone. "A little dizzy?"

"Yes, but I suspect that has nothing to do with my illness." He chuckled. "You are so much fun to tease—you blush like a schoolgirl."

"Only because you say the most outrageous things." Now, how was it possible that she had been with him but a handful of minutes and already, as before, she found herself on easy terms with him? The question could not be answered rationally. "Let me see you walk."

He took a deep breath and began walking across the carpet,

out when he rounded the end of the bed he took hold of a bedpost with his right arm and hugged it—hard. She went to him, looking quickly up at his face. His eyes were closed.

"Good God, the room is spinning," he murmured.

"You must sit down at once." She took his arm and led him to a wing chair near the wardrobe.

He sat down with a thud, leaning his head against the tall back. "Perhaps Marchand was right, I may not be ready to move about just yet, but the thought of spending another second in that bed—!"

"I think you are doing the right thing. You just need to go very slowly. Rest here for a while, then try to walk again. I'm convinced you will do better next time."

She drew forward a footstool for his feet, but when he refused it, she sat down at his knee.

"You are a great comfort to me," he said, looking down at her. "I wish you had come to me long before now."

"It would not have been wise," she said with a slight lift of her chin.

"No, definitely not, more so now that I've seen exactly how tall you are." He appeared charmingly disgruntled. "I'm beginning to understand why half the ladies of my acquaintance never appealed to me. Your height suits me exceedingly well."

She wondered if he was thinking the same thing, that if he were to hold her in his arms, she would be precisely the right fit for him.

He continued. "The fact is, I've nearly driven Marchand to distraction. I know that. I might complain of his ministrations, but I make the worst patient in the world."

"I don't doubt it for a second."

He looked down at her and chuckled. "You didn't have to agree with such spirit."

She smiled up at him.

"You've left off wearing your caps," he stated. "I like your hair dressed in curls like that."

"Thank you."

He met her gaze and her heart began to dance all ove
again. She should leave now and fetch Marchand to tend t
Ramsdell, only she didn't want to. Besides, Marchan
needed a respite from his labors. She rose and offered he
arm. "Come. Let's see if you can walk back to the bed."

"I'm *not* returning to bed."

"I wasn't suggesting you should, only that you walk wit
me and sit on the edge again—just for practice."

He obliged her and found that he was much steadier thi
time.

"Just as I thought," she said. "The dizziness appears t
be a result of having lain prone for so many days. Are you
legs trembling at all?"

He shook his head. "Not a bit." Even so, he sat down o
the bed and remained there for several minutes, then, entirel
without her aid, shuffled slowly back to the chair. "You wer
exactly right. I am only in want of a little practice. I ar
grateful to you."

When he sat down, she eyed him thoughtfully. "What if
had the chaise longue brought back to your chamber, the on
I slept in while I cared for you? You could rest there durin
the day with your legs supported for hours, if you wishe
which would give you some relief from the bed. It also migh
serve to relieve Marchand of some of his worries."

He nodded. "If it wouldn't be too much trouble."

"Not a bit. I do, however, have one request."

"Whatever you ask, I shall do."

"Will you promise for the next three days not to mov
about without someone in the chamber? I can't impress o
you enough how much your servant fears you will injur
yourself again by falling down."

He sighed. "If I must"—here he paused and met he
gaze—"but only if you promise to visit me."

Her heart stopped.

"Now, don't look at me in that manner," he said, a fain
smile on his lips, "as though I have just grown horns."

"You know very well I do not view you as some sort of menace—just a rather disturbing force."

"I disturb you, then?" he queried, his voice having dropped a full tone.

She shook her head at him. "You know very well you do, though I am persuaded it is just your height. In a day or so I shall have grown accustomed to a giant walking about Lady Brook and staring down at me." When his eyes became lit with a familiar fire, which meant his next words would be enticing, she quickly added, "And now I must go to Marchand."

She turned and strode to the door.

He called to her, leaning forward in his seat. "Pray do not neglect me, Miss Pamberley, or I vow you shall arrive one morning to find my valet's corpse on the floor. I am depending on you."

He seemed so earnest, so hopelessly desperate that she couldn't help but smile. "I always keep my promises. I shall be bringing Celeste with me in a short while, and together I'm sure we can contrive to alter your shirts to, er, Marchand's satisfaction, if that is to your liking?"

He slumped against the chair, obviously relieved. "Yes, indeed it is," he breathed. "Thank you—for everything."

Constance left the chamber, her heart in turmoil. She was both ecstatic that she would be seeing more of Ramsdell, yet at the same time she knew she should avoid him entirely. She was horridly susceptible to him, even though he was an irascible patient. She enjoyed the playful rapport they shared, and his fiery gray eyes always seemed to set her pulse racing and her stomach tumbling about as though caught in a whirlwind.

She took a deep breath as she closed the door behind her, summoning her courage and her discipline. Surely she could manage to spend a few minutes each day with Ramsdell without risking her heart's comfort. Surely!

SIX

Three mornings later, just past dawn, Constance stared at the numerous gowns scattered over her bed, thinking the collected lot resembled something of a rainbow. She was being ridiculous, of course, behaving like little more than a ninny-hammer about what gown she should wear for breakfast, for nuncheon, for tea, and for dinner. But Ramsdell's presence in her home had disrupted everything, including her long-held belief that what she wore no longer mattered, only that she should strive to appear prim and proper for the sake of bargaining with the tradesmen.

Now, however, all she could think was that every lady with whom Ramsdell was acquainted undoubtedly wore the latest in Parisian fashions and beside them all she must appear like a country dowd. A single glance at the various costumes before her confirmed this opinion.

The worst of it was, no matter how often she strove within her breast to be sensible about Ramsdell, she failed. He had begged her to attend to him, and she had acquiesced, but the result had proven terrifying since the few minutes she had decided she would spend in his company that afternoon quickly became an hour, then two, and of such sweet companionship that her heart seemed to be in a perpetual state of heightened sensation.

The same few minutes had been repeated later that evening, and several times over during the following two days.

He would recline comfortably on the chaise longue in his bedchamber, and she would sit in a chair adjacent to him.

Her thoughts, subsequently, had become fixed on Ramsdell, on being with him, conversing with him, arguing with him, watching him, reading to him and with him, challenging him, and even defying him.

That morning she had promised to bring his breakfast to him along with a copy of *The Times,* only she couldn't decide what to wear. All her gowns were made high to the neck, designed to give her a stern aspect, except a pale pink frock that was made of a gauzy muslin and required a lacy betsy to become suitable for morning wear. The undermaid had already dressed her hair in a becoming crown of ringlets, which she knew pleased Ramsdell, but which gown should she wear?

She chose the pink one, donning it quickly and carefully, and arranging the white lace betsy over the swell of her breasts. She was ready to pronounce herself prepared to enter Ramsdell's sick chamber, but she made the huge mistake of moving to the long mirror in order to make one last perusal of her entire ensemble.

What she saw there startled her. It was as though the clock had been turned back. She saw the young, excited maiden who had thoroughly enjoyed her first London Season so many years before, a beautiful young woman, just as Ramsdell kept saying to her, whose color was considerably heightened. She pressed her hands to her cheeks, knowing that the rosy glow that lit her face was because her heart was on fire and her whole being was illuminated. She was astonished and distressed. The situation was hopeless, and well she knew it.

"The devil take it!" she cried, shocking even herself at her unladylike choice of words.

She quickly stripped off the pink confection and donned a modest amethyst gown of patterned silk, made high to the neck and trimmed with a small point lace about the cuff of each short puffed sleeve. She then slid one of the gowns from off her bed and draped it over the long mirror, afterward returning the remaining gowns to her wardrobe. If she lingered sadly over the pink muslin, it was for only a brief moment. She refused to dwell on the unfortunate nature of her circumstance with respect to Ramsdell's prestigious rank. She straightened her shoulders, lifted her head high, and ordered her feet to take her about the day's business.

She made her way to the kitchens, and within a few minutes bore a tray, dressed with a deep red rose from the garden, and carried Ramsdell's breakfast to his bedchamber, just as she had promised.

When she entered his room, however, she suffered a shock, for he was neither reclining on the chaise longue nor on his bed, but was standing, fully dressed, by the window. Even his coat sleeves sheathed both arms, though a sling still kept his left forearm supported.

"Do but look at you!" she cried, smiling. "I can see that I have brought you your breakfast to no purpose. Am I to understand that you wish to join the ladies and your cousin in the morning room?"

He shook his head. "I had no such intention, only to show you the progress I have made, though I fully intend to go downstairs with you, but not until I have enjoyed the breakfast I knew you would bring me."

She felt her cheeks tingling with pleasure at his words. "Then, come," she responded brightly. "Sit in the chair and I'll serve you."

He crossed the room, and only then did she realize he was wearing his boots as well. "Your Wellingtons!" she cried.

He grinned. "I have been staring out at your exquisite roses for these past several days and hope you will join me in taking a turn about the garden this morning." He sat down in the chair and watched her.

"Of course I will," she responded promptly, settling her tray on the bed. She drew forward a small cherrywood table by the door and placed it in front of him. She then set the tray on the table and tucked a long linen napkin into the V of his waistcoat so that it flowed over his supported arm. She buttered his bread, she cut up his bacon, she broke up his apricot tartlet into manageable pieces, she poured his coffee, she served him.

The conversation ran first to local events—she had it on good authority that Lady Bramshill of Henley Lodge was planning a ball in a fortnight's time and that all the notables of the surrounding area would be in attendance.

"You will go, of course," he said.

"Yes. Lady Bramshill is a fine young woman with lively matchmaking propensities, which serves to keep the country alive with every manner of speculation."

"Has she succeeded yet in her occupation as matchmaker?"

"Of course. Since she began her campaign to see everyone properly paired, three weddings have ensued in less than two years—a quite adequate showing for a novice, don't you think?"

He smiled. "Undoubtedly."

"Would you attend were an invitation extended to you?" she asked. The query was an impulsive one, but once the words were out, she regretted them.

When the thought had entered her mind, she was only thinking how pleasant it would be to have such a good friend at the assembly to keep her company, but once the words passed her lips, she realized how inappropriate they were. "No, forget I said that. I wasn't thinking, Ramsdell, truly."

"I wish that I could oblige you."

"We both know it would be wholly inappropriate."

He nodded. "Very much so. Besides"—and here he tried for a lighter tone—"I suspect Charles and I will be gone by then, something I have little doubt you are desiring more than anything. It cannot have been easy to have had the care of two invalids in addition to all your usual responsibilities."

Constance blinked at him, considering what he had just said. She realized that though her life had seemed so crowded with her duties prior to Ramsdell's inauspicious arrival at Lady Brook, she hadn't felt even the slightest bit pinched for time. His presence seemed to have filled her with an abundance of energy that kept her moving briskly and happily throughout her usual regimen. The minutes passed like seconds. Besides, Alby had so completely immersed himself in her sisters' chores that he had become more of a benefit to Lady Brook than a drain on her resources.

"How odd," she said, her lips parting slightly.

"What?" he pressed, sliding a piece of tartlet into his mouth.

"It's silly, really. It's just that except for the fatigue I felt while you were ill, I have never felt quite so alive as now." She paused for a moment. He fixed his gaze on her as he took a sip of coffee. She continued. "I know what it is. I've just never had a friend like you before, someone I could talk to about everything. For instance, you seem to understand better than anyone how much I love Lady Brook because I'm involved in every aspect of her care and future development. I can see my own love of our lands reflected in your countenance when you speak of Aston Hall."

"Indeed." He smiled and sipped his coffee.

She nodded. "Your entire expression becomes quite animated when you speak of your ancestral lands."

He clattered his coffee cup on his saucer and leaned back in his chair with a heavy sigh. "You shouldn't do that, you know."

She was instantly distressed. "What have I done now? Have I said something I oughtn't?"

He nodded. "Yes. You have reminded me again why I'm going to miss you like the devil once I leave—which I am beginning to realize must be very soon."

Constance felt her throat constrict into a knot so tight, she felt as though she were being strangled. She looked away from him, rising to her feet and crossing the room to the window. He wasn't even gone and she was already missing him.

She looked down at the rose garden, where she could see Celeste, Marianne, and Katherine busily cutting flowers for the house. Augusta was standing up on a bench and giving directions to Alby for the successful navigation of the maze. She jumped down and Alby emerged, running out of the maze. She watched Augusta check her pocket watch, then begin hopping up and down. She could hear her sister squeal—how unlike Augusta!

Her sisters all paused in their labors, and she could hear them congratulating Alby on his navigation of the maze in a new record time.

She smiled and turned back to Ramsdell, who was just rising from his chair. "Your cousin is trying to set a record for the maze—the fastest time through. Jaspar Vernham holds the record of fifty-eight seconds, but then, he was eighteen at the time."

"Who is Jaspar Vernham?" he asked, crossing the room to join her by the window.

"He used to work in the stables, but he has since made his fortune in India."

"The one you were in love with when you were fifteen?" he queried. "Was that his name?"

"Goodness! Do you actually remember all the absurd things I tell you?"

His face grew somber suddenly. "That's the rub, I suppose. Nothing you tell me seems absurd, or ridiculous." She saw in his face a longing that reflected utterly the desire of her own heart. A faint despondency touched her spirits. He would leave soon, and with his departure he would take part of her heart away forever.

He took a step toward her, his brow knit faintly, questioning.

That particular question she did not want to answer.

"Perhaps we ought to take that turn about the rose garden," she suggested quietly.

He straightened his shoulders. "Indeed," he murmured, "that would be best."

Ramsdell walked slowly beside Constance, his mind and heart torn as never before. He tried to tell himself that the powerful feelings he felt for Constance were strictly because of the artificial intimacy of their situation—he as patient, she as nurse. But the part of him that demanded truthfulness knew that when she spoke of never having had a friend like him before, she was saying something as equally profound about himself. He had never, never known such easy discourse as that which he enjoyed with her.

For a moment, he had toyed with the notion of asking her to become his mistress. But a rebellion broke deeply within his soul at such a thought. Not for Constance to become any man's mistress! Never.

They had gone but a few feet down the hall when she looked up at him and asked, "How does it feel to be mobile once more?"

Even in the dim light of the hallway she was as beautiful as a lustrous summer day. The gown she wore, simple and elegant, only magnified her elegance of person and beauty of face and temperament. He was doused with longings of every kind, uppermost to steal her away from the world, to hold her close to him, and to spend hours communing with her.

He had forgotten the question she posed, so he simply smiled and let her read the contentment he felt in his eyes. He offered her his arm. A tremulous smile touched her lips. She wrapped her arm lightly about his and then, as though it were the most natural occasion in the world, laid her other hand on his forearm. Her touch sent a lightning bolt to his heart. Would it ever be different for him when she was around?

"You must be Lord Ramsdell," a voice intruded at the end of the hall.

Constance turned toward the staircase and saw Alby silhouetted by the light pouring in from the windows above the stairwell. She felt Ramsdell stiffen slightly beside her.

Alby began walking toward them both. "The ladies kept me informed of your condition. I can't tell you how relieved I am that you are walking about and appear to be recovering well."

"Charles?" he queried as though dumbstruck.

"I am known by a different appellation. The ladies call me Mr. Albion, or *Alby*, if you prefer. Am I acquainted with you?"

Even Constance was surprised by his performance. Charles was utterly convincing, appearing not to know who he was or that Ramsdell was his cousin. "Alby," she began, "are you not aware of your relationship to Lord Ramsdell?"

By then Charles had arrived to stand before them. He looked at her, his gaze slightly hazy as he shook his head. "Something about him, even about his name, seems familiar to me, but I do not know him."

Constance looked up at Ramsdell, whose face was hard with observing and suspecting. "You are so changed," he said. "I've never seen your skin so brown before."

At that he smiled faintly. "I have been walking a great deal since I recovered from my accident. All the ladies traverse half of Berkshire every day in the performance of some service or other. I have gotten into the habit of joining them." He turned to smile sweetly upon Constance. "The mistress of the house gave me the opportunity to either idle away my time waiting for her sisters to return from their various tasks or to help them." He glanced back at Ramsdell and his smile broadened a trifle. "I decided wisely to throw in my lot with the prettiest ladies in all of England. I have learned to gather honey, I have collected more berries than I thought existed, and in some of the loveliest copses in the world, I have walked more miles in the past sennight than I vow I have walked my entire life. Farnbury alone is seven miles—one way!" His gaze became strange and otherworldly. "I cannot help but feel as though I have stepped into a dream, a dream from which I do not wish to be awakened—ever. Ah, but I'm keeping you. Are you taking the air? You'll find nothing sweeter. I would beg to accompany you, but my duties lie in that direction."

He gestured down the hall.

Constance smiled, a warmth of appreciation flowing through her veins. "Mama enjoys her time with you more than anything, Alby. I do thank you again for reading to her and talking with her. I know she enjoys your company prodigiously."

He bowed slightly. "It truly is my pleasure, I beg you will believe that."

He nodded to Ramsdell, then walked in a dignified manner toward her mother's chambers.

"Good God," he murmured in a hushed voice. "He is so changed. I vow I would not have known him."

"Indeed?" Constance queried, a little surprised.

"Was he like this from the moment he awakened from the accident?" Ramsdell asked.

Constance shook her head, slowly considering his question. "No, not precisely. He was merry as a grig for a time, flirtatious, depending day and night on the lighthearted ministrations of my sisters. Somewhere, though, in the past sennight, he has been gradually becoming more, I don't know, *older*, I think."

"Is he growing up at last?" he asked faintly as he set them both in motion again.

"You may be right. I had no great opinion of your cousin when he first awakened. He seemed too eager to please and flirted outrageously with each of my sisters until I feared that one or the other of them would tumble head over ears in love with him and elope. Your accident ended my ability to watch him more closely in order to make certain nothing of that sort would happen, but by the time you recovered, I could see that he had tempered his conduct to a certain degree."

He had listened to her carefully, and when he reached the top of the stairs, he inquired, "Your house seems to have cast a spell over both my cousin and me. Or is this your doing? Have you made a man of Charles at last, for I am beginning to think it was brilliant of you to have encouraged him as you did to engage in such homey employments."

"I must confess," she said, beginning her descent yet still holding on to his arm, "that I didn't feel he would be harmed by a little strolling about our country lanes and—"

"A little *strolling?*" he queried, chuckling. "Seven miles to Farnbury and back—a little strolling?"

Constance could not suppress a trill of laughter. "That was yesterday, and if you must know, he retired to bed quite early. My sisters were destitute without his company for the remainder of the evening. For whatever your cousin may have been in his former life, he has brought a great deal of joy to our home in his new one." She was teasing him, of course, referring to new and old lives.

By now they had reached the bottom of the stairs, and she led him by way of the entrance hall and the hallway that led directly to the terrace into the sunshine and light of the beautiful late July day.

"What a beautiful morning," he said. "I feel as though I have not been out-of-doors for centuries." He took in a deep breath. "The air is so fragrant in July."

"Indeed, it is. Everything is so fully leafed that a kind of rich moisture hangs from every branch, flower, and blade. But, come. The rose garden will be intoxicating with the sunshine brightly on the blossoms."

When she arrived through an arched break in a neatly

groomed hedgerow of yew, she was greeted by her four sisters, each of whom bore a general air of contentment, prettily flushed complexions from their labors, and a basket of freshly cut roses.

"May I present my sisters, Lord Ramsdell?"

"I would be most gratified."

Constance made the formal introductions, and each sister greeted him warmly in turn, curtsying slightly, then offering him a hand to shake.

Marianne extended her hand and dimpled a smile. "We are all grateful for your renewed health. May you enjoy many more years to come."

"Thank you, Miss Marianne."

Celeste offered him a pink rose, which he took and held to his nose.

"Congratulations on your recovery," she said sweetly. "Were the shirts to your liking?"

"How can I ever thank you, Miss Celeste? I am wearing one of them now and will do so until the bandages can all be removed." Celeste turned pink with pleasure.

"Lord Ramsdell," Katherine cried. "I cannot credit that you are freed from the sickroom at last! Constance tells us that you are a great horseman. Mrs. Spencer calls you a nonesuch. Are you not longing to feel the reins again?" Her eyes shone with admiration as she looked up at him.

He took her proffered hand and shook it gently. "I have heard that Lord-a-Mercy is one of the finest hacks in the county and that you have an excellent seat. To answer your question, I ache to be flying against the wind."

Katherine nodded her eager understanding.

Augusta dropped a curtsy when he turned to her. "My felicitations as well, m'lord. We were sick with worry for a long time, and I offered many a prayer at the chapel on your behalf."

"Then I imagine it is to you that I owe my life. Thank you—Miss Augusta." Augusta smiled gently, and to her credit her gaze did not falter from his, though Constance could see she was trembling.

Marianne showed an inclination to engage him in conversation, but Constance was before her. "I was taking Lord Ramsdell on a brief turn about the rose garden, after which he has begged to make use of the library. When you have returned from Sandhill, we shall enjoy a nuncheon together."

Marianne showed the barest tendency to pout her disapproval of this scheme, but Constance had for so many years ruled the roost that she merely shrugged and bid Ramsdell farewell until the noon hour. The rest of the sisters followed suit, and once again Constance was alone with her noble guest.

"I am beginning to understand what Charles was saying. Being at Lady Brook does have a dreamlike quality."

Constance looked up at him, noting that his eyes were a little pinched. "Are you fatigued yet?"

"A little," he admitted. "But don't think I intend to take to my bed until much later."

She chuckled, and for the next fifteen minutes she led him up one row of rosebushes and down another. She gave a history of each, from which garden she had been given a slip to start, which of the plants showed a resistance to the pestilent aphids that attacked unceasingly until the fall, and which rose leaves never seemed affected by mildew even on the wettest of days.

When they had reached the end of the garden, he glanced around him. "This is the entrance to the maze, then," he said, gaining his bearings.

"Yes."

"Will you take me through it?"

"Do you feel capable of it, for it is quite large," she asked, a little surprised that he would even suggest such an expedition.

He narrowed his eyes. "Are you provoking me?"

She couldn't help but chuckle. "Follow me. There is a stone bench in the center. You can rest there for a time."

"What a poor fellow you must think I am."

"I think nothing of the sort, as well you know."

He took his time. It would seem he intended to memorize the pathway. With each turn, he glanced left, then right. When they finally reached the center, she turned to face him. "Do you think you could actually find your way out without assistance?"

He turned in a full circle. "Perhaps. Yes, I think I could."

She watched him carefully. She feared that he would collapse, but he showed no signs of any great fatigue.

"Would you like to sit down?" she asked, gesturing to the stone bench. She withdrew a kerchief from the pocket of her morning gown and walked toward the seat. "I think we could brush the dust off sufficiently." She balled the kerchief up and began swiping at the stone.

Ramsdell did not join her, however. She rose up from her labors and regarded him with a smile. "I promise you, your breeches will not suffer in the least. Shall I prove the strength of my convictions by taking up . . . my seat . . . first." Her words had dwindled away, for he was looking at her in a strange, penetrating manner. "Oh, dear," she murmured. She could read his mind, his thoughts. She didn't know whether to be deeply distraught or *aux anges*.

He moved toward her in three purposeful strides. He caught her at the back of her waist with his right arm and drew her roughly against him. "I can't do this properly, my fair Constance, not with one arm in a sling, but I vow I have been longing to kiss you from the moment I awoke to find you asleep in my bedchamber. I know I shouldn't, but I'm going to anyway."

She could have protested. She certainly could have easily fended him off; instead, her right arm snaked tightly about his neck and she leaned against his right side, careful not to put pressure on his injured arm. "Oh, Ramsdell," she breathed against his lips.

Then he kissed her, a searing kiss that sent ripples of pleasure cascading in wave after wave down her neck and side, clear to her toes. Constance lost herself in his embrace and in the feel of his lips pressed against hers. She recalled the moment preceding his accident, when he had stood up on the floorboards of his careening curricle and through sheer brute strength had drawn his team to a halt. She remembered thinking, "My goodness, he's so very tall." She was tall. She fit perfectly against him, just as she knew she would, and she wanted the kiss, the embrace, to go on forever.

A breeze dipped down into the center of the maze, catching at the hem of her amethyst gown and tugging at her ankles. The sun was warm on her shoulders and back. Ramsdell's arm and hand were restless over her waist. He held her in a tight grip, as though he feared she would run away if he released her. He drew back and kissed her eyes, her cheeks, her face. "I shouldn't be doing this."

Her voice caught on a light gasp. "No, you should not. But I am not a schoolroom chit, Ramsdell. I understand that you are giving no promises. So, kiss me again, if you please."

She heard him groan. She parted her lips and he kissed her deeply. She stroked his cheek and his chin and his ear. She knew she was half in love with him as surely as she knew that nothing could ever come of that love were it allowed to ripen and deepen. She drew back and settled her head on his shoulder.

"I wish my arm were not in a sling so that I could hold you against my heart."

She warmed to his words. She breathed deeply and drank each of them in. "Stay with me for a fortnight," she whispered. "Dance with me at Lady Bramshill's ball."

"How you tempt me," he whispered against her forehead. "But the longer I stay, the harder 'twill be for me to leave or for you to let me go."

She knew what he was saying was true. A fortnight would be a long, long time for them. How many conversations and walks and embraces could they share during that time—a dozen, a hundred? Every word would bind her to him more securely than the last, every step she took beside him would link her soul to him more firmly than mortar and bricks, every embrace would marry her spirit to his so that she could never be touched by love again.

No, he should leave.

"I'll go tomorrow and take Charles with me," he stated firmly.

She looked up at him, tears burning her eyes. He kissed the tears. "Constance, I would that our worlds were not so disparate. Will you ever forgive me?"

"There is nothing to forgive. Nothing. So, I beg of you, do not repine. Just kiss me good-bye."

He obliged her, letting his tongue rove her mouth freely and fully. She kissed him back with abandon, taking in every sensation, since it would be the last, of his wondrous height, of his well-muscled shoulders and back, of his hard thigh pressed against her own.

SEVEN

By eight that evening, Ramsdell was exhausted, yet he would not retire to his bedchamber, not for the life of him. This would be his first and last evening spent with the lively Pamberley family, and with Constance.

He was struck by the excellent manners of all the ladies, which surprised him somewhat since they lived such a cloistered existence. Constance, clearly, governed them all with a firm but loving hand, undoubtedly since she was six years Marianne's senior and a full eleven years Augusta's.

She guided the evening with as much grace and skill as any hostess he had ever witnessed in the finest drawing rooms of London. She had an eye to everyone, and with a lift of her hand or her brow was able to direct one of her sisters to offer tea to Charles or brandy for himself, to sing a duet or bring an extra cushion to better support his arm.

Charles—Alby—read a chapter of *Ivanhoe* at the Pamberley ladies' request. He had never heard Charles read before and was surprised at the skill he demonstrated. He was so drawn in by his cousin's storytelling ability that quite often he forgot all about the reader and was disrupted from following the plot only by the frequent bursts of awareness that *Charles* was reading!

Charles was read to, he was never permitted to read.

So little was expected of Charles while under his roof! How much everyone had been deprived because of it!

At Lady Brook, he was beginning to see his cousin as a young man with potential as well as with polished manners

When the ladies wished to dance, he was a prompt and expert partner. His skill had increased since he had arrived at Lady Brook, probably as a result of the lively, encouraging ambiance the house cast over all its guests.

Celeste cried, "How well you have mastered the steps Alby! And you said you were too much of a slowtop to learn What fustian after all!" Charles had indeed remembered all his steps and even showed a grace previously lacking. He was in a fair way to becoming an exemplary partner.

The ladies, in particular Marianne and Celeste, begged to hear his anecdotes of London. The little stories he told were unfamiliar to Ramsdell, yet the clarity of description could not have been feigned. When had Charles attended Astley's Amphitheatre, when had he seen the lions in the Tower of London, when had he been to a masquerade at Vauxhall?

He began to suspect that Charles had in recent years taken to living a secret existence apart from the watchful eyes of his mother, stealing from his town house as often, perhaps, as he disappeared from Aston Hall in the summer and fall months. Whatever the case, Ramsdell could now see that Charles had been on his own course for some time, a circumstance he felt boded well for his cousin's future.

Two hours later, he rose unsteadily to his feet and expressed his need for his bed. Constance immediately joined him as he walked slowly from the room. "I'll go with you," she said quietly.

He suspected she was concerned about his ability to mount the stairs, but he whispered, "Are you hoping for a farewell kiss?"

She glanced up at him sharply as a blush stole quickly into her cheeks. "No, of course not! I—I only wished to make certain you didn't tumble down the stairs. I still can't believe you didn't retire to bed *hours* ago."

His stomach felt wiggly, like jelly, and his legs were trembling.

When he said nothing, she clucked her tongue. "I thought as much." She then stunned him by sliding her arm about his waist and drawing his arm over her shoulders.

He was relieved to settle some of the weight of his body against her, even if but just his arm. He let out a sigh. "You are right. I should have sought my bed shortly after dinner, but I so wanted to be with your family tonight."

She helped him mount the first step. "Slowly will win the day, m'lord," she said softly.

He obeyed her. They took the stairs one step at a time. One step. One step.

"Did you enjoy the evening?" she asked. One step.

"Enormously." Another step.

"Your cousin is delightful company." Another.

"Indeed. But the truth is"—another step—"I have never seen him so"—another step—"animated."

The progress was slow, but she kept him enlivened by complimenting Alby's expressive abilities and his willingness to do whatever was asked of him. Ramsdell was breathing hard.

"Just a few steps more, seven to be exact."

"I'm 'fraid it might as well be a hundred. Am I hurting you?"

"Not a bit!" she cried brightly.

"What a whisker!" he retorted, drawing in a huge breath. "I daresay your shoulders are aching with the strain."

"You offend me," she responded, teasing him. "I told you before, I am a very strong female." He was not humbugged. She might be smiling, but her teeth were clenched.

He laughed. "Only three more."

"Two."

"One."

His breath came out in a long swoosh. "Thank God." He wanted to release her, but he knew very well he would fall

down in a heap if she let go of him. She seemed to understand—that deuced quality that had been dogging him from
the first. She understood so many things, even the fact that
he had to leave, that he couldn't court her with even the
smallest hope that a union between them would result. Damn.
Damn. Damn.

In silence, he ambled slowly down the hall toward his bedchamber, his arm still heavily upon her shoulders.

When he reached his room, she opened the door still holding his waist fast and shoved it wide with the toe of her
slippered foot. Marchand was quick to rise from the chair
by the bed. His face fell as he took in his master's obvious
condition.

Marchand would have cried out, but Constance was before
him. "Look what I had to drag all the way up the stairs and
all because he must be polite and do the pretty among my
sisters." Marchand blinked, and still opened his mouth to
speak, but again Constance cut him off. "No, no. It will be
of no use at all to reprimand him. Just put him to bed as
quickly as you can."

Marchand finally took up her hints and pinched his lips
tightly together. He guided Ramsdell to the wing chair. Constance released him, and he flopped into the chair with a
heavy thud. He closed his eyes. His face was ashen with
fatigue.

"Good-night, Ramsdell," she said.

He opened his eyes and extended his hand to her. She
placed her hand in his, but he addressed Marchand first.
"You may begin prying off my boots. Don't worry, Miss
Pamberley has already seen my feet, so she will not fall into
a fit of the blushes at the sight of my stockings." He was
smiling through his tiredness.

To her he said, "Thank you for a lovely evening and for
all you've done. I intend to leave quite early, with Charles,
so this must be good-bye."

Marchand paused in his struggle with the tight-fitting

boots and glanced up toward Constance before quickly re-suming his most difficult chore. She could see that he was pleased.

Constance squeezed his hand. "Good-bye, then, Lord Ramsdell, may your life be full of surprises and . . . and excellent conversation."

Ramsdell held her gaze for a long time, pinning her hand in a tight clasp. His eyes misted with something close to tears.

Constance smiled tremulously, and when the tears welled up within her chest, she finally withdrew her hand and walked quickly from the room. She did not hesitate, but went straight to her bedchamber, falling instantly across her bed and sobbing into her pillow for a hard quarter of an hour as the pain of the separation flowed through her.

She wanted to crawl into bed and sleep away her sadness, but she remembered that she had not yet bid good-night to her mother, who would be expecting her. She dipped a square of linen into the basin of water on her chest of drawers and sat in a chair with the damp cloth pressed to her eyes. She didn't want her mother to see her unhappiness.

Finally, when most of the redness and swelling was gone, she left her bedchamber and stole into her mother's room. She saw at once that her mother was asleep, and was ready to leave, but her eyes opened suddenly and she blinked, quite purposefully. Constance went to her bedside immediately and tended to her, asking if there was anything she needed.

Her eyelids fluttered. Constance swallowed. Her mother wanted her to talk. She knew her parent well enough to pre-sume that she had detected her sadness and asked if that was what she wanted to know. A single steady blink followed.

Constance's shoulders sagged, and she pressed a hand to her face. In a quiet voice she told of her blossoming affection for Ramsdell and of the hopeless nature of what she believed to be his returned affection for her. She saw tears of sympathy in her mother's eyes, which was her undoing. She let the tears flow once more, and though her mother had lost the use of her arms and hands, still Constance picked up her mother's hand and held it to her own cheek.

Little sobs escaped her several times and probably would have continued had she not felt a faint movement of her mother's fingers against her cheek. She drew back and stared at the thin, gnarled digits as though they had become living snakes.

"Did you move your hand, Mama?" she asked, astonished. She glanced at her mother and saw a single steady blink, then heard her groan a single harsh groan as her lips moved ever so slightly.

Constance stared at her mother for a long while. The doctor had said she could regain her facility at any time, or never, during the remainder of her life. Why now? In seven years there had been not a single movement or the smallest sound, but now she had moved her fingers and somehow forced air through her vocal cords.

"Oh, Mother," she cried, fresh tears flowing down her cheeks now. "I must get the others—"

But Mrs. Pamberley's eyelids fluttered, then she blinked twice quite firmly and moaned again.

"All right. Whatever you wish. Whatever you wish. Mama, when did you start feeling your hands and using your voice? Yesterday? Two days ago? Five?" Only with five was there a single blink.

"Oh, Mama. How marvelous. How utterly, utterly marvelous. I can't be sad now." She chuckled. "You've saved me." Then she watched as her mother's lips twisted into what she knew was a smile.

Constance arose and dressed on the following morning with a light heart. The grief she had felt at parting with Ramsdell had quickly been replaced by the extraordinary knowledge that her mother was showing signs of recovery.

She made her bed, still unable to credit the truth. She placed a hand to her cheek where she had felt her mother's fingers stir, and a melody rose in her chest.

She might have broken into song, but the sudden rise of male voices stopped her before the first strain of "Fly Not Yet" struck the air.

She paused in fluffing a pillow and listened. Her heart began to hammer against her ribs. She recognized Ramsdell's voice. But he was gone! He said he would be leaving before first light. She could not have been mistaken in that.

A joy suddenly rose up in her heart and exploded into a thousand prickly, teasing sparks of pleasure. He was not yet gone! She could see him again, speak with him, touch him perhaps, one last time before he left Lady Brook forever.

She quickly checked her appearance in the looking glass, not to determine if she was fashionably gowned—for she was not!—but to make certain that her hair was tidy and her morning gown of plain blue calico did not show any tears or conspicuous worn patches. Fortunately, the fabric was still reasonably woven together, and she left her bedchamber on a light tread.

She was a little surprised when she stepped into the long hallway and saw that her sisters, their heads covered in mobcaps, were peeking from their doorways and exchanging looks of shock and curiosity. Only then did she realize that something untoward was happening.

Marianne, sharing the room next to Constance's, queried, "What is it, Constance? Why are Lord Ramsdell and Alby shouting at each other?"

"I don't know," she responded. She paused in her footsteps and listened in earnest this time. Good grief! The cousins were arguing with such force that she was certain the plaster in Ramsdell's bedchamber must be cracked by now.

She quickly made her way to scratch on the door, then entered the chamber without permission or ceremony.

Both men paused abruptly in mid-shout. Ramsdell's expression was mulish beyond permission and Alby's face was flooded with color. The latter moved to the window and remained there with his arms folded across his chest, staring down at the rose garden and the maze.

Ramsdell sat fully clothed in the wing chair in the same place Constance had left him the night before, his face blazing with rage. He turned his glossy beaver hat agitatedly in his hands.

"My lord." She greeted him softly with a nod. To Charles she said quietly, "Mr. Albion."

Alby shot a quick, volatile glance, whereupon she straightened her shoulders slightly and cocked her head at him. "You have disturbed our home, which I'm sure could not have been your intention when you arose this morning."

The rebuke was softly but clearly spoken, which brought Charles turning toward her and bowing stiffly. "I beg your pardon, Miss Pamberley. It will not happen again."

Lord Ramsdell watched him from narrowed, unhappy lids before he also offered his apologies. "Our—my conduct was unconscionable. I do beg your pardon." He scarcely met her gaze. She had never seen him so distressed.

"Where is your man?" she asked.

Ramsdell spoke to the floor. "Marchand is waiting in my town coach on the drive. He has been doing so for the past hour. We were preparing to leave—"

"*You* were preparing to leave," Alby broke in, his tone quiet but firm.

Ramsdell clenched his fingers about the brim of his poor hat and clamped his lips shut. He was clearly beside himself and did not speak for a long while. After a moment in which Constance watched his teeth grinding away rather methodically, he said, "I will tell you again, Charles, *you are my cousin,* and I will not tolerate your Banbury tale a moment longer about not knowing who you are or who I am. I insist you gather your things together—or let Marchand attend to it—and leave with me on the instant." Only then did he glance at Charles, his face hard as marble.

Alby, however, apparently had other ideas, and turned to face him fully as though prepared to do battle once more. "Whether I am your cousin or not is something I cannot dispute since I do not recall my name or my relationship to anyone. What I do know, however, is that I am not leaving Lady Brook until Miss Pamberley tells me to, or until I recall with complete confidence precisely who I am. I am happy here, happier than I have ever been, and the mere thought of leaving Lady Brook causes me great pain."

Constance had never seen Charles Kidmarsh so adamant before, nor apparently had Lord Ramsdell. She had previously suspected that Charles was shamming it, but now she was not so certain.

Ramsdell turned to Constance for support. "Will you tell him to leave with me, for his sake as well as for mine?"

She saw the haunted look in his eyes and believed with her whole heart that he was not thinking about Charles at all, but about himself. This knowledge made her decision an easy one.

She took a deep breath and plunged in, "No, m'lord, I will not. Mr. Kidmarsh—Alby—came into my house because of that wretched bend in the lane, and from that moment on I have felt deeply responsible for him. I can see that you are distressed, but I will not allow him to leave unless either he wishes for it or until Dr. Kent deems it best, given his protracted loss of memory. As it happens, I am all too well acquainted with Dr. Kent's opinion on this subject, and ever since *your* accident I have come to rely most strictly on his judgment."

Ramsdell's expression grew mulish once more. "Dr. Kent may attend to him at Aston Hall. As for your sense of responsibility, I will say only that I think you are being absurd! Any obligation you owed my cousin ended once I arrived at Lady Brook. You know very well it did."

"I know nothing of the sort. Besides, you don't seem to be taking into account that your cousin suffered a blow to the head that might possibly have caused some permanent injury. Dr. Kent has had considerable experience with such cases, which was why Dr. Deane summoned him to Lady Brook in the first place. I know his mind on this subject, for I once tried for over an hour to persuade him to allow Alby to be moved to Dr. Deane's house in Four-Mile-Cross. He would have none of it, insisting that the patient's contentment in cases like Alby's was the primary factor in a complete recovery. He insisted he remain in my house until he regained his memory."

"There is only one flaw in your tidy history," he said piercingly, rising to his feet somewhat unsteadily. "You don't believe *Alby's* memory is in the least deficient!"

She glanced at Alby. "Yesterday I had serious doubts, but today I must confess that I see nothing in his eyes, or in his expression, that tells me he knows himself to be your cousin."

Ramsdell threw up his right arm in exasperation. "Leave it to a woman to be swayed by a beautiful face and . . . and good breeding!" he retorted nonsensically.

Constance could only smile as she watched him, a little swirl of affection rising in her chest. "You have spoken the truth," she said, "more than you know, I think."

He glanced at her, startled. She could see that he was completely taken aback by her remark. He scrutinized her face for a moment, and she saw a slow realization dawn on him as he came to understand she was speaking of him and not of Charles.

His demeanor changed as though she had pricked a large soap bubble with a very sharp needle. "The deuce take it!" he cried. He sat down in his chair again and, settling his elbow on the arm, propped his chin up with his hand. "I can't battle the pair of you. I shall send for Dr. Kent and then we shall have this matter settled once and for all."

"I believe that would be for the best, given the circumstances."

Charles moved forward and looked down at Ramsdell, holding his gaze steadily. Constance could see that he was trying to work something out in his mind, but what?

"You are my cousin," Ramsdell stated, but in a kinder tone than he had heretofore been employing.

"So you say," he returned slowly. Before Ramsdell could offer a retort, Charles turned to Constance and again offered his apologies. "I promise you I shan't engage Lord Ramsdell in another shouting match while under your roof. And now I must beg leave to withdraw, since your mother has been waiting for me this quarter hour and more."

"Of course," Constance said softly. "And again I thank you. Your efforts on her behalf are appreciated more than you'll ever know."

He smiled at that and quit the room.

Once the door was shut, Ramsdell, his brow furrowed with worry, said, "I should leave Lady Brook—now. I know I should. But I have been his guardian for so long—"

"I had thought," Constance began slowly, "that the bulk of the coddling came from your staff and your aunt. I'm beginning to think I was mistaken."

He glanced up at her sharply. "Whatever do you mean?" His tone was abrupt.

"I know very well that you do not hover over him, but you are always there to rescue him from his scrapes and to follow him on his adventures to make certain he's safe. Were I Charles, I would take pains to lose my memory as well."

He appeared ready to argue, but she lifted a hand and said, "I'm sorry, perhaps I shouldn't have said that, and though I can see you wish to argue your point, I must demur. I have numerous tasks to attend to this morning, so if you will excuse me, I'll leave you to sort out what must be done next. You are welcome to remain at Lady Brook for as long you wish, as is Mr. Kidmarsh. Please, make yourself at home and . . . and perhaps I'll see you at nuncheon. If you choose to leave, well, we have already said good-bye."

Ramsdell fumed the entire morning, a circumstance that robbed him of much of his precious energy. He informed Constance by way of a formal missive that he had sent for Dr. Kent and that he would not be leaving Lady Brook until Charles went with him. The response she scribbled hastily made no reference to his staying, or even her interest that he was, but, rather, indicated that Stively, her head groom, and Jack, the stable boy, had brought down a buck in the home wood not an hour past and that Cook would soon be putting a haunch of venison on the spit for dinner. *Wasn't that fortuitous?* Her exact words.

He laughed for the first time in the course of a rocky morning. How like Constance to get over rough ground lightly by speaking of venison for dinner, when she knew damn well he was furious about having to stay and wanted nothing more than a reason to brangle with her.

Besides, he did not want to be beholden to her, and he hated trespassing on her kindness. But worse, staying at Lady Brook meant he risked becoming more attached to her than ever. Damn and blast!

He considered Constance's pithy comment about his own role in Charles's lack of development. Perhaps what she had said was true, that he was partially to blame, though he wasn't certain what might have happened to Charles if someone hadn't interrupted the four hapless elopements he had become entangled in over the course of the past several years. Still, Constance's words carried some merit.

Besides, Charles was different at Lady Brook—a blow to the head notwithstanding. His conduct had become humble and helpful. He had even cared for the chickens alongside Augusta and Katherine, actually making repairs in the fence that made up a portion of the coop.

The fact that earlier Charles had stood his ground about not leaving Lady Brook also gave him pause. His cousin appeared to be growing up in the feminine environment of Lady Brook. Who was he, then, to thwart the workings of fate, since so far the results had been exemplary?

By noon he was so reconciled to this avenue of thought that he found some of the knots in his shoulders, chest, and arms unwinding. By dinnertime, with the smell of venison reaching every hallway in the mansion, he was well disposed to enjoy a second evening among the Pamberley ladies.

The next day, Dr. Kent arrived and examined both gentlemen. He pronounced Ramsdell's wounds as healing faster than anything he had witnessed before, and recommended some mild exercise—a stroll in the gardens twice a day—to encourage his health. As for Charles, he remained adamant that until he regained his memory, he should stay where it was obvious to a simpleton he was thriving.

And that was that.

Secretly, Constance was *aux anges* that Ramsdell would remain under her roof, yet she knew she could not possibly resume their former intimate discourse. The mere sight of him, however, had the ability to rob her of breath, to send her pulse racing, to make her dream of sugar plums and fairies and poor country maidens wedding dukes, earls, and even viscounts.

These romantical sensations and musings, however, she could ignore or dismiss at will and afterward go about her business without being much affected. However, let her once more fall deeply into conversation with Ramsdell, and suddenly those dreams seemed laced with a deal too much reality to be kept entirely at bay.

She knew what the future must be, so in order to protect her heart, she avoided any serious conversation with Ramsdell. She also knew he understood, for he avoided being alone with her, or even, when in company, engaging her in any lengthy discussion.

How proud she was of her discipline and common sense and how grateful she was that the daily requirements of keeping the manor running smoothly occupied most of her time. As the days began creeping by, she became more and more accustomed to his presence at Lady Brook, at mealtime and during the evening hours when both gentlemen and ladies joined together for song, for card games, for reading, dancing, and tea.

How Ramsdell occupied himself throughout the day, and what his thoughts were, she could not know, except that she suspected he spent a great deal of his time in the library, since Augusta said she had found him there more than once over the course of the week.

"And did his lordship seem content?" she asked Augusta on the fourth day, her curiosity besting her.

"As to that, I couldn't say," her softly spoken youngest sister replied. "He was always reading and upon my arrival would exchange a few polite sentences with me. Afterward, he would resume reading, I would fetch the books for which I was searching, and then would leave. I suppose one could say he seemed content. Certainly he was quiet in his endeavors."

Constance found Augusta's report less than satisfactory. She would only have to glance at him to assure herself of his content or discontent. Augusta, it would seem, was not endowed with such perception. In the end, she could only sigh, wonder, and go about her usual duties.

Ramsdell was miserably discontent. He was not used to lying about quietly for hours on end, and the one diversion that had come to mean everything to him—Constance's company—he could not have by dint of the way his heart quickened just looking at her.

He knew her gowns were old and some of them even dowdy, a fact that made him smile. He suspected she had been wearing the ugliest of them for his benefit. But even this humorous thought made his heart ache. Constance understood the rules and was abiding by them with enthusiasm. He found himself wishing she had less self-control—or that he did.

More than once he had awakened from a dream in which he had been kissing her with *both* his arms wrapped about her tightly. His body had been on fire with desire, and something more, a powerful sensation in his chest that spoke of the true nature of his feelings toward her. He tried to tell himself that the intensity of his interest in Constance was solely because he knew he couldn't have her, either as wife or mistress. But another possibility badgered him, that he had at long last found the woman for whom he had been waiting all these years.

With a brisk snap, he closed the book he had been reading, arose from the comfortable leather chair near the fireplace, and crossed to the window. The library was situated on the first floor and overlooked both the southern and the eastern vistas. He had a clear view of the rose garden and the maze, a great deal of the home wood, which sloped up a southern hill to disappear beyond, and a view of the downs that rolled eastward.

The Lady Brook property included several wooded copses scattered along the borders of numerous fields. The berry vines were found to the southeast, something he now realized because the younger ladies and Alby, er, Charles, had just appeared, each carrying a small basket slung over their arms. Charles, on the other hand, had a shotgun propped over his shoulder, probably in hope of bringing down some small game.

How much he wanted to be anywhere but indoors. The July sun—no, it was August now—shone brightly over the verdant fields and woods. He could hear the ladies' laughter

float up to the window as they passed through a gate covere
with a rose-laden arch and began winding along the pat
toward what had been described to him as the merriest littl
brook in all of England.

The dancing stream bubbled and laughed for miles alon
the northern and eastern borders of the property and ha
been the source of the name for the Pamberley mansio
Lady Brook had been built in the late sixteenth century b
a romantic husband who had made his fortune in trade an
erected his home for the love of his life, or so Miss Mariann
had told him last night between rounds of whist. The Pam
berley ladies were distant relations of the original owner.

He supposed that the present house was owned by a mal
relative who had kindly allowed them to continue living an
directing the affairs of the estate until such a time as Mrs
Pamberley passed away or one or more of the young wome
were situated in prosperous marriages.

Not much chance of that, he thought with a shake of hi
head. Portionless Ladies of Quality, however beautiful, rarel
married well, if at all. Such was the unhappy state of thei
society. A lady without a dowry was as likely to marry wel
as was a second-, third- or fourth-born male likely to marr
an undowered female. There would be no basis for financia
security. Even if such an alliance resulted because of a lov
match, chances were poor that the couple would enjoy a
happy marriage, since the man had no fortune by which to
keep his wife in the fashion to which she was accustomed
He had seen it happen time and again.

If the thought occurred to him that were he to wed Constance he could change all their fortunes with a blink of a
eye, he quickly dismissed the thought. He knew his duty to
his title, to his family's extensive heritage, to his coffers, anc
to his estate. He could command a half-dozen ladies of his
acquaintance with a snap of his fingers, ladies who possessec
by birth the right combination of qualities. His wife woulc

be the next Lady Ramsdell. She would enjoy wealth and privilege, something the lady would have known all her life.

The rub seemed to be that the only lady who had ever appealed to him as the sort of companion he had been hoping for all these years was a country miss whom he could not have.

He watched Charles and Augusta fall behind the others, walking more slowly, apparently caught up in a conversation that the elder sisters found tedious. A few more minutes, and all of them disappeared into a tangled copse.

With the sight of them gone, Ramsdell was left alone again. Impatience and agitation welled up within him. He was sick to death of shuffling about the house, of dawdling over a book in the library, of walking alone about the garden and the estate, of staying out of Constance's way. He was not used to so much inactivity. He detested being idle and could hardly wait until he could mount a horse again.

He made up his mind quite abruptly. He would follow Charles's lead. He would search out Constance and find out in just what way he could be of service to her.

EIGHT

Constance stared up into one of the cherry trees and saw what had been concerning Finch. "Shall we have Mr. Hook smoke all of them?" she asked. The blight had come to attack her orchard, and steps needed to be taken immediately.

" 'Twould be best, miss. Sooner the better." He suddenly looked past her. "Well, wot d'ye think o' that. 'Tis his lord ship, if I don't much mistake."

Constance turned in the direction of his gaze and saw that he was right. Lord Ramsdell was coming straight for them from the direction of the house.

"So it is," she murmured.

"A man o' his stamp canna sit around fer days. In a fort night, he'd go stark, staring mad."

Constance smiled faintly. "That he would." She turned to the business at hand. "Well, you had best have Jack fetch Mr. Hook, then."

"Aye, miss." He paused, waiting wordlessly, but his eyes formed a question he didn't want to put into words.

She sighed and laughed. "Very well. Yes—Jack may ride Lord-a-Mercy again."

Finch nodded and smiled a toothless grin. "Thankee, miss He'll be that pleased, he will."

He ambled past her on a quick country tread and doffed his hat to Ramsdell as he walked by.

Constance watched the viscount approach, wondering why

ie had waited so long to venture out-of-doors. She knew he
must have been bored to tears these past several days, with
nothing to do but kick his heels or open a book or two.

She smiled as he advanced on her, but cloaked her heart
with her common sense. She extended her hand to him.
"Have the books been crawling off the shelves and making
you think murderous, darkling thoughts?"

He chuckled. "It is almost as though I never have to explain anything to you. Why is that?"

"Because, m'lord, as I have said before, we are very similar in temperament, at least that is my opinion. Idleness
drives us both to distraction, but tell me, what possible
amusement have you sought by coming to the orchard?"

"I was hoping to find some way of being of use to you
while I complete my recovery. Charles has clearly benefitted
from entering into the routines of Lady Brook. I am hoping
to do the same. Besides, I see you at all hours of the day,
marching upstairs and downstairs, running about the estate,
quite independent from your sisters, and I am all agog with
curiosity! What, for instance, were you doing here? I am
convinced it was not to enjoy the beauty of the orchard."

She planted her hands on her hips and directed her gaze
back up into the trees. "We've a problem with the blight, as
you can see." She cast an arm upward. "There and there.
I've just ordered our stable boy to fetch Mr. Hook from Sandhill to come and smoke the orchard. There are also a few
wasps' nests near the stables I want him to blow up as well."
She glanced at him and smiled. "It would seem you and Mr.
Hook have a great deal in common. Though he could spend
his days leisurely reading, since he is retired, he far prefers
to be employed in some manner."

"Hence, his interest in blight and wasps."

"Precisely."

"So, Miss Pamberley, how can I best assist you and
thereby end the weariness of my idleness?"

She smiled at him, struck by how greatly he was improv-

ing. Much of the color had returned to his complexion, an
the shuffle was almost completely gone from his step. H
did not in any way look like a man who had battled deat
just a week or so past. If a certain tightness in her stomac
accompanied her perusal of his face, she ignored the sensa
tion. Common sense would win the day!

"Would you like to attend me while I deliver a few basket
to the poor? Cook has demanded more berries of my sister
and Alby, so I was left to make the trip. Since I am goin
without them, I can easily manage the gig and be back in
little over an hour. With your help, even less, for you ca
hold the reins while I deliver our packages."

He breathed a sigh of what sounded very much like relie
and agreed readily to the scheme. By the time she reache
the stables, Stively had harnessed the gig for her, and th
large wicker basket strapped to the back was burgeonin
with the various articles the ladies had assembled to be dis
bursed that week for the poor—loaves of bread, jars of pick
les, preserves, and honey, children's smocks, and wooden to
whistles that Jack had carved in his spare time.

"You have nice, light hands," he commented after she ha
set Old Nobs at an easy trot heading toward Sandhill.

"Thank you. I take that as a great compliment *if* even hal
of what Mrs. Spencer has said of you is true." She turne
and smiled at him. His beaver hat shaded his face agains
the strong sunshine, but already a sheen of perspiration wa
beaded on his brow. He was clothed in a corbeau coat, a
white waistcoat, buff pantaloons, and glossy Hessians. The
neckcloth he wore had been tied if not with precision at leas
with some order, the work of Marchand, undoubtedly. He
was probably very warm engulfed from head to foot ir
proper clothing as he was, while she was comfortable in her
serviceable gown of primrose yellow cord muslin, half-boots
and a wide-brimmed bonnet tied beneath her chin with a
yellow ribbon.

He smiled in return and settled back more comfortably in

his seat. She realized he had been, until then, wary of her skill, which made her chuckle.

She tended to her horse, to the reins, and to the lane. She let him view the pretty Berkshire scenery as she kept Old Nobs at a moderate pace. She might have worried about sustaining a polite conversation with Ramsdell, but in the end she decided the less said between them the better, since even a small resumption of their former rapport would give her heart far too much encouragement.

She heard him huff a sigh several times as beautiful farmland, islands of woodland, and a dozen signs of wildlife all passed into view. Every now and then he made a comment about what he was seeing—enclosures richly set with oak, ash, and elm, a flock of geese being prodded along by a little girl with a stick tied up with a pretty blue ribbon, a caravan of handsome Gypsies. She responded in kind, the beauty of the day and the somnolescent heat of the sun filling her with a lazy kind of peacefulness.

In less than half an hour she drew the gig up in front of a fine brick house. Ramsdell lifted his brows. "The inmates of this dwelling are in need of your bread and honey?" he queried.

She chuckled. "Of course not. Do you see the path beside the fence?"

He nodded. She went on. "An old woman, who raises the most pitiful ducks you have ever seen, also cares for her two young great-grandchildren on the most meager of incomes. I *trade* her a few things for one of her ducks each week. Only, it is quite uncanny how the duck escapes my gig and waddles all the way home before I know what has happened to it!"

He caught her hand as she began to descend. "Are there no rough edges about you?"

She was surprised. "I am stunned you would say such a thing," she cried, "when I seem completely unable to keep from speaking my mind to you at every turn."

"Have I complained?"

"You are trying to turn me up sweet," she retorted play
fully. "I know full well you are hoping to take the reins i
your one useful hand for the drive home."

He was smiling in just that way of his, with his eye crinkle
catching up sunbeams and showering them into her eyes. "
haven't fooled you a bit, eh?" he murmured on a caress.

Her heart fluttered almost to a standstill as she shook he
head and dropped lightly to the ground. She gathered up th
various articles from the wicker basket and on a brisk trea
made her way to the hovel some quarter-mile distant at th
edge of a pond.

She brought the poor duck back with her to show Lor
Ramsdell. He saw the unhappy, thin creature, and his smil
of amusement made the entire journey worthwhile. She the
set the duck at the top of the path and immediately watche
it start its journey home, quacking irritably all the while
Apparently, he was tired of his part in the weekly charade.

She drove the gig a little farther up the street in front o
a narrow house with a well-swept walk and porch and carefully tended flower garden. "Mrs. Applegate has just birthe
her fourteenth child. Mr. Applegate, the farrier, was kicke
by a horse two months ago and is just now recovering from
several broken ribs. We have a number of smocks for the
new baby and some honey."

"Are those her children swarming about the landlord o
the Turtle Inn?" His gaze was directed to the other side o
the street.

She eyed them for a moment. "Most of them."

"They are remarkably tidy."

"Do you see the oldest girl?"

"The fair one with a red ribbon catching up her curls, wit
the fat toddler on her hip?"

"Yes. She is just turned fifteen and has been in charge o
her younger siblings from times out of mind. She has taught
them their numbers and letters and keeps them bathed and

fed. She has an amazing ability to let them run about as children ought, yet she keeps them tending to their sums and doing their chores without hardly a complaint." The girl recognized her suddenly and waved to her. Bidding good-bye to the publican, she began a swirling progress toward her with her siblings scrambling for the right to possess her free hand as she began crossing the street.

When some of the older children recognized Constance, a general shouting ensued and a free-for-all running commenced. Constance handed the reins to Ramsdell and made a quick descent. She was soon knee-deep in children, who all babbled quickly, informing her of the arrival of baby Tom. She listened politely to each who would speak, then addressed the eldest. "And how does your mother fair, Alice?"

"She's a bit of a fever, but otherwise well enough. She said ye would be callin' today."

"I have brought a few things—gifts from my sisters. Will you see if your mother is well enough to receive me?" Alice disappeared into the house but not before she handed the toddler to her. Constance held up the year-old child and watched him kick his legs and laugh down at her. She drew him close to her side, and he snuggled his head against her shoulder.

Ramsdell thought he had never seen a prettier sight than Constance Pamberley cradling the child gently against her shoulder as she then addressed the other children in turn, from smallest to biggest, and asked specifically after their favorite pasttimes. *Did John enjoy the book she sent over? Could Emily still beat them all at spillikens? Where was David? Working at the Twyford farm?*

There were no rough edges about Constance, he concluded. She was a polished jewel, a diamond of the first water in every respect, a gem that took in the sunshine and reflected the rays in a thousand exquisite directions at once. He had never seen a lady so in harmony with her family, her home, her land, and her neighbors. He wanted such a woman at Aston Hall, but for the life of him he couldn't picture any of his present female acquaintances picking up the village children and cuddling them so sweetly.

She took the excited brood around to the wicker basket and made presents of Jack's carved whistles in honor, she said, of baby Tom's birth. The air was soon filled with a variety of tones as each child happily blew into the small wood devices. Old Nobs took exception to the noise, however, and stepped forward a pace or two. But Ramsdell quickly tugged on the reins and spoke a firm, "Whoa, old fellow!"

Old Nobs, hearing the master's voice, obeyed at once and settled down to a mere flickering of his ears in protest to the whistles.

A moment more, and Alice came back, bidding Constance to come inside. Constance glanced up at Ramsdell and said, "I'll be only a few minutes."

"I am in no hurry," he stated with a faint smile.

He glanced around and noted that the publican across the street bowed to him before disappearing hurriedly inside his establishment. Within a minute he returned bearing a tankard of ale.

Ramsdell knew the good man was bringing him a bit of refreshment and because of the heat, even though the equipage was resting in the shade of a thick-leaved chestnut tree, he had never been more grateful for the sight of ale in his life.

"Wi' me compliments," the man said grandly, "and in honor of yer recovery, if it pleases ye, o' course." He held the tankard toward Ramsdell.

"My good man," he said seriously, extending his hands toward the heavy ceramic cup, "you've no idea how grateful I am, and I thank you."

He took the tankard and drank deeply, aware of the fine brew of which the publican was clearly quite proud. "I vow I've not had better in all the south of England," he exclaimed.

Mr. Rose beamed, his chest swelled, and even his balding pate showed a rosy hue of pride as he stood on the cobbles and watched Ramsdell find the bottom of the tankard. While he enjoyed the brew, he related several histories of the village and offered a description of the various notable inhabitants of their neighborhood.

He then spoke of Constance. "Is she not, m'lord, the very best of women? I've never 'eard a cross word pass her lips, and though we call her The Gentleman, 'tis not without a great deal of affection and pride, for she does the work of a man, seeing to Lady Brook the way she does. She could 'ave wed a dozen times too, even though she is two inches taller than most of the men 'ereabouts. But Mrs. Spencer, the vicar's wife, says 'er 'eart weren't engaged sufficient-like to take on the mantle of Cupid, as it were. And one of the gent'men were a lord, the Earl of Upton, I think it were."

Ramsdell was stunned. Had he heard correctly?

"The Earl of Upton, you say?"

"Aye. 'Twere the subject of a great many debates, I can tell you. But hush now. 'Ere is the lady herself."

Ramsdell turned and watched beautiful Constance emerging from the house with yet another child in her arms. His mind went numb, and everything he knew about the universe seemed to shift and dim a little.

The Earl of Upton had offered for Constance Pamberley and she had refused him? He knew Upton, and though he had no great opinion of the man who had married an ambitious daughter of Viscount Woodburn's, he couldn't credit that Constance had refused a match that would have given her every advantage, for herself and for her family.

He watched her cross to the carriage, carrying a child who appeared to be about four years old, a girl with long, blond ringlets, a stubborn chin, and the merriest eyes Ramsdell had ever seen. "I'm Mary," she stated, her gaze leveled at Ramsdell.

"How do you do, Miss Mary?"

"Fine, thank ye. Miss Pamberley said I could ride to the top o' the street and back. 'Tis my turn, ye know."

Constance queried above the girl's head, "Do you mind very much? It has become something of a tradition when I come to the village in my gig."

"Not at all," he said, handing the tankard back to Mr. Rose. After again proclaiming the publican's brew the finest he had ever had, he shifted the reins back to Constance, who had settled Mary between them.

Mary glanced at Ramsdell with wide blue eyes. "Aw you really a lord?" she asked.

"Indeed, I am."

"Wot 'appened to yer arm?"

"I was in an accident and broke it."

"Did it 'urt wery much?"

"I don't remember. I bumped my head at the same time and didn't wake up for ten days."

Mary looked up at him, her brow furrowed deeply, considering what he had just told her. Finally, she made her judgment. "Wot a whisker!" she exclaimed at last, breaking into a smile.

Ramsdell chuckled and politely asked Mary if she had ever broken her arm. As Constance slapped the reins, Mary replied that she had not, but then launched into a cataloging of every bruise or cut she had suffered in her brief but apparently adventure-riddled existence.

After a time, when Mary was safely returned to her family and all the bread and honey, and pickles and whistles had been distributed among the needy, Constance turned the wheels of her gig toward Lady Brook and silently passed the reins to Ramsdell.

"You trust me, then!" he exclaimed.

"Well," she drawled. "We shall see, shan't we?"

He growled faintly, which set her to chuckling.

She watched as he deftly threaded the left ribbon over his forefinger and the right over his ring finger. She watched him guide the horse at a brisk trot along every bend in the road as though he were using both hands.

"Mrs. Spencer was right!" she exclaimed when he maneuvered the horse expertly around a tight curve in the road. "You are a nonpareil!"

He smiled with pleasure at her compliment, surprised at how delighted he was that she thought well of at least this accomplishment.

She added, "But then, you are used to managing four, even six horses at once, aren't you?"

"Yes, I daresay I am."

"Have you ever driven a mail coach?"

"Several times."

"Indeed!" she cried enthusiastically. "Was it thrilling for you? I had heard that members of the Four-in-Hand Club were often given to paying the coachman for the opportunity to handle the ribbons, but I've never met one before who had done so."

"I will confess, it is one of the most exhilarating experiences in the world," he returned. He then began slowing down as a heavily laden cart appeared at the top of the road, seemingly inclined to use up most of the lane.

"Oh, dear," Constance murmured, catching sight of the cart.

"Never fear," Ramsdell stated. "I've been hunting the squirrel since I was breeched and I've never locked wheels yet."

"Grazed a few, have you?" she asked, chuckling as she stiffened with the approach of the cart.

Ramsdell gave the reins a slap, and Constance let out a squeak.

"Henhearted?" he asked.

She looked up at him, her eyes wide. "Abominably so." She seemed convinced a collision was imminent and closed her eyes.

Ramsdell let out a crack of laughter, slapped the reins

again, and the next moment breezed past the cart with inches to spare. "You may open your eyes now," he said. "The danger is past."

He watched her eyes pop open, and in obvious disbelief she turned around, apparently to ascertain there had even been a cart on the road.

"And you did that with one hand?" she cried. She turned back to him, "Ramsdell, I'm amazed. Only, tell me how you fell to mischief around Lady Brook Bend, for I am convinced you could have navigated that particular turn with your eyes closed."

"Thank you for the compliment," he responded. "As it happens, a deer darted in front of my horses and frightened them. They bolted to the right, and the next thing I knew we were barreling across your lawn. But that is all I recall. Why didn't my curricle suffer injury?"

Constance explained his heroics, turning the horses at the very last moment, but he responded by shaking his head. "I have no recollection of having done that. I remember standing up, even shouting a curse to the air, but nothing after that. What a spectacle I must have made!"

"Yes, you certainly did, but a welcome one. The horses were wild-eyed with fright as they bore down on us. Both Dr. Kent and I thought we would perish with you. You saved us all."

He glanced down at her as he guided Old Nobs up the tree-lined drive toward the front of the brick mansion. He recalled his conversation with the publican and decided to broach the subject that had been teasing his mind since leaving the village. "I had it in the strictest confidence that the Earl of Upton offered for you."

Constance chuckled. "I take it Mr. Rose gave you more than just a tankard of ale."

He maneuvered the gig past the front of the house and set Old Nobs heading toward the stables. "He told me a great many things but none more surprising than your refusal of Upton's hand in marriage."

"Why were you surprised that I refused him?" she asked, tilting her head so that she could see his face beyond the wide brim of her bonnet.

"Your circumstances—your family's circumstances— naturally. Or did Upton offer for you during your Season when you had less need of contracting a good, nay, *brilliant,* marriage?"

She shook her head in response to his last query.

"Why, then, did you refuse him?" he asked.

She was silent as the carriage house loomed near. "Do you know Upton well?" she queried.

"Tolerably so," he responded.

"Then need I say more?"

He knew from the subdued tone of her voice that he had offended her. He drew the gig to a stop as Stively emerged from the stables, trotting forward to take care of Old Nobs, who was fidgeting in his harness, ready to be released from his duties.

Constance quickly descended the gig. Ramsdell stood up, placed his right hand on the side of the carriage, and leapt easily to the ground. He caught up with her just as she reached the gate leading into the kitchen gardens.

"Constance, are we to quarrel now? Pray, forgive me if I have given offense. I hadn't meant to. To be a countess would have afforded you every manner of opportunity and connection."

She whirled back to him, her color much heightened. She dipped her chin, then lifted a blazing countenance to him. "I want an excellent husband for myself and for each of my sisters. Given my—our circumstances—the gentlemen we consider must be in possession of at least an easy competence. But if you think a mere fortune would persuade me to accept any offer that came my way, or to allow my sisters to accept a hand in marriage when that hand was tainted

with . . . with a propensity to flirt with every manner of crea
ture so long as she wore a skirt, then you have greatly mistaken my character! Or did you perhaps believe that I
couldn't have known he kept an opera dancer in Mayfair and
a Drury Lane actress in Bloomsbury?"

"I don't know what I thought," he responded, taken aback,
"except that as Countess of Upton you would have been able
to bring out each of your sisters in the height of style—"

"Having set for them the worst possible example? What
foolishness that would have been." She wrung her hands.
"Have you taken the sum of my character in this manner
because I wished Charles, with his lack of fortune, out of
the way of falling in love with one of my sisters? Is that
what caused you to think all that mattered to me was the
size of a gentleman's income?"

"No," he stated firmly. "You misunderstand me completely. You sacrifice in so many ways for your family that
I naturally presumed you would have sacrificed by accepting
the hand of a man you could not esteem because of what he
could provide for your sisters."

Some of her feathers began to settle down. "Had he been
in possession of *one quality* I could have admired, believe
me, I would have gladly made such a sacrifice as you suggest." She pressed a hand to her forehead, and her shoulders
slumped slightly. "I shall tell you the truth, though I am loath
to confess it. Upton offered for my hand only after I had
refused a carte blanche from him, not once, but thrice. Believe me, his offer of marriage was not a compliment to me."
She laughed a trifle hysterically. "In defense of my refusal,
I shall add only that had I wed such a man, and been forced
to endure his defects of character, I know one day I should
have murdered him. I have not the smallest doubt of it."

Ramsdell was sorry he had brought forward such an obviously painful subject and slipped his hand beneath her chin,
forcing her to look up at him. "I beg your pardon most hum-
bly, Constance Pamberley. I had no idea." Then, because it

seemed the proper thing to do, the tender, humble thing to do, he placed a kiss on her lips.

He meant to comfort her, but the moment his lips touched hers, he felt as though a bolt of lightning struck him, traveling through his entire body in an instant.

He drew back and looked at her. How wide her eyes were! How sweetly parted her rosy lips!

She blinked up at him slowly and leaned toward him as though off balance. He caught her about the waist with his right arm and pulled her against him. He untied the ribbons of her bonnet and pushed the wide brim away from her forehead. He kissed her properly as she slung her right arm about his neck, placing a hard, demanding kiss full on the lips. When she parted her lips, he searched the depths of her mouth with his tongue and felt his heart melt into a euphoric liquid fire.

He felt lost in a place so wondrous that he could no longer put two thoughts together. All he felt of the moment was her tall, perfect body pressed full-length against his, the swell of her breasts softly against his chest, and the strength of her arm wrapped about his neck. Soft musical sounds caught in her throat as he explored the moist depths of her mouth. The kiss became a summer's adventure, lush, full, rich. He wanted to go on kissing her forever. Forever and ever.

Eventually, however, the sounds of the stable yard and the orchard and the gardens all broke through the still bounty of the passion he felt for Constance. Chickens clucked, horses called to one another, meadowlarks and robins chattered away, bees buzzed close to her yellow gown. He drew back and stared into hungry eyes. "Why do you always end up in my arms?" he asked on a hoarse whisper.

"I don't know," she breathed. "It is too ridiculous, isn't it? I behaved this way only once in my life, when I was a chit of fifteen. And how old are you to be kissing a wholly unsuitable female of whom your family could only disapprove?"

"I am seven and thirty, but I feel as though I'm eighteen if a day," he whispered. "Constance, I will try very hard not to kiss you again while I am staying under your roof if you will try very hard not to find yourself alone with me."

She let him kiss her again. She hadn't meant to, but his words were so sweet and so full of desperation that she raised her face to him and he obliged her.

She no longer considered where his kisses would end. She knew the answer—in the hopelessness of her attachment to him. Yet kissing him as she was seemed to satisfy her need to be connected to him, even if the gesture was both transitory and woefully incomplete.

As to his wish she stay away from him, she was not certain that was what she would do.

NINE

When Constance left Ramsdell to prepare the day's entries for her ledger books, she had great difficulty concentrating on the task at hand. She enjoyed being with him so very much, more than she ought, but she could not escape a faint uneasiness that had seeped into her mind.

She knew he had meant only what would have been best for herself and her sisters by questioning her judgment in having refused Upton. Her strong reaction to his criticism had not been directed toward him, but toward the memories that the conversation had invoked in her. Upton's offer had been a deep insult to her. She had been angry when she refused him. She was angry when Ramsdell hinted she should have accepted him.

Then he had been deeply apologetic and had meant to express his heartfelt regret at having recommended Upton by kissing her. She leaned her elbow on her desk, her mind falling backward. She could taste him still. Mr. Rose's ale had been a pleasantly bitter flavor on her lips.

How thoroughly he had kissed her! How easily she had let him! How much she had wanted the kiss to go on forever. Forever and ever.

Yet, he was far, far above her touch and always would be.

She allowed herself to dream for a moment, that he was her equal and love had blossomed fully between them. She tried to imagine being swept into the usual course of events—

a sweet courtship, a brief engagement, a wedding breakfast and formal nuptials shared with their immediate families, perhaps in the blue drawing room. She would leave with him on a honeymoon and return—where? Not to Lady Brook, but to his home.

The thought spun strangely through her mind.

Not to come home to Lady Brook?

How odd that would seem, how foreign, how unwelcome.

She found herself a little surprised by her thoughts. She remembered her former suitor, who had declared she would never love and never marry because she was already wed to Lady Brook Cottage.

But what unpurposeful musings were these? What nonsense!

Ramsdell had already made it clear that he would never wed beneath his rank, so she was safe.

Why safe?

She felt so confused, even distressed in a way that made no sense to her.

She gave herself a strong shake and returned to attacking the ledgers. Within a few minutes, her inexplicable qualms were gone and her devotion to Lady Brook was fully upon her once more.

Two hours later, Constance was disrupted from her labors when Katherine peeked in and called to her, "There you are! You must come to the kitchens at once and see how many berries we found. We went to the usual place, the copse behind Whitley Wood, but you can't imagine what happened!"

Constance replaced the lid on the inkpot and laid her pen on the silver filigreed tray directly in front of her. She rose from her chair, welcoming the domestic diversion. Her shoulders ached from having sat scribbling her numbers for such a long time.

"Tell me all," she responded with a smile, aware of the sparkle in Katherine's hazel eyes.

"You'll never guess. Alby pushed through a particularly

thick part of the copse, and found an old lime pit, now dripping with moss and ferns and the sides hanging with goose-
berries. You've got to come see! The vines have probably
been untouched for centuries. I've never seen such lush fruit!
The ground everywhere is deep with mulch."

Constance accompanied her to the kitchens, where Cook
was exclaiming over the size and obvious succulence of the
berries. All five of the adventurers showed signs of scrapes
and stains from having invaded a new land, but each cheek
was flushed with excitement, pleasure, and the happy effects
no doubt of having sampled the fruit without restraint.

Was there anything quite so pretty as four damsels in
gloves, straw bonnets, and beribboned summer gowns showing in mood, gesture, and expression that summer was richly
on Berkshire? Nothing, surely!

Alby, she realized, was not wearing his hat. His face was
becoming quite bronzed from his daily excursions with the
ladies. His hair was damp across his forehead, his smile
broad, and his beautiful eyes sparkling with life. Augusta
was beside him.

"No, no! Just one more, I promise," he was saying to the
youngest Pamberley sister. "Now, open?"

Augusta blushed and parted her lips, tilting her head in
embarrassment. Alby popped a fat gooseberry into her
mouth. She chewed and smiled and giggled. Her eyes shone
like stars as she stared up at him.

While this romantic vignette was transpiring, the scullery
maid was gently spreading the berries out and separating
them with care, Cook was setting a large copper pot on the
stove, Katherine was examining her plunder, and Marianne
and Celeste were arguing about who had collected the most
berries. All were oblivious of Charles's flirtation with
Augusta.

Katherine accidentally knocked over one of the smaller
baskets and began shrieking and dancing about in an attempt
to keep the berries from rolling onto the floor.

All the while, Constance was fixed on only one sight—of Alby slipping his hand under Augusta's chin and staring down at her as though he were looking at her for the first time. Through the clamor of the bustling kitchen, lightning passed between Augusta and Charles as tangibly as if a white bolt were actually visible. Had they been alone, Constance was convinced nothing would have stopped Charles from kissing young Augusta.

She whirled around to leave, to collect her stunned thoughts, but collided with Ramsdell, who apparently had been standing behind her for quite some time. He steadied her with a hand to her elbow, but his attention was equally caught, as her own had been, by the sight of his cousin dallying with Augusta. Constance turned back to watch them as well.

Augusta had fallen into a fit of the blushes and turned away from Charles to tend to one of her baskets, but Charles moved to stand behind her and whispered something in her ear.

Constance felt as though she were eavesdropping and could no longer bear to watch. She slid past Ramsdell and headed back to her office.

After she had been there just a few seconds, his voice startled her. "What do you mean to do?" he asked.

Constance, who was standing behind her desk, her fingertips resting on one of the black ledger books, glanced sharply at him. "Oh! What a fright you gave me! I didn't expect you to follow me."

"Follow you? Of course I followed you. I wish to know what you mean to do."

She stared at him. "Of the moment, nothing."

"Are you saying you don't intend to disrupt this wholly inappropriate flirtation?"

Constance turned more fully toward him and straightened her shoulders. "What? In front of Cook, the scullery maid, and Augusta's three older sisters? You must be mad!" She laughed, but the sound of her voice was slightly hysterical.

The truth was, she didn't know what to do. She had had sufficient warning that Augusta might be in the throes of a calf love, but she had scarcely been prepared for the light that suffused her face when she stared up at Charles.

"At the very least, Miss Augusta ought to be admonished," Ramsdell stated, flustered. "At once!"

"Oh, *at once,* he says," she responded sardonically, but did not budge from her place behind the desk.

He leaned into the hallway and glanced back at the kitchen. "Good God! They are leaving together—going into the garden! You must stop them!"

"Why don't you stop them?"

"But don't you understand," he said, turning back to her, "anything might happen in a garden."

Constance bit her lip and felt her heart soften. "Yes," she agreed quietly. "Anything might."

Ramsdell's eyes narrowed, and, seeing the direction of her thoughts, cocked his head and glared at her. "That was very different."

"Enormously so."

He grunted. "You and I are both of an age."

She considered this for a moment. "According to your calculations, if you and I are of an age when eight years separate us. Therefore, Charles and Augusta must be of an age, since just a little over eight years separate them. Augusta will be nineteen in September."

"You are splitting hairs," he snapped. "You know very well such a comparison is ridiculous. You and Augusta might as well be twenty years apart in age."

"Yes, yes, you are right, of course," she acquiesced. "However, I have no intention, at least not at the moment, of admonishing my sister. Later, perhaps—probably. If you are so set on disrupting their tête-à-tête, might I suggest you go to the gardens and perhaps ring a peal over Alby's head about dallying with chits just out of the schoolroom?"

He seemed horrified by the suggestion. "I could not possibly do so."

"Why not?" she pressed him. "Or is it because he is a man and as such must be allowed his flirtations without redress?"

"You can be very provoking—"

"And rational, which is why I daresay you diverted the subject back to my character when I had brought forward a basic dictum of society. No, no, pray don't eat me. Rest assured I shall speak with Augusta. May I hope that you will do the same with Charles?"

He nodded once curtly. "Very well." He slapped the doorframe and disappeared down the hall, but not in the direction of the kitchen or the kitchen gardens.

Constance watched him go, relieved by the exchange. Perhaps her acerbic tongue would serve to put him out of patience with her and thereby end some of their wretchedly pleasant camaraderie. Perhaps.

Oh, the devil take it—unlikely!

Later, Augusta sat on the end of the chaise longue in the library, her hands folded primly on her lap. Her cheeks bore two spots of bright color. "I have told myself these very things every day from the first moment I laid eyes on Alby, that his clothes and the state of his curricle gave strong indication of his impoverished state, that there couldn't possibly be anything serious or of a permanent nature between us, but then I but look in his eyes"—here she lifted shining blue eyes to meet Constance's gaze—"and I am lost. Constance, I never thought of myself as a particularly romantic female—Jane Austen always appealed more strongly to me than Lord Byron—but ever since Alby lay on the nursery bed so white-faced and so very beautiful, my heart has ceased to beat properly.

"I suffer from palpitations and feel nigh to swooning when he draws near. And . . . and I think he is beginning to feel the same way about me."

Constance wrung her hands. "But it is hopeless, my dear. You do understand that much. Ramsdell told me he hasn't a feather to fly with. He has been his guardian for years, you know, and he is perfectly knowledgeable with every aspect of what constitutes, I daresay, a pitiful competence. That, combined with your own undowered state, you do realize that such an alliance would prove disastrous."

Tears filled Augusta's eyes. " 'Tisn't fair," she murmured. "If only he had not crashed through our fence and landed in our petunias! If only I had married last fall, when I had the chance." She pounded a fist against the palm of her hand determinedly. "I should have accepted Joe Chaddleworth's hand, then I would never have even met Alby!"

Constance's heart felt pressed into the size of a cherry pit. Her chest ached for her dear sister. She dropped down in front of her and gathered up Augusta's hands within her own, larger clasp. "But, dearest, do but think. Mr. Chaddleworth is an extremely portly man, and I daresay any of the children you bore him would have looked like toads."

A chuckle burst from Augusta's throat, but fresh tears raced down her cheeks. "Constance, whatever am I going to do?" she wailed softly. "I am in love with Mr. Albion!"

Constance gathered her close and held her tightly. "I know, I know."

Constance suffered with her sister's unhappiness for a full hour, during which time she determined to speak with Charles herself, in order to hopefully persuade him to cease encouraging Augusta's heart toward him. She found him in the music room, idly plucking at the strings of Celeste's harp.

He was clearly in a brown study, which could mean only that Ramsdell had made good on his promise and had already spoken with his ward.

She viewed him from the doorway, his body half draped over the harp, his expression somewhat inscrutable. He appeared lost in thought and none too content.

She closed the door behind her.

"Hello, Alby," she called to him, straightening her shoulders a trifle as she entered the chamber.

He glanced at her and drew into a more upright position. "Good afternoon, Miss Pamberley.

He was only two years her junior, but in experience she suspected he was not much older than Augusta, which in many ways made him an excellent match for her sister. A measure of melancholy descended on her as she took up a seat on the piano stool near him, a reflection perhaps of his own misery.

He shifted slightly to meet her gaze squarely, a gesture that pleased her. "I hope you have not come to comb my hair—I have already received a severe dressing-down for my conduct from, from my guardian."

She studied his face carefully. His large blue eyes were heavy with concern, but there was none of the petulance she might have expected from a man who had been so wretchedly cosseted during the course of his life. "Is your heart engaged?" she inquired. She hadn't meant to begin with such a bold question, but there it was.

He seemed a little taken aback. "I don't know," he responded honestly. "I will confess to you that since my arrival I have enjoyed the company of each of your sisters prodigiously. Only in the past two days have I found that my attention wanders more and more to Augusta, which seems odd to me since she is not the prettiest nor the liveliest nor even the most accomplished. But there is something in her expression, of sweetness and intelligence, which I have come to find distracts me."

Constance felt a small measure of relief pour through her, both that Alby was not simply toying with her sister and that his affections clearly were not fully engaged. A disruption of the romance at this point, therefore, would not be an impossibility. "You have spoken forthrightly, and for that I am gratified. Are you aware that my sister believes she has tumbled in love with you?"

A look of surprise and pleasure darted into his eyes, then quickly disappeared, replaced by his former heavy concern. He gave himself a shake, his blond curls dancing about his forehead. She was again reminded of Renaissance paintings and sculptures. Was it any wonder that all of her sisters were half in love with him?

But at this thought, the reins of her mind drew her up sharply. She realized with a start that Marianne, Celeste, and Katherine had showed decreasing interest in Alby over the past several days. Only Augusta had sustained her enthusiasm over his presence at Lady Brook. She was not comforted, however, by this rumination.

Alby rose from his seat behind the harp and moved to stare out the windows. "Did Augusta confess as much to you, that she held me in some affection?"

"Yes," Constance said. "She said she loves you."

His shoulders slumped slightly. "Then I have behaved unconscionably."

"You mustn't repine," she said, "or even berate yourself. After all, 'tis summer in Berkshire, and though some may say that the springtime brings thoughts of love, I myself have never been unaffected by the bounty of the fruit-, nut-, and wheat-laden season. The rose garden alone intoxicates every sense."

He turned back to her, a faint smile on his lips. "I believe you are right."

"You have but to conduct yourself with discretion until you are completely well, and I am persuaded Augusta's attachment can easily transform into a profound friendship."

His brow knit with piercing concentration. "Though there are only a few scattered parts of my memory that have not fully asserted themselves, I do recall that no one has ever spoken to me as you have just now, as though I could hold a particle of sense or intelligence in my brain. Not even Ramsdell."

"He was all scold and little tolerance."

A bitter expression crossed his face, darkening his angelic beauty. "He spoke solely of responsibilities to my position and to our family, nothing of Augusta's abilities or virtues."

Something about this remark did not entirely make sense to her. "Your position?" she asked.

"Yes. I may not recall Ramsdell entirely, but I do know that I am heir to Kingsholt."

The name was a pistol ball fired from his lips to ricochet about the walls of the music room to finally pierce her ear and her brain. *"Kingsholt?"* she asked with fainting heart.

He turned bitterly away from her, leaned his hand on the upper frame of the window, and stared down into the countryside below. "Yes."

"But I thought—Alby, when you arrived, your curricle, your clothes, with the exception of your boots, were ragged."

At that he gave a chuckle and turned back to her, a crooked smile on his lips. "Apparently, the only way I could escape from Ramsdell's house as well as the notice of the entire county of Bedfordshire was if I donned the appearance of a young man, with pockets to let, traveling about England after the fashion of the romantics."

Constance felt any number of emotions surge through her. Alby was a man of means and could therefore take on an impoverished wife. Yet, Kingsholt was a mansion of enormous proportions, whose attending wealth was one of the finest in the kingdom. None of the Pamberley sisters was suited to reign over such a property. Alby's mother and aunt had great ambitions for him, the alignment, for instance, of Kingsholt with a duke or an earl's daughter.

Yet, why had Ramsdell insisted Alby was impoverished? She recalled very specifically that he had said his cousin had no portion to speak of.

So he had purposely lied to her!

She understood, or thought she understood, and found herself furious. With every ounce of restraint she shoveled her ire into the back of her mind and addressed the matter at hand. "All that I ask, Alby, is that from this point on, you protect Augusta's heart. I am convinced you are a gentleman, not just in breeding and form, but in conduct as well, and I have every confidence you will not encourage my sister's love for you beyond what you are willing or able, by the nature of your circumstances, to return to her."

He seemed to grow several inches in height during her brief speech and promised his obedience to her request. She believed him.

She then excused herself and went in search of Ramsdell.

However, Marchand informed her that he was resting and was not to be disturbed the rest of the afternoon.

Her heightened anger, finding no outlet, demanded that Lord-a-Mercy be saddled.

She donned her riding habit and took enormous pleasure in settling well into the saddle, speaking a few provoking words into his ear, then giving the fine bit of flesh and blood his head. Soon, the August air was rushing madly over her heated features as she made her way to the vicarage of Hartfield.

Ramsdell watched her from the infrequently used parlor on the first floor of the mansion. He had a fine view of her bonneted head as she dug her heels into Lord-a-Mercy's flank and sped down the drive and into the lane. He was torn by what he saw. His admiration of her abilities rose with each day he spent at Lady Brook. He could also see, however, that she was in the devil's own temper, and he thought he knew why.

Marchand had told him she had been speaking with Charles in the music room, and he had little doubt she now knew the truth of Charles's circumstances, that he was nearly as rich as Croesus.

He sighed deeply. She would not forgive him for having confirmed her belief that Charles was impoverished. He could not recall the day precisely, but he believed it was during the first few days of his recovery, when she had come to visit him and converse with him. She had asked if Charles had always resided at Aston Hall, indicating she felt the gesture magnanimous. For some reason, he had said, "Poor Charles! He hasn't a feather to fly with."

Why had he told such a whisker, when all that was truly required of him was to help her continue in her belief that the lad was impoverished? He shook his head at his own stupidity. But then, he was frequently quite stupid around Constance Pamberley. He frequently did and said things that were ridiculous in the extreme, like embracing her and kissing her.

Now she was as mad as fire!

So much the better, he thought. His stay at Lady Brook, along with his cousin's, was becoming more and more complicated with each passing hour.

And what had he been thinking in the garden? Nothing had been further from his purpose in touching his lips to hers than evoking the lightninglike passion that blossomed so quickly between them. Yet how typical of his relationship with her that with nothing intentioned, fireworks tended to follow!

He shook his head. Lady Brook must have cast some sort of spell over him, he decided. He had never felt such a lack of self-control in his life. Constance had but to show her spirit a little and his chest felt like exploding. She had but to walk into a room and he swore he heard a heavenly chorus.

Even while arguing with her about Charles and Augusta, he had experienced the worst impulse to cross to her, drag her into his arms, and kiss her—again. And again.

He didn't like feeling this way, for the sensation was miserably familiar. His view of the world, when he first set foot in London, was far too romantical. He had set *amour* on a pedestal and knew that once Eros touched him with his golden arrow, he would know perfect love forever. He had been a lad of only twenty at the time, and too green by half, to know that the temptress who pursued him with every artifice known to womankind had motives other than love in mind.

What a nodcock he had been!

And what an avaricious miss my lady Alison had been, for though she had been born into his rank, she had possessed the soul of a courtesan. Yet what did he know of the potential difference between women? Nothing.

Seventeen years later, his heart was severely hardened to the possibilities of love. When Lady Alison had eloped with the Duke of Mercer—after having accepted his own hand in marriage the day before—he had promised himself never again would he be taken in by *love.* He would use his common sense, he would scrutinize the character of each lady he courted with the same finesse with which he employed his quizzing glass to scrutinize her gowns, and he would certainly never, *never,* discount the inherent greed of the fairer sex.

He grimaced slightly. Constance may be in possession of many fine qualities, but she was impoverished, as were her sisters. Why wouldn't she be hoping, expecting, even encouraging him to fall in love with her? Certainly he was a far better man than the Earl of Upton, and even Constance had admitted that she would have gladly married the man if he'd had even one acceptable quality.

What were the true ruminations of Constance Pamberley's heart? Now that she knew of Charles's wealth, would she encourage Augusta to set her cap for him?

The unhappy turn of his thoughts was exhausting him and setting his nerves on edge. He decided to head to the stables and seek out a horse of his own. A hard ride would benefit him greatly, though he intended to travel in quite the opposite direction!

Constance sat in Sophia Spencer's parlor, her brow beaded with perspiration from her vigorous ride to the vicarage. "But why did you say nothing to me?" she asked of her long-standing friend. "I was never more shocked when I learned of Charles Kidmarsh's true prospects!"

Her good friend merely smiled in the most knowing, the most infuriating manner as she passed her a cup of tea. "Because I know you better than anyone else, that your scruples regarding wealth are even more antiquated and determined than your scruples concerning poverty—"

"Any great disparity in fortune or rank only leads to marital unhappiness. I have seen it a dozen times."

"Since you have brought forward your usual argument, I shall respond with mine—any great disparity in character only leads to marital unhappiness. Rank, fortune, have little if anything to do with it in my opinion. I can cite you a dozen examples if you like."

"Pray, do not," she responded with a laugh.

Sophia chuckled. "I can see no harm in any of your sisters tumbling in love with Charles Kidmarsh—and marrying him. I wish only that you shared my opinion, though I think I ought to add that he has nearly as great a fortune as Golden Ball Hughes, in case you were in doubt of precisely how wealthy he was."

"Dear God," she breathed, her heart failing her as she took another sip of tea. Golden Ball was the richest man in England.

"And Charles Kidmarsh, in my opinion, has come to the

Pamberley household by divine guidance and nothing less—
of that I am persuaded."

Constance was astonished. Sophy Spencer was as practical
a woman as was ever born. Her husband was an excellent
man and a warm, loving clergyman who gave sermons each
Sunday that kept his congregation in awe of the spiritual
realm. Here, however, his ability to guide his flock ended,
for his concepts were high-minded, having little to do with
making or buying loaves of bread to sustain the life and
health of his parish.

Sophy was a perfect balance for him, since she never spoke
of heavenly things. She worked hard to see that the details
of life were attended to with great care. The entire parish,
as well as her own children, all eight of whom were kept in
the finest of apparel and possessed the best of tutors, benefitted from her unceasing labors. So to hear Sophia speak
of Charles's arrival as divine was doing it up a bit too brown.

"By *divine* guidance? You cannot be serious!" she cried,
blinking over the rim of her teacup and watching for even
the smallest smile to break her friend's otherwise serious
demeanor.

Sophy was silent apace, meeting Constance stare for stare.
At last she said, "I have been praying for a miracle for years
now, for when you refused the Earl of Upton—yes, yes, for
entirely understandable reasons—I knew that only the angels
could provide proper husbands for yourself and your sisters."

Constance felt the blood drain from her face. "Then you,
too, believe I was wrong in refusing to marry him?" She
was stunned and demoralized all at once. Upton would have
been all the entrée she and her sisters needed to create a
great stir in London. He had even suggested the marital
agreements include a dowering of her sisters.

Again Sophy was silent, but finally she said with a twinkle
in her eye, "I am still out of temper that your refusal of him
meant I would not be a frequent guest at Beauford Hall. You've
no idea!"

Some of Constance's despair left her. Sophia was teasing her about the earl's county seat in Lincolnshire, which was one of the oldest and finest in the country. "He was such an offensive man, Sophy. Had I married him, I am persuaded you would have paid me a visit only once and then refused to cross his portals again except to make a mourning call."

"A mourning call?" she inquired.

"Yes, as I told Ramsdell, I am fully persuaded I would have murdered Upton before the first twelvemonth had passed."

Sophy blinked several times and her mouth fell slightly agape. At last she said, "You . . . you said that to Ramsdell?"

Constance considered her friend's surprise and wondered how she could possibly explain the extent of the rapport she felt with him. "Yes. It would seem we share the same sense of the absurd. Oh, now, pray, take that light from your eye. We laugh at the same things, that's all." She could not meet Sophia's gaze.

"That is not all," Sophy responded with deadly perception. "Oh, Constance," she drawled and *tsk*ed. "Whatever has been going on at Lady Brook besides Augusta's *tendre?*"

For the first time since her arrival, Constance realized she had erred in coming to the vicarage. Mrs. Spencer was far too perceptive to be humbugged by anything Constance might say.

She searched her mind for a full minute before finally responding reluctantly, "Were I to draw up the figure of a man, with a certain quick intelligence, a proper manly force of will, a sense of humor, and an adventuresome attitude toward life—all designed to please me—that man would be Ramsdell."

Sophy drew in a long, slow breath that sounded like a tea-kettle ready to sing. "Ramsdell," she breathed. "Of course!"

"No, no!" Constance cried, laughing and rising to her feet at the same time. "You are not to begin even the smallest matchmaking effort. Ramsdell is above my touch, and well I know it."

"But . . . but, Constance! You are not considering, not by half! Such a man does not come along twice in a lifetime."

Constance shook her head. "If you are suggesting there is the smallest hope, I assure you there is no such thing. Ramsdell agrees with me wholeheartedly that though he admires me, a—a deepening of love between us would be ridiculous in the extreme."

Sophy slumped into the back of her ivory sofa. "My poor child," she murmured.

Constance glared down at her. "Sophia Spencer! I will not allow you to speak to me in that odious manner! I am not a poor *child,* nonetheless *your* poor child."

"I beg pardon," Sophy responded, also rising to her feet. A smile edged her lips as she continued. "Well, then, since you appear to have settled your unhappiness in your own mind, let me change the subject briefly before you depart. You are attending Lady Bramshill's ball, are you not?"

"Yes. I wouldn't miss it for the world. All my friends will be there, and because of having labored to see both Ramsdell and Mr. Kidmarsh returned to health, I have missed my usual rounds of visits."

"Excellent." Her gaze took on a faraway expression that made Constance's heart quail a trifle. She knew her friend well, and whenever Sophy Spencer looked just that way, very soon the entire neighborhood was in an uproar. Sophy added, "Lady Ramsdell, the viscount's mother, is she currently fixed at Aston Hall?"

Constance shook her head. "No. I believe she is traveling on the Continent with Mrs. Kidmarsh."

"Hmmm. It seems to me Lady Bramshill was telling me something about her the other day. Now, what was that—oh. Oh, well, it is nothing to signify." She rounded the table that separated her from her friend and slipped her arm through Constance's. She walked her slowly to the front door, where her horse was tethered. "I'm very glad you came to visit. Only I wouldn't refine overly much on Ramsdell having kept

the truth from you, especially since the result is the same—
you are still disapproving of Mr. Kidmarsh's involvement
with any of your sisters."

That particular slant on the subject brought a greater sense
of peace to Constance's mind than anything else that had
been shared that afternoon. She rode the three miles back to
Lady Brook less likely to strangle Ramsdell than when she
left, which was, after all, a very good thing.

Sophy Spencer adored her role in the world. She saw herself
as a messenger of sorts, a link between forces, needs, and
desires. She sat down at her writing table, delighting in the
late afternoon sun that poured over her vellum at a delicious
angle. She wrote three letters, one to Lady Bramshill, one to
Lady Ramsdell, and one to Mrs. Kidmarsh, the two latter of
which she knew to be ensconced in the pavilion at Brighton
since the ladies were visiting the Prince Regent. Well, well,
Brighton was not so far away from Berkshire after all!

She understood well the limitations of people, which she
felt to be the best of her unique gifts because through that
knowledge she could create bridges over chasms previously
thought too deep to cross. She was acquainted with Lady
Ramsdell, who had a stern managing reputation, and wondered just what that lady would think of Constance. Of
course, there would be no way for her ladyship to form an
opinion unless she actually met Constance.

People were so simple, really. Times might change, but
the nature of humanity remained unerringly true, which naturally made her chosen vocation a matter of poetical simplic-
ity. She had but to design her bridge and labor to construct
it in a timely fashion—something at which she excelled—
and the deed would be done.

Besides, how hard was it to write three letters?

TEN

"Why did you lie to me?" Constance queried, her riding whip clutched in her right hand and both hands planted angrily on her hips.

Ramsdell had met her in the drive as she was handing Lord-a-Mercy's reins over to Jack. The viscount had just returned from his own excursion when he had happened upon her.

"Lie about what?" he asked, evading the question and trying to ignore how much the heat of exercise added an exquisite bloom to her complexion.

Constance huffed an impatient breath. "I am certain," she said, lowering her voice, "that if you will but search your mind, you will discover precisely that to which I am referring, although I will give you a hint and tell you it concerns Alby."

"Ah," he breathed, dropping in step beside her as she walked back to the house.

"You said he hadn't a feather to fly with."

"Yes, that is true. But I was very ill at the time. What if I told you I had been speaking while yet in the grips of a fever—"

"I believe I should flay you severely for telling such a whisker."

"You are angry, then."

She stopped in mid-stride and turned to glare at him. She

tucked several strands of her light brown hair beneath her riding hat. "Yes—quite."

His lips twitched. "I can see now that you are."

"Did you think me so mercenary that you must keep the truth of Alby's inheritance from my knowledge?"

He shook his head. "No, of course not. Well, perhaps I did a little, at first, when I told you that particular rapper, but my opinion was based on the obvious circumstances of your family and house, not upon your character. Later, I felt I could only increase your agony were you to learn that Alby, er, Charles, was a wealthy man yet by the nature of his position could never become aligned with any of your sisters."

She nodded, another well of irritation bubbling up like a hot spring inside her. "You were being merciful then, hoping to spare me further misery?" she inquired facetiously.

He grunted and grimaced at her. "Do come down from your high ropes, Constance. None of this would matter had I been allowed to take Charles away when I wished."

That much was true, she had to admit. Still, she could not like that he had lied to her, and said as much. "For then I cannot help but wonder what other whiskers you have told me and in what other ways you have bamboozled me in an attempt to display your magnanimous mercy."

"None, for I promise you I am not such an inventive man that I could easily conceal more than one lie at a time."

She believed him. She slapped her crop against the heavy velvet skirts of her habit and continued her march toward the house. Her boots crunched loudly on the gravel.

"So tell me," he said, once again falling in step beside her. "Has the truth distressed you further?"

She shook her head. "No, of course not. It changes nothing, only the nature of the reason by which Augusta must guard her heart and Charles protect it."

"What do you mean, Charles protect it?"

"I asked Charles not to encourage Augusta if he could help it. He said that though he was inclined to favor her, he had not fallen in love with her and would take every care to guard her heart."

At this, Ramsdell paused in his tracks and hooked her elbow with his own, forcing her to stop beside him. "What did you say?"

Constance was confused by his odd response and reiterated, "We spoke of his interest in Augusta and her strong feelings for him. He promised to behave the gentleman for her sake, since an alliance between them could not be countenanced."

He shook his head, clearly bemused. "This is not at all like Charles," he muttered. "And he agreed to this, you say?" He seemed stunned.

"Why, yes, just as I suspected he would. Your cousin is a fine young man, though I must say he seems a great deal healthier since his arrival at Lady Brook, even since he first regained consciousness so many weeks ago."

"He has improved a great deal," Ramsdell said, nodding slowly. "In many ways. He used to fall in love at random and was much given to eloping with any pretty face that seemed inclined to go with him."

"Indeed," Constance responded, considering this statement. "I would have to say I saw something of the gentleman you describe when he first left his sickbed. But of late, particularly from the time he began helping my sisters with their daily chores, he has been much more reserved and gentlemanly."

Ramsdell looked around him—at the house, the gardens, the tall tips of the elm trees that fronted the cherry orchard in the distance. "Your home has a restful, sublime quality one does not find everywhere."

Constance followed the path of his gaze. "Thank you," she said, her spirit softening. "I have heard Mrs. Spencer say much the same thing of your home, of Aston Hall. She is, I believe, acquainted with one of your mother's younger sisters and visited your house many years ago. I would presume your estate is in immaculate condition?"

"It is," he responded without arrogance. "As Lady Brook is."

Constance also looked about her. "Yes," she murmured. "Though I must confess there are a dozen improvements I would love to make, which I will as soon as I've enough saved."

"What, for instance?" he inquired.

She forgot many things at that moment, especially that she had forbidden herself to be alone in his company again. As it was, since the subject was so near to her heart, she immediately launched into her plans to drain the bottom land and plant a peach orchard. He asked her many questions, then shared with her his own experiences with a portion of land he bought five years earlier to the south of Aston that had required a great deal of soil renovation to bring even the smallest blade of grass to life in its rocky soil.

The subject of haying was not far distant, followed by horse and sheep husbandry, the possibilities presented by the use of canals and succession houses, a discussion of orchards, poaching in the home wood, vagrancy, the plight of the poor, the troubles in the North with machine smashing in some of the new mills, the impact of so many modern inventions on society in general, and whether King George III would live another year.

So delightful was the general flow of the conversation that Constance didn't even realize they were sitting together on a stone bench to the side of the kitchen garden until Cook suddenly appeared on the steps and called to her.

"Miss Pamberley, there ye be! Yer mother 'as been callin' fer ye fer some time. We couldn't find ye anywhere!"

Constance immediately rose to her feet, as did Ramsdell. "Is she ill?" she called back, quickly gathering up her long, velvet train and moving up the path toward the door to the kitchens.

"Nay," Cook said. "But 'twere Mr. Albion wat sent fer ye. He said 'twere most important. He's with her now."

Constance turned to Ramsdell. "You will excuse me, won't you?"

"Of course. Do you wish me to attend you, for I can see you're shaken?"

She nodded. "Mama rarely sends for me, you understand. She will request all of my sisters before sending for me—she knows I am continually pressed with concerns about the estate."

"Then I can understand your trepidation. I will accompany you."

"Thank you."

Constance entered her mother's chamber and found Alby standing near her, a glow on his face. She looked down at her mother, who was sitting up in bed with only a pillow behind her to support her head. She had never been able to do so before.

"Mama!"

She took a step forward, but Charles prevented her from doing so with a lift of his hand and a softly murmured "Wait!"

Mrs. Pamberley opened her mouth and said in a slurred but distinguishable voice, "Con-nie."

She had not heard her pet name in seven years. The sound was not of this earth.

"Mama," she murmured, tears springing to her eyes. "But how? When?" She glanced at Charles. "Alby, was this your doing?"

"I only encouraged her a little. You must remember, I know full well how frail the body grows when it remains unused." His eyes flitted past her shoulder, reaching Ramsdell, then returned to her face. "We are practicing all your sisters' names as well, but I felt certain you, most of all, since you carry the burdens of your family on your shoulders alone, would want to hear her progress."

"Thank you—yes. Thank you so very much." Remembering Ramsdell, she brought him forward and introduced him to her mother. Ramsdell bowed. Mrs. Pamberley lifted a finger in his direction by way of acknowledgment. She lifted a finger!

"Mother!" she cried.

Constance pressed her hands to her cheeks and finally moved forward to sink on her knees beside the bed. She took her mother's hand in hers and felt a stronger pressure than ever return the squeeze of her fingers. She lowered her forehead to the coverlet and began to weep. She suddenly felt the burdens of the past seven years flow over her in a monstrous wave. An awareness came to her that she had never allowed herself to be sad in all these years, about the direction the course of her life had been forced to take until that very moment, the moment when hope had just flown in the window.

She felt she could weep forever and was grateful when the gentlemen quickly retired. Her mother's fingers continued to press hers in comforting response as she gave herself for a few minutes to the strong, unexpected emotions that ravaged her heart.

Finally, she felt able to dry her eyes. She drew a chair forward and spent the next half hour looking at her parent, drying the tears that tracked down her mother's cheeks, and listening to her name spoken at least a dozen times.

She owed Charles everything for the miracle he had somehow wrought in her mother. Somehow she would find a way to repay him.

Constance could not find her feet when she moved down the hall. She was floating with a happiness she could hardly express. Her mother gave every evidence of finally recovering from her illness after so many years. She went to her chamber and, after calling for a bath, began the process of dressing for dinner.

That night she found herself watching Charles more than was usual for her. She was still awestruck by the changes he had wrought in her mother, and the amazement she felt found expression in her need to look at him and wonder.

During dinner, after she had searched his face for the twentieth time, she suddenly shifted her gaze to Augusta, who she found was very quiet and composed. She was unable to discern the nature of her present thoughts, or how strenuously she was working to keep her heart in line, except that a faint tic worked beneath her left eye. No wonder she loves him, she thought, for his spirit walks with the angels, surely.

Later, when Marianne was noisily teaching Alby, Katherine, and Augusta the intricate steps of the quadrille, with Celeste doggedly playing the pianoforte in accompaniment, she asked Ramsdell to tell her in more detail of Alby's life.

"What do you wish to know?" he responded quietly, drawing her away from the dancers and toward a settee near the fireplace.

Constance sat down, refusing his offer of a footstool. "Thank you, but my limbs are sufficiently long, as I'm sure you've noticed."

He nodded, taking up a seat beside her. "Yes, that I have noticed," he responded. He turned in to her, resting his right elbow on the back of the settee, and watched her closely. He was dressed in elegant black evening wear, his neckcloth folded intricately, his coat of black superfine molded to broad shoulders, and his black silk pantaloons revealing the shape of muscular thighs and calves. Even his arm was supported in a black silk sling.

She had recognized something provocative in his tone, but her mind was too caught up with the extraordinary events of the day for her to do more than smile faintly.

"Are you thinking of your mother?" he asked after she remained silent.

She nodded, turning toward him. She saw that the lace of his shirt was caught beneath the sling. She thought nothing of what she was doing as she extended a hand and began to straighten out each portion.

She spoke quietly. "What has happened to my mother is nothing short of miraculous. You cannot imagine the thoughts that have filled my head—my heart—since Alby sent for me and I saw my mother lift her finger and actually speak my name." She slowly plucked another crushed edging of lace and with the tip of her finger pressed it against the V of his waistcoat. She continued plucking and speaking. "My mind has been consumed with Charles and how he managed to accomplish in just a few days what even several prominent physicians could not over the course of many years. I am overwhelmed with gratitude." She worked her finger under another line of lace.

"Constance," he whispered. "What are you doing?"

Constance slid her gaze to his face and saw that his eyes were hazy with an expression she had seen at least twice before. She wondered what on earth she had said to have brought such a look to his eye. "What is it?" she asked. "What have I said?"

A pained smile crossed his face. "I think my lace ought to be left where it is for the present, don't you."

She looked down at her hand, which was searching and plucking the lace, but which also at present was resting over his heart. She gasped as the heat of his chest suddenly communicated to her fingers and then as rapidly to her brain. She withdrew her hand and felt her cheeks begin to burn.

"I would have permitted you to continue had we been alone," he murmured, "for I have felt nothing so wondrous in years as the touch of your hand on me."

"I do beg your pardon, Ramsdell," she whispered, folding

her hands primly on her lap. "Only pray did any of the others witness my idiocy?"

"I think not. Can you not hear their laughter?"

"It is very difficult through my embarrassment. I don't know what I was thinking."

"You were caught up in your usual housewifery, I think. Ever in search of that piece of your home that is not in order and setting it to rights without a second thought. Maybe later you can finish this chore, say, if we took a stroll in the gardens?"

"What?" she said, a warmth stealing over her in swift, pleasant waves again. "In the moonlight? How very dangerous, to be sure."

"Indeed," he murmured throatily.

She met his gaze again. Longing stole into his eyes and wouldn't depart. A lethargic dizziness pervaded her body at his silent request. They had agreed to remain in company, to prevent the very thing that was rising again between them. In the distance she could hear Celeste's careful notes on the pianoforte, Marianne's masterful instructions, Alby's murmured "yes" and "I see," and the giggles and chatter of Katherine and Augusta. Yet, so far distant were the sounds that she might as well have been on an island with Ramsdell and her sisters and Alby on a distant shore.

"Later," he said softly. "When your sisters are abed. Come to me in the rose garden."

She sat on the settee, knowing she could not possibly oblige him. When she spoke of the danger of such actions, she had spoken the truth. She would refuse him, of course. She paused, she waited, she grew dizzy again. "All right," she whispered.

She was stunned by her traitorous vocal cords, tongue, and lips! She was supposed to refuse him! To do anything else was madness!

Then the evening began to drag and seemed to resume the normal ticks of the clock only when Katherine and Celeste yawned simultaneously. A half hour later, Constance accompanied Alby and her sisters up the stairs. Ramsdell had previously excused himself.

Constance waited in her bedchamber for a half hour until all the noises in the adjoining bedrooms ceased—the creaks of the floorboards, the laughter of her sisters as they crisscrossed the hall exchanging bits of lace or hairbrushes or borrowed earbobs, the good-night calls, sister to sister. She rocked in a chair by the window and waited for the last voice to fall silent.

At half past eleven she stole from her room, the only light in the hall a trickle of moonbeams that shone through the muslin at the far window.

She wore a shawl against the damp, cool night air. She found Ramsdell in the shadows, but he pressed a finger to her lips, caught up her hand, and began guiding her away from the house, through the formal garden, past the maze, and into the wood beyond. He didn't stop until they reached an old bench beside Lady Brook Stream from which her father had fished for trout so many years before.

"I found this on one of my rambles. I think we can enjoy some privacy here."

Beyond the stream, the wood disappeared and a rolling section of the downs could be seen in a moonlit view that appeared as if snow had fallen on the land.

He sat down and cradled her close in the circle of his right arm. She did not even demur, as she meant to. Instead, she leaned her head on his shoulder and let go of a deep sigh.

"You may repair my lace to your heart's content now," he said.

She giggled. Tears were near the surface though. Her heart was full to breaking. Why was it so easy to be in his arms? She thought of all the men she had refused, marveling that she had at last met one who could command her so easily.

"Constance?" His lips were lightly on her forehead. She leaned back and let him cover her mouth with his own. She parted her lips. The world disappeared. Her thoughts became a brilliant rope of images, of being a child and enjoying a carefree life in this very wood, of kissing Jaspar when she was fifteen and standing with him barefooted in the stream, of sitting with her father and angling for fish, of her first London Season, of her numerous beaus, of her love for the manor that had become the focus of her existence—until then.

Ramsdell's lips were warm and moist on hers, his tongue a joining that swelled her heart. She forgot about everything except the feel of his kiss and the strong arm that surrounded her protectively. She touched his face with her hand, letting her fingers drift lightly over his cheek and the firm line of his jaw. He left her lips to kiss her fingers. The exact shape of his features was hidden in the night shadows that surrounded them both, but she knew the exact color of his eyes, the curved line of his nose, the shape of his high cheekbones. She let her lips trace each shape, memorizing with small dragging kisses the flow of his face. She heard him breathe and a low, hoarse sigh escaped his throat as she touched and kissed him.

"Damn," he murmured into her ear.

"What?" she responded, her throat aching.

"This sling and my wounded arm. I can't hold you or kiss you properly."

She drew back and smiled at him and kissed him. "I have begun to believe that is for the best."

He chuckled, then caught her lips with his own and kissed her maddeningly. "Constance," he said, his voice anguished as he drew back from her. "I know I'm taking sore advantage of you."

"Not by half," she murmured. "I am merely storing up for myself a host of memories that will keep me warm during the winter. Don't repine, I beg you. There can be no harm in a little kissing."

Ramsdell kissed her and felt his heart stretching at every seam. He was fond of Constance, he was drawn to her, every turn about her home made him wish he would find her around the next bend. When she had drifted her lips over his cheek and brow and slid kisses over his eyelids, he felt driven to distraction. His thoughts kept turning to having her beneath him, as his wife, making love to her, planting his children in her womb, having them grow up beneath her gentle, orderly eye. Futile thoughts, but sensual ones that kept him holding her close to his side and searching the depths of her mouth.

A rustling nearby diverted Constance's attention, and when she shifted her gaze past his shoulder, she nudged him and hushed him. "Do but look," she murmured against his cheek. "Slowly."

A magnificent buck, some ten yards away, had come to lap at the stream's edge. The branches of the trees overhead permitted a dappled moonlight to pattern his back and flanks. His ears twitched. He took only two or three sips at a time, then lifted his proud head to scrutinize his surroundings.

"Extraordinary," Ramsdell murmured.

The buck's head shot up and stared in the direction of the bench. His entire body shook with the tension of waiting and suspecting. He sniffed the air.

Ramsdell chuckled, then spoke to him. "We are but a harmless pair. You've nothing to fear from us."

The buck needed no further encouragement. He wheeled about and in a pig's whisker disappeared into the woods.

Ramsdell squeezed her shoulder and drew in a deep breath followed by a satisfied sigh. "I could remain with you, in this lush, fragrant spot, until the sun rises."

She again leaned her head against his shoulder and stared at the beauty of the downs. "I too," she responded.

She remained with him for an hour, by which time the

fatigue of the day's events laid claim to her comfort. She must seek her bed.

He walked beside her the entire way back to the house, holding her hand and choosing a route that kept them in shadow most of the way. Once inside, he did not immediately relinquish her, but drew her into an antechamber near the foot of the stairs and kissed her soundly. She didn't know which sensation was finer, the cuddling on the bench or the feel of the entire length of his body against hers as he held her close.

"Tomorrow night?" he asked softly, drifting the words over her lips.

"Yes," she breathed into his mouth just as he kissed her again.

A half hour later, she made her way to her bedchamber.

ELEVEN

Over the next several days preceding Lady Bramshill's ball, Constance no longer forbade herself the enjoyment of Ramsdell's company. During the day she frequently included him in her chores, whether delivering foodstuffs to the poor in neighboring villages, or inviting him to walk into the wood along with Stively to dismantle newly planted poaching traps, or discussing with him various tedious estate problems, knowing how intimately he was involved with every aspect of Aston Hall.

The evenings brought a different sort of communing, of dancing, even with his arm still cradled in a sling, of companionable competition at cards, and later, in the warm, secret embraces shared beside Lady Brook Stream. Each day took on a vibrant, dreamlike quality that caused her to awaken with excitement, and close her eyes at night to the sweetest slumber she had ever known.

If she feared her attachment to Ramsdell might become generally known, she was much mistaken, for what her sisters thought of Ramsdell was summed up succinctly by Katherine, who whispered to her one evening, "Won't you be relieved when Ramsdell departs? I know you must despise having to wait on him hand and foot when you are so very busy. Of course, were he *younger* . . ." Her sister had then giggled at her little joke.

Were Ramsdell younger . . .

Constance had smiled to herself but made no effort to disabuse Katherine's mind about her true sentiments toward the *aged* Lord Ramsdell.

Sir Henry Crowthorne had also helped to enliven their evenings. Having returned from a trip to York, where he had visited his uncle for a fortnight, he had joined in their nightly revelries with Constance's blessing, particularly since he had quickly gained the favor of both Lord Ramsdell and Charles. The baronet's manners were so easy and so pleasing that before long a fast friendship had formed among the men.

One day, with hunting rifles in hand, they had spent hours scouring his estate for deer. Ramsdell and Charles had returned late that afternoon with a fine haunch of venison for Cook as well as several brace of pheasant.

The next morning, however, Celeste received a missive from Sir Henry stating that he had gone to Bath for several days but would hopefully return on the day before the Bramshill ball. He also expressed his hope, his fervent wish, that Celeste would go down the first two sets with him at the ball. How like Sir Henry to leave nothing to chance.

Everyone felt the loss of his congenial company, including Celeste, who, Constance noted with some encouragement, did not seem quite so lively as when Sir Henry was present.

Here was hope, she thought with a smile.

Still, she could not help but wonder just what Sir Henry would have to do—in addition to his daily exhibitions of a fine character, gentle address, and grace in the drawing room—to make himself acceptable to Celeste.

Three days after Sir Henry left for Bath, an event occurred that filled Constance's cup to overflowing. Lady Bramshill sent two additional invitations to Lady Brook for her ball, one for Lord Ramsdell and one for Charles Kidmarsh.

All the Pamberley ladies were ecstatic. Alby, on the other hand, was faced with a moral dilemma. Having refused to adopt his proven identity since he still could not recall his own name, he hesitated accepting the invitation. The ladies pressed him fervently, but he held fast to his convictions until Augusta begged him to seek Dr. Kent's advice.

The good doctor was summoned, though he did not arrive at Lady Brook to put everyone out of their misery on the subject until late the following day—the day before the Bramshill ball.

However, when the dilemma was placed before him, he pleased all the ladies, as well as Alby, by stating that in his professional opinion, Charles—er, Alby—would do well to attend the event since he would be in the company of the Pamberley sisters. With such support, Dr. Kent felt assured that he would be sufficiently well protected from suffering a shock that might set him back in his recovery.

With that question settled, the only thing that remained was the horrible task of waiting for the day to turn to night and the night to end so that the long-awaited event might be fully upon them.

That evening, Sir Henry made good his promise and arrived at Lady Brook to join everyone for dinner. He entered the drawing room, smiling congenially as always, but his gaze was restless until he caught sight of Celeste. Constance watched him, faintly amused by the color that crept into his complexion as he greeted everyone politely, all the while working his way to his beloved, who sat beside Katherine.

Celeste was the last one he addressed, a sweetmeat after a dinner of several entrees. She gave him her hand and he lifted her fingers to his lips. She smiled up into his face but gave only the smallest indication she favored him. Constance sighed. Would Celeste's heart ever be turned toward so excellent a man?

He exchanged a few words with her, then sought out Alby. Constance was a little surprised that the conversation between the men became quite animated, even hushed, as though they had some great secret between them.

She glanced up at Ramsdell, who was standing beside her, and asked, "What do you make of that?"

Having procured himself a glass of sherry, he sipped the wine and followed the line of her gaze. After a moment he shook his head. "Haven't the faintest notion, but both fellows seem inordinately pleased." He smiled after that, which made her believe he knew more than he was letting on.

Dinner was excellent. Cook had outdone herself, as usual. Thin slices of ham, trout, potted pigeons, boiled cauliflower, and broccoli teased the palates of all. A fine East India Madeira accompanied the feast. With but Morris and one footman to serve, the dinner was enjoyed with only one remove consisting of chicken, lobster patties, fried sole, and apricot fritters. A plum pudding, apple tarts, and a sweet custard concluded the meal.

The gentlemen remained to enjoy their port while the ladies retired to the drawing room. The subject among the sisters soon became a thorough discussion of the ball gowns each would be wearing to Lady Bramshill's ball. Celeste had fashioned Constance's gown for her, having taken apart an old dress of deep purple satin that had hung in her wardrobe for three years untouched. She had covered it with a sheer gossamer tulle, while at the same time cutting the neckline quite low so that her eldest sister would appear very à la mode.

Constance was immensely pleased with the result and could hardly wait for Ramsdell to see her in the beautiful confection. For the present, however, she began to wonder where the gentlemen were. It would seem they were tarrying longer than usual over their port.

She had just begun to worry that some disagreement or other had detained them, when the door of the drawing room slid open partially.

Alby, a warm glow to his face, stood on the threshold quite dramatically until every eye was upon him and each feminine voice had fallen silent. Neither Ramsdell nor Sir Henry had yet come into view, but Constance could hear their voices in the hallway beyond.

"We have a surprise for you," Alby said at last.

Constance felt her heart flutter. She knew her mother was somehow involved.

He slid the door open the rest of the way and there, sitting in a Bath chair, was their mother, dressed in an evening gown of dove-gray silk with her peppered hair caught up in a knot of curls atop her head. She looked absolutely beautiful, though decidedly thin and frail. Even her white silk gloves hung quite loosely on her arms.

All the ladies froze in their seats, and a moment of electric tension swirled in the blue drawing room. Alby availed himself of the opportunity to speak. "Mrs. Pamberley has something she wishes to say to you."

Constance heard her sisters gasp and exclaim.

"Speak?" Marianne cried. "But how?"

Constance's vision shimmered with tears.

"Good . . . evening, my . . . daughters" came from slowly moving, crooked lips, but the words were sufficiently clear to cause the youngest sisters to leap from their places and rush toward the Bath chair in a rustle of silk, satin, and lace.

Constance, who had already been blessed with the knowledge of her mother's progress, went instead to Charles and hooked her arm about his. She kissed his cheek, thanked him, and blessed him. She held his arm tightly, her gratitude causing her limbs to tremble. He covered her hand with his own and gripped it in a wondrously painful clasp as the sisters pelted their mother with every manner of question.

Mrs. Pamberley was not yet capable of responding, except with lifts and squeezes of her fingers, which elicited further excitement.

Constance glanced at Ramsdell but found that he was looking at his cousin with an odd expression on his face, one of distance, surprise, and admiration. She felt he was beginning to see Charles as a man and not a man-child, which she thought boded well for Charles's full recovery.

When a quarter of an hour had passed in the ladies' affectionate assault on their mother, Constance watched Celeste remove herself to address Sir Henry.

"Did you have a part in this, then?" she asked quietly.

Sir Henry beamed and nodded.

"Is that why you went to Bath? To fetch the chair?"

"Yes. When Mr. Albion made his request known to me, I knew I had to go. I would do anything for your mother, who has always been an excellent friend to me as well as to my father when he was alive." He then softened his voice slightly as he continued. "And . . . I would do anything for you, Miss Celeste." He gazed into her youthful eyes, which were shining back at him with intense gratitude.

"I have never known such a kindness as this," she responded quietly. "Sir Henry, I will be honored to go down the first set with you at Lady Bramshill's ball, if—if you still wish for it."

Sir Henry lit up like a firework exploding at Vauxhall. He lost all ability to speak, but his face gave full expression to every thought. When he took her hand, Celeste did not demur, but allowed him to lift her gloved fingers once again to his lips and to place a kiss on the back of her hand. "I am most honored!" he declared.

It was some time before Celeste actually withdrew her hand from his enamored grip, something Constance felt certain bespoke a settled future for her sister. Her belief was further confirmed when Celeste permitted Sir Henry to keep her locked in conversation in a dimly lit corner of the withdrawing room for the next hour, until her sisters demanded she play the harp for their mother.

Constance stayed at her mother's side, as did Augusta. Alby sang ballads with Marianne and Celeste, entertaining them all with his rich baritone voice.

Constance tilted her head as she watched him. His shoulders had broadened during his time at Lady Brook with so much physical exertion, the color of his face was a beautiful healthy bronze, and his legs in black pantaloons appeared stronger and more shapely than ever. He had transformed from a lovely blond cherub into a man of excellent proportions and athletic presence. He was no longer a child figure with wings, but a mythological Adonis.

She glanced at Augusta, whose face had lost its studied passivity and at that moment was openly rapt in admiration as he sang "Her Hair Is Like a Golden Clue."

Oh, dear, she thought, what would be the end of this *tendre?*

On the following morning, the day of the ball, Constance emerged from her study near the morning room at the same moment that her sisters and Charles entered the house through the wide carpeted hallway leading to the terrace. Summer light poured through the glass doors, which caught the sprays of water that spilled around Charles when he removed his hat. She realized he was soaked from head to toe, a circumstance that explained in part why all the ladies were laughing.

As she surveyed her sisters, she realized that Augusta as well was damp nearly to the shoulders of her walking dress.

"What on earth happened?" she called to them, cradling several black ledgers in the crook of her arm.

Katherine immediately responded. "You cannot credit what happened! I had persuaded everyone to cross the stream near the large oak tree by way of the fallen log, which, as you know, has blocked the stream and created a deep pool. Everyone was willing to do so, even Augusta, who is generally hen-hearted, but only because Alby said he would help her. But what must she do but slide on a bit of moss and Alby, in trying to keep her from falling, actually tumbled her into the pool. She had enough sense not to lean with her shoulder, but jumped lightly with her feet, whereas poor Alby went in headfirst!"

All the ladies then added their particular rendition of what happened—how Augusta shrieked, then Alby tried to steady her but only served in pushing her, how Augusta's gown flew up to her knees, and how Alby stood up in the waist-high water with his hat about his ears.

"And when he lifted his hat, a trout flew out and back into the water!" Marianne cried.

"*No!*" Constance exclaimed. "You're telling whiskers again!"

Celeste added her laughing voice. "We all saw it, Constance, a small trout with such a wiggle of panic that it glided down Alby's arm and dove off his elbow."

The hall rang with laughter, which echoed off the white walls for a full minute. When the last of the chuckles and giggles died away, a woman's voice was heard at the end of the hallway coming from the entrance hall.

"But that is my son's voice! I know it is!"

"Madame," Morris was heard to say in response. "Please. I beg you—"

"Nonsense! I *will* see him!"

Everyone had fallen silent as a petite woman with suspicious blond hair appeared in the doorway.

"Charles!" she called to Alby. "It is you! My poor child, my poor son! When I heard of your accident from Mrs. Spencer, I had to come!" The lady walked briskly down the hall, casting away from her a swansdown muff and matching reticule. With her arms outstretched, she descended on the group clustered around Alby. A stunned silence fell abruptly as all eyes turned toward the woman, who, it would seem, was Charles's mother.

Mrs. Kidmarsh further exclaimed, "Dearest God in heaven! What has happened to you, Charles? You are damp from head to foot! Come! Let Mama care for you!"

The effect was nothing short of a burst of grapeshot fired from a cannon! The aftermath was the smoke in Alby's eyes and the stillness of the bruised air surrounding the five Pamberley sisters and Charles Kidmarsh.

Constance had been stunned by the sight of first Mrs. Kidmarsh descending on her son in a furiously brisk stride, and
now at how Charles eyed her with an expression of nothing
short of rage.

The sisters parted before the lady like Moses lifting his
staff over the Red Sea. She flung her arms about her son's
neck and instantly began to weep and exclaim, "You shall
contract an inflamation of the lungs and then you shall be
no more!" The wailing of her voice nearly made the paint
peel from the walls.

Constance was frozen with shock, consternation, and disgust. She understood so many things about Alby at that moment, had he professed to be Zeus himself when he awoke
from his coaching accident she would not have been surprised.

His features were stiff with ire as he placed his hands
forcibly on his mother's shoulders and detached her from
him in a single, hard movement.

"Contain yourself, madam," he said in a clipped voice.
"For I haven't the deuce of an idea who you are!"

Constance watched him closely as he looked down into
the smaller woman's eyes. She knew then he was indeed
feigning his amnesia. The only emotion he should have felt,
given the circumstances, was one of confusion about who
the lady was who was hanging on him. The rage, in her
opinion, exhibited certain knowledge.

Another woman arrived at that moment in time to gather
a now-weeping Mrs. Kidmarsh into her arms. "Eleanor, what
are you doing? I thought we had agreed—"

"Did you hear what my son said to me?" Mrs. Kidmarsh
wailed, cutting her off.

"Yes, yes, and you've suffered a shock."

"My son. My poor, poor son!" Mrs. Kidmarsh wailed.

Constance watched the older woman with growing interest. She was quite tall and her gay eyes wore a concerned
apologetic expression as she met her gaze over Mrs. Kid-

marsh's head. To Constance she whispered, "I'll take her back to the drawing room. Please come to us when you can spare a moment."

Constance nodded her acquiescence.

Mrs. Kidmarsh continued to weep.

The older woman murmured, "Yes, yes, dearest. Now, pray, collect yourself, for you are giving all these nice young ladies a fright." She turned her toward the foyer and began guiding her up the hall. She continued. "Mrs. Spencer was very clear in her letter about how it might be, and I must say, you were a bit foolish to throw yourself on Charles before he knew what you were about, but I won't remonstrate further. Do you wish me to send for a physician, for I can feel you are trembling." As they reached the swansdown muff and reticule, the older woman stooped and picked them up before continuing on.

"Yes," Mrs. Kidmarsh responded. "I wish to speak with Dr. Kent immediately. Though I have no great opinion of him, Mrs. Spencer said he has been consulted throughout the course of both their accidents."

Once the ladies disappeared back into the entrance hall, only silence remained. Constance realized she was clutching her ledger books as though they might fly away should she loosen her grip. The edges, however, were cutting into her arm, so she slowly relaxed her fingers and turned to address the matter at hand.

She saw that her sisters were decidedly downcast, and Marianne, always full of spirit, gave voice to the general opinion as she turned toward Charles. "Alby, she spoke to you as though you were six years old!"

"Don't I know it," he responded bitterly, then hurriedly cleared his voice. "That is, if that is how she normally speaks to her son, I don't wonder he didn't leave for the Colonies long before this—or India!"

Augusta spoke in hushed accents, shaking her head somberly. "And you! A man of seven and twenty! It is not to be endured!"

He glanced at her and smiled softly as she turned to look at him. A warm glow lit up her face in response.

"Thank you for saying as much, Miss Augusta. You give me courage. Indeed, you've no idea how much."

The color on Augusta's cheeks turned the precise shade of the pink roses in the garden by the maze. Constance thought she had never looked prettier—or more completely in love.

"Alby," Constance said, addressing the sorely tried young man, "why don't you seek your bedchamber and I'll send Marchand to you."

"I believe that might be best."

After the group sallied up the hall and turned into the foyer in order to mount the central stairs, Constance made her way quickly to the kitchens. She sent the footman with a message to Jack to please take Lord-a-Mercy and to bring back Dr. Kent, who she knew would be at Four-Mile-Cross today.

Morris, much distressed, arrived at that moment and explained how he had just settled the ladies in the blue drawing room and was going in search of her, when Mrs. Kidmarsh— even against the strong protests of her ladyship—followed him into the entrance hall. It would seem Charles's laughter, along with her sisters', could be heard all the way to the front door.

"Don't fret yourself, Morris. Mrs. Kidmarsh has been under a severe strain and I have just given orders for Jack to bring Dr. Kent back to Lady Brook."

"An excellent notion," he said. "She's quite a jinglebrains, isn't she?"

Constance bit her lip. His comment was wholly inappropriate but far too insightful to be heard without agreement and suppressed amusement. She swallowed her laughter, however, and begged him to bring a tray of refreshments to the drawing room—peach ratafia, macaroons, and an assortment of fruit. "And, Morris, would the other lady be Ramsdell's mother?"

He nodded. "Indeed, that she would."

"Where is Ramsdell?" she asked.

"I last saw him leaving through the terrace doors toward the home wood, I think. But that was two hours past. He is partial to walking the paths."

"I see. Well, it would seem we have guests to attend to. Would you also have Fanny prepare two more rooms for the night? I feel Mama would wish me to invite them to stay."

"Aye, that I will."

Constance then squared her shoulders and headed toward the blue drawing room. Her heart was pounding in her chest as she thought of Lady Ramsdell waiting for her to come to her. If she understood correctly, her *good friend,* Mrs. Spencer—whose head she would have on a platter in the not too distant future—had told her ladyship all about one Constance Pamberley of Lady Brook Cottage, who had been caring for her injured son.

TWELVE

Constance entered the blue drawing room and found to her surprise that Ramsdell had returned from his walk in the woods and was even at that moment greeting his mother and kissing her on the cheek. His brow was damp from his exertions, but she thought he looked most handsome with so much vigorous exercise warming his features.

His mother's gaze, fixed on him, was full of affection and pleasure, and she did not immediately release the hand she had placed on his arm. She was saying, "Eleanor became so uneasy that I decided we should begin our journey home quite beforetimes, though I did insist we could hardly return from Europe without stopping at Brighton and paying a call on the regent. Prinny, of course, insisted we stay for at least a fortnight, then we received an invitation to Lady Bramshill's ball, which I know was Sophia Spencer's doing."

"The vicar's wife, here, in Berkshire?" Ramsdell asked, a frown furrowing his brow. "I didn't know you were acquainted with her."

Constance, who did not want to intrude on this conversation, remained unnoticed in the doorway. Mrs. Kidmarsh was reclining on the sofa beside the fireplace, her eyes closed and a vinaigrette held to her nose. Someone, presumably Lady Ramsdell, had closed the shutters of the two nearest windows, which darkened the chamber considerably.

She then noticed that a slight blush was on Lady Ramsdell's cheeks as she responded to her son's query. "Yes. I—I used to know Mrs. Spencer many years ago. Her letter mentioned your accident, as well as Charles's, so we both felt it imperative to leave Brighton that day, which was yesterday. But you know how carriage sick Eleanor becomes. We had to stop near the Berkshire border for the night—and here we are."

Constance chose this moment to step into the room, feeling that to continue pausing and listening would very soon border on eavesdropping. "I trust I have not kept you waiting long, Lady Ramsdell," she said.

"No, not at all. Hugo has just returned from his walk, as you can see." She turned to her son. "Will you perform the introductions? Miss Pamberley and I have not been properly introduced."

Ramsdell performed this office with some formality, though the true ceremony of the introductions were lost when Mrs. Kidmarsh merely opened one suffering eye and barely inclined her head to her hostess.

Constance did not feel insulted, however. She had already taken Mrs. Kidmarsh's measure and knew that everything in that lady's life, including basic manners and common sense, would always give way to her overrefined sensibilities.

After Mrs. Kidmarsh closed her eye and moaned a little more, Constance addressed her ladyship. "I have ordered a little refreshment for you. Morris will be bringing it directly, if that would suit you."

"Why, yes, it would—very much, thank you. The drive from Sussex was rather stifling and I find I'm parched."

"I don't wonder, ma'am, with the days as hot as they are, though I think you'll find most of the house will be comfortable throughout the remainder of the day. The elms give us profuse shade against the afternoon heat."

"I can see that they do. You have a lovely home, Miss Pamberley. You are to be congratulated on the condition of the house and lands. Everything seems to be in remarkable order. I was given to understand by Mrs. Spencer that you are the present owner of Lady Brook?"

Constance nodded. "I inherited the estate upon my father's death. The entail, most fortuitously, was not exclusive of heirs female.

"Rightly so," Lady Ramsdell stated with some finality. "I see no reason why any woman should be excluded if there are no sons born to the family."

"I couldn't agree more," Constance responded with a smile.

"You *own* Lady Brook?" Ramsdell asked. He turned toward her as though seeing her for the first time.

Constance glanced at him and realized with a start that for all their conversations regarding the property, somehow Ramsdell had assumed she merely served as housekeeper and bailiff for a male relation. "Don't tell me you didn't know?" she asked, dumbfounded. "After all our discussions!"

"I supposed—I presumed that you merely had a love for your home."

"Well, I do."

Lady Ramsdell chuckled. "It would not be an unusual mistake to make, Hugo, since it is so rare that a woman owns property these days. But tell me, are you feeling well? Mrs. Spencer said that you were violently ill for apace."

"I was," he said. He struggled to take his astonished gaze from Constance but eventually was able to return his full attention to his mother. "Quite ill, but Miss Pamberley—and Marchand—nursed me back to health. There was a great deal of infection, you see, for the bone"—here he lifted his bandaged arm slightly—"pierced the skin when it was shattered."

Lady Ramsdell pressed a hand to her mouth. "I don't know whether to be grateful or deeply distressed that I was so ignorant of your illness all these weeks."

Ramsdell leaned over and kissed her cheek. "Don't give it another thought. All's well that end's well."

Lady Ramsdell smiled suddenly. "I won't," she stated again with finality.

Constance had the impression that when Lady Ramsdell made up her mind about anything, the object was immediately accomplished.

Mrs. Kidmarsh rose to a sitting position, the shift in conversation having caught her attention.

"And did you care for my poor Charles as well?" she asked, addressing Constance.

"Dr. Deane of Four-Mile-Cross attended to your son. He remained by his bedside that day and was quite pleased when Mr. Kidmarsh regained consciousness, I believe around four o'clock. He then sent for Dr. Kent. By the next morning Mr. Kidmarsh appeared to be in excellent health except for a mild headache. He remained abed for a fortnight and was tended to, most assiduously, by my four sisters. Ramsdell's accident occurred on the fifth day, and all my attention was given to him."

"So Charles remained in bed a full fortnight, you say? Well, thank goodness for that. I'm glad he showed such excellent sense." She wafted the vinaigrette beneath her nose one more time. "But why didn't he know me just now? Mrs. Spencer's letter stated that he had suffered some loss of memory, but how is it he did not know his own mother?"

"He's been suffering from amnesia, a peculiar disorder of the brain that sometimes attends a blow to the head. This is the primary reason he has remained at Lady Brook all this time instead of returning to Aston Hall, as both Ramsdell and I would have preferred. Dr. Kent refused to let him depart, believing that the recovery of his memory would be severely hampered were he to change his surroundings. It would seem, and I hope this will give you some comfort, that Mr. Kidmarsh has been very happy at Lady Brook."

Mrs. Kidmarsh's expression took on a pained aspect. "I almost didn't know him," she said. "He is greatly altered, and so very *brown,* but why was he wet?"

"Your son and my sisters had all just returned from

Wraythorne, which is four miles distant. They had taken a shorter path home, but one that involved crossing a stream by way of a fallen log."

"I don't understand," Mrs. Kidmarsh said. "How can a carriage cross a log?"

Constance paused for a moment and blinked "Oh, I see . . . no, no, they walked to Wraythorne—and back again. They did not take one of the carriages."

"Walked? *Walked?* My poor Charles walked four miles, you say?"

"Well, that would be more like eight by the time they returned to Lady Brook."

Mrs. Kidmarsh appeared ready to swoon again. "He has never done so!" She glanced at her sister, her eyes wide with horror. "I should never have left Aston Hall! Look what has come of it! Charles, walking! His health will be ruined. Ruined, I tell you!"

"Nonsense, Eleanor. Charles looked the picture of health. Indeed, he seemed very much a man and not the little boy we left behind in Bedfordshire."

Mrs. Kidmarsh's mouth fell agape. "Are you to turn against me too?" she cried, aghast.

"My dear sister, I love you very much, but you can be such a ninnyhammer. Charles has not suffered here at Lady Brook—he's grown up. *Grown up.*"

"You are greatly mistaken," Mrs. Kidmarsh said with a decided sniff. She turned as one who has suffered mightily in this life and begged Constance to continue. "So, he was walking across this log—"

"Yes, he, along with my sister Augusta, slipped from the log and fell into a pool of water. But I shouldn't refine overly much on it. The day is so warm, I sincerely believe there isn't the smallest concern that he will suffer because of it."

"You don't know Charles's constitution as I do. He was always a sickly babe." Her face puckered up, and she began to weep again.

Constance didn't know what to say to her and so changed the subject. "I know that Mama will insist that you both stay the night, Lady Ramsdell, and longer if it would please you. She told me that she knew you from seminary so many years ago."

"Indeed, I did," she responded quietly. She looked very conscious, just as she had earlier, when Ramsdell questioned her about being acquainted with Sophia Spencer. "But I don't wish to intrude. I understand your mother is quite ill, that her apoplexy has robbed her entirely of her speech and movement."

"That *was* true," Constance said, "until Mr. Kidmarsh arrived. It would seem your nephew has had a miraculous effect on my mother. She has in recent days, under his supervision, begun speaking again and has even shown signs of regaining her mobility."

"Good heavens!" Lady Ramsdell cried. "Is this true?"

"Charles?" Mrs. Kidmarsh exclaimed, astonished. Her weeping stopped quite suddenly. "How is this possible, when he knows nothing of such things?"

Constance could not resist saying, "He mentioned to me that he was so well acquainted with the attending exigencies of the sickroom that he knew precisely how my mother was feeling and apparently set about to help her regain the strength of her limbs and her voice."

Mrs. Kidmarsh's color rose on her cheeks, and she trembled as she spoke. "I have been a good mother to my son. No one knows the trials! From the beginning, I—"

"You are greatly mistaken," her sister interrupted. "We are all too familiar with your sufferings, Eleanor, so pray take a damper." She then addressed Constance. "We should be exceedingly happy to accept of your invitation."

Since at that moment Morris arrived with a beautifully arranged platter of biscuits and fruit along with an aromatic carafe of peach ratafia, Constance left the ladies and Ramsdell to enjoy their refreshment. She sent the footman to bring in the baggage and Stively to tend to Lady Ramsdell's fine traveling coach and two pair of horses.

She then went in search of Charles.

She found him just emerging from his bedchamber, dressed in a brown coat and buckskin breeches. His hair was still damp but arranged in his usual curls across his forehead.

She led him to the library, which was as far from the drawing room as any two chambers in her home. She could see his heart was weighted with concern. The former amiability and joy of his countenance had given way to a paved look that boded ill for his health and his joie de vivre.

She confronted him with what she believed to be the truth, that he knew precisely who he was and that Mrs. Kidmarsh was indeed his mother. He denied it at first, but when she expressed her sympathy, he was undone and spent the next half hour unburdening his soul to her. She was sickened by the lengths to which his overly devoted mother had gone to keep her son from all evil but made every effort to remain passive as his voice gave way to the numerous miseries of his former life.

"I can't go back there," he stated at last with a strong shake of his head. "Now that I've known what my life can be, I will never place myself in her hands again. She sees me as an infant. She will never see me as anything more."

"You must make her see that you are a man now," Constance said.

He turned toward her, his hands outspread in an appealing gesture. "But how? How? I have but to sneeze and she puts me to bed with leeches and a warming pan even if the day is as hot as Hades."

"You are a man now, Charles. Have you considered an establishment of your own, apart from her?"

His shoulders slumped. "If you knew the caterwauling that would ensue, that always ensues when I mention my own town house in London."

"Then you are doomed," she said provokingly.

He cast her a scathing glance, which made her smile. "The choice is yours. Undoubtedly, she will fall into a fit of hysterics at first, but eventually—especially if you press her with your true age—she will have to accept your decision. What other course is open to her? To disown you?"

His face grew mulish. "If only she would!"

Constance chuckled. "I have seen her kind before, and I truly believe that at the base of her overzealous mothering is a genuine, if misguided, love for you. In time, that love will assert itself probably with greater balance and proper intent—but only if you press her."

"Do you think so?"

She nodded. "With all my heart." She then recalled Ramsdell's explanation that Mrs. Kidmarsh was not the only one to blame, that his entire staff was maniacal about Charles, whose cherubic visage had enchanted them all from the first. She added, "Though I daresay, you oughtn't to return to Aston, at least not until you are prepared to battle Ramsdell's battalion of retainers as well as your mother."

At that, Charles smiled crookedly. "You've no idea what my upbringing was like in the hands of so many good-intentioned people."

"You must also blame your kind heart. If I know you at all, Alby, I know that you were unwilling to hurt those who have loved you so profoundly."

"You do me too much honor in saying so. I would rather set down my entire conduct to a lack of courage."

"I would not be so harsh in summing up your character, but if that is what you believe, then it is time to take up your sword and defend your soul."

He met her gaze and his smile broadened at her words. "You are right. I shall begin at once."

Nuncheon was a lively affair, since Charles had grown more used to having his mother close at hand. He seemed to have decided that she must grow accustomed to him in his newly awakened state and therefore behaved as he had almost from the time he recovered from his accident—in an enthusiastic, helpful, joyous manner. He let his wit run rampant and teased all the ladies, including his mother, until even she could not keep from smiling.

Constance watched Mrs. Kidmarsh, who in turn rarely ever let her eyes stray from Alby. Her expression underwent several changes from the moment she sat down to table, from pensive and even curt in her responses to anyone, to almost confused as her son began cutting an apple for her and one for Augusta, to amused when he teased Katherine about loving the stables more than the drawing room.

"Of course I do!" she cried. "Who wouldn't prefer the wind in one's face to the stuffy confines of a receiving room?"

Lady Ramsdell addressed her. "You sound very much like my son, Evan. Once he discovered the delight of the stables, he was never anywhere else, which at least had the advantage that I always knew where he was. The disadvantage was the abhorrent language he would try out on all of us, strictly for the purpose of seeing our shocked and disapproving expressions. He was such a saucebox in those days. Now he loves his horses. Hugo, did I tell you he is considering selling out? We visited him in Brussels in late June. Since the war ended, he says he is fagged to death with sitting about in the most useless manner day in and day out. I should be happy to see him come home, only I wonder what he shall do to keep occupied."

"He will probably tend to his property in Worcestershire and breed racing horses."

A heavy sigh erupted from Katherine that first set all the eyes to landing on her, and then a swift, general laughter followed. "I don't see why any of you are in the least amused. I couldn't imagine a happier fate and wish only that I had a horse or two fit for the Newmarket races. Lord-a-Mercy has some good strides in him, but he is too short of bone to gather any real speed." She began speaking to the air as her audience settled in for a long listen and began cutting slices of cold chicken, fruit, and slivers of Cook's excellent pigeon pie.

When her diatribe ended, Ramsdell addressed his mother. "And what will you be doing this afternoon?" he asked. "Though I would suppose you will spend much of it resting for the ball tonight."

"Perhaps later," she said, smiling, her eyes bright. "From my bedchamber window I noticed the most beautiful rose garden and maze. I'm very good at mazes, and I intend to spend the next hour or so solving it. Eleanor, do you wish to join me?"

Mrs. Kidmarsh nodded, her expression a little rapt as she was savoring the pigeon pie. "How on earth did your mother acquire such an excellent cook?" she asked, addressing Constance. "I vow I've never had better pie, and earlier the macaroons equaled the ones at Brighton!"

All the ladies chuckled their pleasure. "Cook is a delight," Augusta said, smiling sweetly, "but a stickler for the ingredients. She has an herb garden that she tends to personally and will not use a piece of meat that is not fresh."

"Well! I vow if I remain too long at Lady Brook, I shall become quite high in the flesh. I now understand why my son looks as though he's been feasting on ambrosia. It's because he has!"

Constance watched as Charles turned toward his mother and offered her a genuine smile. Mrs. Kidmarsh looked at him, responding in kind, though sudden tears sparkled on her lashes. His expression then grew wholly sympathetic, which was nearly Mrs. Kidmarsh's undoing. She immediately began clearing her throat and hastily swallowed a gulp of Madeira.

Charles, for his part, grew a little more subdued, his thoughts inscrutable except for the pinch of his lips and the faint working of his jaw. She knew that he loved his parent but suspected he was steeling himself against her extreme affection in order to succeed in making his own way through life.

When nuncheon concluded, the party broke up into several portions. Alby stole away with Marianne and Augusta to return to their favorite berrying copse, Katherine commandeered Celeste to help her put the finishing touches to her ball gown, Ramsdell took Stively into the home wood to view the latest poaching trap he had uncovered, Mrs. Kidmarsh and Lady Ramsdell retired to the terrace, the rose garden, and maze, and Constance made her way to her mother's room, where she intended to spend the next hour.

She read to her parent for some time and discussed at length her previous acquaintance with Lady Ramsdell. Constance learned that though Lady Ramsdell had been a year her mother's senior, she had always been kind to her as well as to all the younger girls.

"Was that when she met Sophia?"

"Yes . . . Sophia knew . . . her younger sister. Good . . . friends. We . . . were all excited for her . . . when she married the fourth . . . viscount. A brilliant . . . match."

"Indeed?" Constance queried more out of politeness than anything else.

"Poor as . . . church mice . . . Mary's family. Daughter of . . . country squire . . . in Wiltshire."

Constance heard the words but couldn't quite make them fit into her brain. "Poor?" she queried.

"Yes. Very . . . much so."

Constance couldn't credit what her mother was saying.

"Was she undowered?" she asked.

"Yes. Pockets to let."

Constance was completely dumbfounded.

Ramsdell's father had married a woman of unequal connections and wealth? How was that possible, given his son's determination to do otherwise? She had always felt that Ramsdell's convictions had been learned within the structure of his family, handed down to him from his father, and his father before him. Now, learning that the dowager Lady Ramsdell had been an impoverished miss from Wiltshire set her own heart beating strangely in her breast—not of hope, but of fear.

From the first, she had known a certain sense of ease with Ramsdell for the very reason that he was completely unattainable. She had nothing to fear from him.

Yet what was it she feared?

She felt sick with anxiety suddenly and recalled yet again the prophecy of her former suitor. He had told her she could never love a man for Lady Brook and her family would always be uppermost in her mind and heart.

Yet, she hadn't believed that—at least not exactly. She had always thought that her heart had simply remained untouched these many years, that the right man had simply not come to Lady Brook. Now, with the knowledge that in some manner Ramsdell was not quite as unattainable as she had thought, nothing but fear raced through her.

Constance wanted to know more, to pelt her mother with a dozen questions about Lady Ramsdell and the fourth viscount, but she could see that the lengthy conversation had fatigued her parent. "I should go," she said at last.

Lady Ramsdell stayed her with a lift of her hand. "One . . . moment. Connie . . . do you love him? Tell . . . me."

Constance felt a sudden warmth flood her cheeks. "Yes . . . no . . . I don't know! But it hardly signifies. We don't suit, we can't suit. The disparity in rank—"

"Means . . . nothing. Do . . . you . . . love . . . him?"

"Oh, Mother, don't ask. All these weeks I haven't permitted myself to even wonder about the depth of my sentiments for from the first I knew—we had both decided—that ours would be a simple, summery country flirtation, and nothing more."

She saw a crooked smile touch her mother's lips. "How . . . very foresightful . . . of you . . . both!"

She knew her mother was laughing at her, and that made her smile. How different it was to have her parent speaking and making sport of her! How wonderful it was!

She rose from her chair and leaned over to place a kiss on her cheek. "I intend to end this quite useless conversation right now. I have several things I must do before the ball—for one thing, I have yet to cut the flowers for our guests' rooms. So, if you will excuse me, I'll let you have your afternoon sleep and, pray, forget about Ramsdell."

"Love . . . you," her mother said, her eyes softening in expression.

"I love you too, dearest. Sleep well."

She reached the door, but her mother could not resist one parting thought. "Don't . . . be a . . . goosecap. Marry him if you can."

She merely laughed, though uneasily, at the absurdity of it and quit the room.

Constance made her way to her own bedchamber, intending to fetch a pair of gloves suitable for cutting roses. She eventually found them on the table by the window and noticed above the tops of the silver fir trees in the forest across from Lady Brook, a billow of dust that shaded the deep blue sky. The creation of the new lane had been under way for some time but probably wouldn't be complete for months, not until sufficient crushed rock could be laid a foot in depth to create a suitable macadamization. Without the rock the lane would turn to mud during any rain and would become virtually unpassable.

Change.

She didn't want anything to change, she realized with a start. She wanted Lady Brook Bend to remain as it was, but the dust in the air told her that was now impossible. She had effected the change herself when she had hired Mr. Bellows to cut a gentler arc through the forest.

Now she had learned that Lady Ramsdell had been even poorer than herself when she had wed her husband. Again, an inexplicable fear coursed through her. She felt threatened as never before, as though destiny was hovering over her and demanding she acquiesce to a marriage that had not even been offered to her. After all, the precedent had been set within Ramsdell's family. History could repeat itself.

But she didn't want change. She wanted everything to remain the same. The dust rose higher into the sky, and a chill shook through her body.

But this was ridiculous!

She gave herself a strong shake. She told herself her fears were absurd, that she was the master of her own fate, and that whatever Lady Ramsdell's life had been did not mean hers must follow suit. Not by half!

She squared her shoulders. She lifted her chin to fate. She would live her own life as she saw fit. The fears, the anxiety, the inexplicable tremblings in her legs, left her—that is until from the corner of her eye she saw Augusta and Charles emerge from the shrubbery near the lane.

Change.

Even from that distance she could see that her sister was overset as she wiped a tear from her cheek. Her shoulders were slumped, so unlike Augusta. Charles stood over her, speaking. Augusta listened and wrung her hands. He cupped his palm beneath her chin and lifted her face to his.

Then he kissed her!

Augusta would surely push him away, perhaps even strike him a blow across the face. Surely!

Instead, Constance watched in stupefaction as her sister forgot entirely where she was. She leaned into Charles and slid her arms about his neck and kissed him back. The incredible truth hit her fully in the face—she had kissed him before!

Constance could watch no more but turned away from the window, her former anxiety wreaking new havoc in her body. She felt dizzy and queasy. Her heart raced. She could hardly breathe. She could barely keep her balance.

Change.

She didn't want change. She loved her home, her family, just as it was. She had clung to the routines of Lady Brook for so long as her primary security in such a wretchedly insecure world that she couldn't bear the thought of a lane being cut through the fir forest, or of Lady Ramsdell having been an impoverished miss, or—heaven forbid!—of Augusta in love!

She sat down in a chair and forced the frightening sensations away. She spoke rationally to her overwrought mind. She forced her limbs to relax. She took a hundred deep breaths.

Even so, she was not able to leave her bedchamber for a full half hour, and only then after she had reminded herself again and again that she was the master of her fate.

She was.

She was.

THIRTEEN

Ramsdell knew he had made the trek back into the home wood, Stively at his side, not so much to help dismantle another poaching trap but for the strict purpose of being apart from the rest of his family and Constance, at least for an hour or so. He had needed time to adjust to the truly unsettling news that Constance was the owner of Lady Brook Cottage.

The walk had calmed his disturbed sensibilities, and now, with Stively having returned to the stables, he made a slow progress back to the house and began to determine just in what way Constance's property changed things, if at all.

She owned Lady Brook.

The moment his mother had made this fact clear to him, he had been in a state of stupefaction. He couldn't think with any degree of precision, and thoughts of Constance reigning over Aston Hall kept vying with his long-nurtured ideal of exactly the woman he would take to wife.

Constance did not fit that ideal. She was not the daughter of a peer, she did not have sufficient London experience to be an immediately successful hostess, and regardless of her property, she was not well dowered.

But she did have Lady Brook and he could no longer ignore that her possession of the property changed how he viewed her. The question rose in his mind, how fixed were his ideals, and was it possible that he could set them aside in favor of Constance?

The very nature of the question, however, disturbed him deeply, and Lady Alison, his first love, rose suddenly to mind. Had she viewed him in a similar manner? Did she ask herself, does he have enough wealth, enough potential, a high enough rank?

He felt sickened suddenly, because for the life of him, he could see no difference between his thinking and her scheming. Yet that had not been his intention when he laid out the particulars of his notion of a proper wife. He had merely wanted to fulfill his father's strictures and to protect his own heart.

Surely these were admirable objects?

Still, he could not differentiate between Lady Alison and himself, not in this situation.

After all, was Constance truly worthy of him now only because she could bring Lady Brook with her? His stomach churned and burned his throat. For one of the few times in his life he was ill at ease with himself and his beliefs.

He turned these arguments over in his mind again and again until he reached the terrace and the rose garden, where he found his mother and aunt enjoying the beautiful vista. He felt relieved to see them, for then he could set aside a debate he could not seem to resolve.

Both ladies reclined in chaise longues that were shaded by a large elm. His aunt, he discovered, was fast asleep and snoring gently. Between the sisters was a teapot, two cups and two saucers, and a plate that might at one time have held either biscuits, tarts, or perhaps a cake but which now was nothing but a gravel bed of crumbs.

Lady Ramsdell greeted him in a hushed voice. "Do draw forward a chair, Hugo. I should enjoy a few minutes of your company."

The terrace was laid out with several wooden chairs and lounges for the purpose of taking the air and viewing the gardens. Ramsdell settled a chair close to his mother's chaise longue.

"Were you much shocked to learn that Charles had stolen away from Aston Hall—*again?*" he inquired.

Lady Ramsdell hid a yawn behind her hand, then responded. "Poor Charles," she whispered. "He's been desperate for years to take his own life in hand. With no one to fend off the excessive ministrations of your staff, I daresay he escaped from Aston as quick as the cat could lick her ear."

Ramsdell huffed a sigh. "I know that I am partially to blame for all that has happened. I ought to make changes, oughtn't I?"

"Yes, but I couldn't begin to tell you what you could do. Our servants are all so *devoted.*"

Ramsdell chuckled. "Don't I know it."

Lady Ramsdell glanced up at her son and gave the subject a turn. "You know, Miss Pamberley would be wise not to manage her house with such excellent efficiency, and she ought also to get rid of her cook, otherwise she will tempt me to remain at Lady Brook through the remainder of the summer."

"Mama!" he cried, laughing. "What an odd thing to say."

She eyed him carefully for a moment. "She strikes me as a superior young woman."

"Indeed, she is," Ramsdell responded.

Lady Ramsdell sighed. "Should we be dressing for dinner soon, for I imagine we will need to leave for the ball at a timely hour?"

"I don't know, but I am persuaded Con—Miss Pamberley will send a servant round to gather everyone up at the proper time."

"Of course you are right." She glanced at her sister. "I don't like to wake her," she continued, lowering her voice. "She is entirely overset as much by her son's conduct as by the fact he doesn't recall who she is."

"I'm sure in due course he will remember her. As to his conduct, I find him greatly improved. Don't you?"

She nodded. "Remarkably so. He seems very *manly* these days. But what if he doesn't want to remember his mother? The mind is a curious thing and, though I am deeply fond of Eleanor, she has not been the best of parents."

"I have little doubt he will one day know who she is." He lowered his voice conspiratorially. "He is half in love with the youngest daughter, you know."

She nodded. "The pair of them do smell a great deal of April and May. It is Miss Augusta, is it not?"

"Yes."

"A delightful child, to be sure, very gentle in spirit, which I believe would suit Charles well."

He heard the approval in her voice. "You would not object to such a match?"

She glanced up at him. "Why would I? She is a Lady of Quality, clearly of excellent breeding. The lineage, though not noble, is quite unexceptionable. All that Miss Augusta lacks is a dowry, which can be of no consequence to Charles, after all."

He stared down at her, feeling the color drain from his face. There it was again, the truth he had not seen before. He held the prejudice deeply in his own heart, of who he should marry and who he should not. His mother, clearly, held an entirely different set of dictums close to her heart.

His father, on the other hand, had made known his expectations from the time he could remember. His strictures rang in his ears—*add to the property, make wise investments, marry the daughter of a peer.* His father had even left a letter for him in his will, which he had memorized.

Aston Hall is given to you in trust. Never betray that trust. And for God's sake, don't let your head be turned by a provincial miss or any lady living on the fringes of tonnish society. You will regret it infinitely, for she will never function well as Viscountess Ramsdell and all that that position en-

ails. *You will have need of her abilities as your responsibilities to Parliament increase through the years. This is the advice I give you, the advice my father gave me and his father before him. One day you will pass along the same wisdom to your son, I have little doubt. For now, know that I love you and God be with you.*

The advice had been sensible. He had seen no reason to part with a basic philosophy that had served his family well for generations. His mother, though not the daughter of a peer, had brought a handsome dowry to her marriage, some fifty thousand pounds. She had been presented at court by the Marchioness of Glyndebourne at the age of eighteen and had had a score of beaus. His father had tumbled in love with her, married her, and had been exceedingly happy.

"Your father meant well," his mother intruded as though having read his mind, "but the truth is there is something he kept from you, something I think you ought to know."

Ramsdell felt as though every nerve in his body had suddenly been lit on fire. He sensed that from that moment, his life would change. "Yes?" he encouraged her.

"My dowry was fabricated."

He blinked, pondered, and shook his head. "What?"

She nodded and laughed. "I have always detested the whisker George and his father concocted in order to make our union more acceptable to the beau monde—that a wealthy distant cousin, upon his death, had quite fortuitously bestowed fifty thousand pounds on me. The money, of course, belonged to the Ramsdell estate. Have you ever heard anything more absurd?"

Ramsdell felt for the second time that day as though he had been knocked flat by a heavily laden wagon. "You were poor, then, Mama?"

"Very. And we had hardly any connections worth mentioning except my father's distant relation, the elderly Marchioness of Glyndebourne, who by some miracle actually agreed to present me during my first Season."

Ramsdell couldn't believe his ears. He stared at her through her, into her. "I don't believe it," he said.

"It is all too true, and at the moment I'm excessively relieved to finally have revealed the truth to you—especially to you. Having received a letter from Mrs. Spencer and then actually visiting in the home of a woman with whom I attended seminary was quite uncomfortable for me, you've no idea! I felt the truth would out at any moment, and then where would I be? What would you think of me?

"I know your father wanted to prevent a fortune hunter from enticing you into an inappropriate marriage, but I have long since believed that his intentions harmed you. I have never known such a stickler as you. I also think your notions of an acceptable bride have kept you from forming a serious attachment long before this—that is, until now."

He sat back in his chair, his neckcloth suddenly feeling a great deal too tight. "What do you mean?"

"Were I to judge what I have seen thus far, I would say your affections have been engaged. Am I mistaken?"

His mouth fell agape. "Why would you say such a thing, especially since you have been here only a few scant hours?"

"The way you look at Miss Pamberley, with your expression so tender! Upon my soul, Hugo. I had come to believe you were impervious to Cupid's golden-tipped arrows." She lifted a hand to gently feather his hair. "Oh, my darling, you are so much like your father, more than even Evan, who has a great deal more of his temper than you. Your papa used to look at me in the very same way I have seen you look at Miss Pamberley. But . . . she will not do?"

He held back a deep sigh. "No, of course not."

"Why are you never satisfied, my pet?"

He started and blinked. "I beg your pardon? Are you somehow inferring that I ought to marry Miss Pamberley?"

"I have said only one thing to you over the years, well, two perhaps—that your bride be a Lady of Quality and that you love her. Have I ever said more?"

"No."

"Then, for God's sake, Hugo, marry Constance, or you will regret it the rest of your life. And now I see that the very servant you prophesied has come to inform us of the hour."

Ramsdell turned and saw that young Fanny was indeed approaching them. He wanted to continue the conversation, but already his mother had risen from her chaise longue and was even now gently prodding his aunt's shoulder and calling softly to her.

There was only one thing to do, then—return to his own bedchamber and begin the process of dressing for Lady Bramshill's ball.

Having completed her toilette, Constance stood before her long looking glass gowned in the ball dress Celeste had created for her. Her light brown curls were drawn into a chignon atop her head with dozens of tiny ringlets allowed to cascade behind. She ought to have been pleased with the result, for truly the coiffure suited her immensely. She looked young— though distressed—and, yes, she could even admit this much, she looked beautiful. She knew Ramsdell would approve heartily of her appearance.

Yes, he would approve and he would offer her several delightful compliments and he would especially like her gown.

Celeste had once again performed magic with her needle. The amethyst gown, covered in a sheer tulle and cut low at the neckline, fit her to perfection. In the mirror she could see the young woman she once was, who had danced until her feet ached nearly every night during her London Season.

She knew an impulse, however, to drag her fingers wildly through her hair and ruin Fanny's beautiful chignon and ringlets. She no longer wanted Ramsdell to see her like this, to see her at her very best. She wished he had never come to Lady Brook, for his presence had brought change to her house, and the very thought of her home altering even one minuscule degree caused the air to escape her lungs and her limbs to tremble.

But then, nothing had changed really. The only difference was that she now knew of Lady Ramsdell's true circumstances. Perhaps Lord Ramsdell didn't know of the relative poverty of his mother's origins, or perhaps he did know but felt it unwise to follow his father's suit and marry a country miss.

If only her heart would stop racing like the wind!

She drew on her gloves slowly and took a long last look at herself in the mirror. Tears suddenly smarted her eyes, for another truth asserted itself—she *did* want Ramsdell to see her like this, to see her, to dance with her, to embrace her, and to kiss her.

What was she going to do? What was going to happen to her? If only she had remained in ignorance of Lady Ramsdell's family, then she could be at ease again!

She squeezed her eyes shut and forced all her thoughts away from the forefront of her mind. She had several duties to perform at the moment—to order the proper number of carriages, to arrange the places for dinner, to make certain that her guests had been properly attended to.

She swallowed her fears, therefore, and left her bedchamber.

Ramsdell stared at himself in the mirror settled atop the chest of drawers. He had completed dressing for the evening and was satisfied with what he saw, at least with regard to the careful styling of his hair, the intricate folds of his neckcloth, the smooth black silk of his coat and white waistcoat, his breeches and silk stockings, his black dancing slippers.

His heart, however, was another matter entirely. Why, for instance, did his chest feel as though it were being squeezed by the hands of a giant. What was it about a formal ball that forced a man to confront his life?

The ritual of dancing was an ancient one, but his society had been bringing man and woman together more closely than ever before—the waltz was considered scandalous by many, an excuse for hugging. But dancing performed at a function such as a formal ball changed everything. Adherence to social strictures was more forcibly guarded with matrons lining the walls ready to pounce on those who broke the rules. He wasn't inclined to break the rules, that was not what was troubling him. He had always approved of the ceremonies and order of rank that attended such an assembly.

What he was considering was larger and more involved— how the attendance at such a ritual was a sort of promise, a promise to sustain the very society that would concoct such a ritual in the first place. He was a responsible man and would keep that promise; he had always wanted to keep that promise, to choose a bride from among dozens of Ladies of Quality, to leave an heir to the viscountcy of Ramsdell, to enhance the affluence of his estate.

The thought shattered his mind—he did not want to attend this ball with Constance. To do so was to come far too close to keeping his promise to his forebears. He wasn't ready, she wasn't the appropriate bride for him, she didn't fit his requirements.

His mother had been an impoverished miss from Wiltshire and her dowry fabricated!

He felt utterly overwhelmed. Good God! His father had lied to him. His father had married precisely the sort of woman he had insisted Ramsdell should never wed. His father had set the worst sort of precedence especially since his heretofore exacting son had fallen into the hands of a woman who could undo him in the most exciting way with just a glance, just a word from her rosy lips, just a soft, warm, inviting embrace.

There was no reason now, he realized, that he could not take one Constance Pamberley to wife. No reason at all, especially since . . . he loved her.

The thought rushed through his mind like a strong wind sweeping down a hollow. His heart burst into flames and sent sparks throughout his entire body and mind. He felt dizzy, yet alive as never before. All the images he had had of her—beneath him, sharing his bed, ruling over Aston Hall—suddenly poured over him in a wave of excitement and pleasure. The thing he had never allowed himself to feel now became a torrent of sensation that engulfed him—how happy, how exhilarated he would feel marrying Constance Pamberley.

Oh, God!

"M'lord?" Marchand called to him. "Is anything amiss? Are you feeling poorly again, for if you don't mind my saying so, your color is a trifle high."

Ramsdell chuckled and turned to look at his most faithful valet. "No," he said. "Nothing is amiss. Nothing that cannot be repaired by an honest clergyman."

When Constance had performed her duties, she made her way to the blue drawing room. Her anxieties had become considerably diminished in the steady work of ordering carriages and seeing that the dinner was ready for her guests. When she arrived at the drawing room, however, instead of finding that at least one or two of her guests and the same number of her sisters had made the descent down the stairs, she found only . . . Ramsdell.

Her heart lurched, sputtered, kicked, and shouted at the very sight of him. He was in full evening dress, blacks and whites like the famous Beau Brummell, and had never appeared to greater advantage. He was framed by the red brick of the fireplace and the blue silk damask of the walls beyond and was undoubtedly the most handsome gentleman who had ever lived.

She smiled, almost tremulously. His answering smile was soft, inviting, enticing. The look in his eye was strange, however, even otherworldly. She felt her panic rise in her breast. He was speaking silent mysteries to her. He was speaking silently of change.

Change. She knew it was coming. She felt a sudden impulse to turn on her heel and run, to run away from Ramsdell, from the drawing room, even from the house, to run and never to stop.

She might have done so, but at that very moment he extended his hand to her and said, "Come to me, Constance, before the others arrive."

Her fears departed swiftly upon his words, upon his gesture, upon the wicked invitation he was extending to her. Only desire for him, to be with him, to be held by him, to be kissed by him swelled her heart. She began walking toward him as one mesmerized. She took his hand, and he drew her into the circle of his right arm.

"The deuce take it," he murmured hotly, and with a slow movement slid his hand from his sling and surrounded her carefully but fully with both arms.

"Oh," she breathed against his lips.

He kissed her as he had never kissed her before, engulfing her entirely in the flames of his desire. She received his kiss, responding to his unspoken will. She kissed him madly, wrapping her arms tightly about his neck, letting the fires in her rage and burn and leap to terrible heights. She felt consumed by her love for him, by her desire for him. Forgotten were all her fears.

Time stopped yet moved at lightning speed. His tongue became a wild search and she let him explore to his heart's content. Every intention of being circumspect, sensible, and orderly disappeared with each tick of the clock.

After a time, she drew back and looked into his eyes. Gray had smoldered into black coals. "Constance," he murmured. "I—"

Voices intruded. Unkind, thoughtless, heartless voices disrupted her communion with Ramsdell. She drew back abruptly, her head dizzy with kissing him.

"I have much I wish to say to you," he whispered, catching her arm as she turned quickly away from him. His fingers slid along her glove and caught the palm of her hand in a gentle squeeze before letting her go entirely.

"Later, then," she murmured. She seated herself on the sofa beside the fireplace and began slowly pressing imaginary wrinkles from her gown. Each glide of her fingers down the tulle and silk took her farther from Ramsdell and hopefully returned her complexion to a more normal hue.

Augusta entered the drawing room along with Katherine.

The fiery, love-drenched moment was now at a complete end.

The drive to Lady Bramshill's large mansion near the border of Kent was as pleasant as any summer journey could be. All three traveling chariots were well sprung and comfortable. The early evening weather was bright and clear without a single cloud in the sky to threaten the enjoyment of the evening.

Constance found herself in a daze. Even through dinner the memory of Ramsdell's kiss had remained in the forefront of her mind and would not be dismissed, even with the sternest of mental commands. Presently, she sat between Ramsdell and Katherine in her mother's small traveling coach, the narrowed confines affording her the supreme pleasure of being jostled by Ramsdell whenever one of the wheels hit a dip in the highway. That he took each opportunity to slip his right arm about her and protect her from the bounce made every hole in the road a thing to be anticipated with delight.

The postillions having been given orders to "spring 'em" accomplished the ten-mile journey in little over an hour. Once arrived at the imposing gray stone mansion of Henley

Lodge, the excursion took on the misty quality of a dream for Constance. So rarely did she leave Lady Brook to enjoy a holiday that the simple occupation of having another woman's butler take her cape without at the same time requesting quiet instructions as to the rest of the party made her feel like a princess.

Constance walked beside Ramsdell up the stairs to greet Lady Bramshill and her husband, Sir Richard. She was a delightful creature of thirty, while he was a dignified, silver-haired man in his late forties. Constance saw in their marriage a contentment not generally found, but she believed Sir Richard was responsible for much of their joint happiness, since he never had anything but a kind, loving word for his young wife.

As she greeted her hostess, who was smiling brightly, she was a little startled when Lady Bramshill leaned forward and whispered into her ear, "I have a surprise for you later."

Constance would have immediately asked for at least a few of the particulars, but Lady Bramshill was sly and quickly turned her full attention to Marianne, who followed behind her.

More guests flowed in behind the Pamberley party, and Constance soon found herself swept into the ballroom, which was alive with a Handel contredanse and the glitter of dozens of couples going down the lively set. Constance heard Marianne exclaim over the beauty of the ballroom, which was hung with yards and yards of a silver-spangled gauze and laced with fresh green ivy from Lady Bramshill's extensive gardens. The effect was Grecian and quite pleasing.

Katherine was immediately drawn away by a captain of the Horse Guards whom she had met at another of her ladyship's balls, and who insisted the next dance must be his.

The music drew fortuitously to a close, and Sir Henry offered his arm to Celeste as the previous dancers began leaving the floor. Alby and Augusta took their places as well, this time for the intricate quadrille.

Ramsdell turned to her. "I refuse *not* to dance," he stated with a smile, and offered his arm to her. "Even though I will appear quite awkward with my sling. Will you do me the honor?"

Constance was certain now that she was dreaming as she laid her hand atop his arm and began walking out onto the ballroom floor beside him. As she passed several ladies, she heard their hushed exclamations. " 'Tis Ramsdell!" "I had heard he might be coming, but I didn't believe it!" "Is he not a handsome creature?" "Is that Miss Pamberley with him?" " 'Pon my word, she seems much changed. Amethyst suits her, for I vow I've never seen her in better looks!"

Constance felt younger and more alive than she had in years and was not surprised by this last comment. She was feeling just as she had so many years before in London, gay and carefree, a sensation that was too sweet not to be enjoyed to the fullest. She gave herself, therefore, to Lady Bramshill's ball, to her friends whom she so rarely saw except on occasions such as this, to the delights of dancing with a dozen different partners, and to the great pleasure of being often in Ramsdell's company.

FOURTEEN

A little past ten o'clock, Constance searched the mansion for Ramsdell. The waltz was quickly forming, and he had previously instructed her to save this dance for him, since he felt he could manage a few turns about the ballroom with his healing arm encircling her back. Presently, however, he was nowhere to be found. She made inquiries along one passage and then another, greeting friends and exchanging quick histories as her eyes continually swept over each principal room and connecting antechamber.

She was about to enter the billiard room, from which chamber a general masculine laughter and badinage could be heard emanating, when Sir Henry appeared in the doorway.

"Hello, Miss Pamberley. I say, do you intend to play a game or two?" His eyes were lit with enthusiasm. "Celeste has just beaten Mr. Weatherby all to flinders."

"Indeed?" she queried. "I didn't know she played at billiards?"

"I have been teaching her," he stated, his chest puffing up a little. "She has considerable ability. I was just going to fetch an iced champagne cup for her since the room has become rather stifling, but you will find her within." He then stepped aside and swept an arm in a grand arc toward the doorway.

"Actually," she said, "I have been searching for Ramsdell. He was supposed to go down the next set with me, but I can't seem to find him."

His brow puckered and he considered. He snapped his fingers. "I saw him earlier with her grace, the Duchess of Mercer, perhaps ten minutes past. Now, where was that—near the conservatory, I think. Yes, Miss Celeste and I had just strolled in from the gardens—" The color on his cheeks became quite heightened and he coughed nervously. He apparently felt he needed to explain. "You see, Miss Celeste was feeling rather warm from the lively reel she had just danced and I felt a bit of air would be of use to her, because it is not a good thing to become overheated in a ballroom."

Constance kept her expression as serious as Sir Henry's, but the whole time her heart was alive with laughter. "You did very well by her," she told him. "Undoubtedly."

He seemed a little suspicious of her remark, narrowing his eyes at her slightly, but finally ended with "And just as I held the door wide for her to reenter the house, I recall having seen Ramsdell and the Duchess of Mercer walking toward the conservatory."

"Thank you. You've been a great help. I shall search for him there, then."

She would have turned away, but he said, "By the way, I just heard the most astonishing news and cannot conceive how I, or any of us really, have remained in ignorance of it this past sennight."

"What is that?" Constance asked, curious.

"The Priory has been purchased," he stated. "Have you heard of it?"

"No, indeed, I haven't," she stated, stunned.

"Well, it would seem it has, and the new owner has been in residence for the past week. Apparently he brought with him a mountain of furniture and an army of servants who have been turning the house out-of-doors these many days and more."

"This is quite astonishing," she remarked, wondering herself why she hadn't heard the news beforehand. "Where did you learn of it?"

"I just had it from Mrs. Spencer, not a few minutes ago. She said that he wished to keep his presence a quiet matter for a few days."

"How very mysterious," she murmured, but her thoughts had gone down a different road toward the field she had hoped to purchase from the estate that marched along Lady Brook's border. Perhaps if she became acquainted with the new owner, she would be able to make arrangements to buy the parcel that had been tempting her all these years. "Do you know his name?" she asked. "Have you met him? Is he here, perchance?"

He rolled his eyes a little. "Mrs. Spencer refused to tell me anything about him, yet teasingly informed me he was, indeed, in attendance at the ball."

"What absurdities are these?" she asked, feeling a faint annoyance that was reflected in Sir Henry's expression.

"I don't know. But you know how much Mrs. Spencer enjoys funning and joking and keeping all of us in suspense if she can."

"That she does." She then groaned. "I can hear the waltz and I was so looking forward to dancing. Well, you had best fetch the champagne for Celeste and I shall see if I can find Ramsdell."

Constance left Sir Henry and found that the closer she drew to the conservatory, the harder her heart pounded in her chest. She was not acquainted with the Duchess of Mercer, but Mrs. Spencer had more than once said that in her youth she had been a gazetted fortune hunter and was now reaping a sad reward for her avaricious pursuit of her present husband. That she was apparently acquainted with Ramsdell did not surprise her, since undoubtedly they traveled in the same circles. However, she was a little startled to think that her grace had kept Ramsdell pinned to her side while he should have been dancing with her.

The door of the conservatory was ajar, and a rush of moist, earthy air greeted her as she drew the door wide. The sight that met her eyes, however, dumbfounded her, for a woman with blond hair—supposedly the Duchess of Mercer—had her arms wrapped securely about Ramsdell's neck and was presently weeping into his neckcloth.

She didn't know quite what to think, except that his lordship did not at all seem to be enjoying the encounter.

His expression even made her smile as he stared down at the blond curls presently tickling his nose. His face was pinched with something close to disgust, and his uninjured arm was doing its best to tug her grace's left arm from about his neck.

Constance, being of a sensible turn, merely cleared her throat in order to draw the couple's attention to her.

She nearly laughed aloud when Ramsdell met her gaze above her grace's head with an expression of immense relief. "Miss Pamberley!" he exclaimed in a strong voice. "Do allow me to present the Duchess of Mercer to you."

The lady fairly flew from his arms, and Constance could not help but note that her eyes were amazingly unaffected by her display of tears.

"Oh!" Lady Mercer whispered. "Oh, no! Is my husband with you?"

Constance saw how it was in an instant and almost felt sorry for the former Beauty. She responded blandly, "I am unacquainted with your husband. However, I am presently unescorted."

"Thank God," her grace breathed.

Ramsdell cleared his throat and finished the introductions. "Your grace, may I present Miss Pamberley of Lady Brook Cottage."

Constance moved forward and offered her hand, which Lady Mercer took in a faint clasp. She found the duchess was trembling.

Lady Mercer undoubtedly had been a great beauty in her day, for the remnants of several lovely features could still be seen in the harried, thin bones of her face. Tonight, however, she was a collection of nerves and flesh, and the quick dart-ings of her eye toward the doorway spoke its own tale. "I should take my leave," she responded breathlessly, and with-out saying good-bye, fled the conservatory.

When the last of her ball gown of peach silk disappeared through the doorway, Constance turned toward Ramsdell. "I am sorry for her, indeed, I am."

"Don't be," Ramsdell responded, his voice hard.

"And pray, why shouldn't I?" she queried, curious.

His laugh was bitter as he responded, "Because she could have had a very comfortable life at Aston Hall with a husband who adored her. Instead . . . she chose Mercer."

Constance was deeply astonished. She had conversed with him at length over the past several weeks, but not once had he mentioned the Duchess of Mercer or any other lady whom he had been even close to marrying. "You . . . you meant to offer for her at one time?"

"I *did* offer for her. She even accepted my hand, but the next day eloped with Mercer." He looked at her and gave himself a shake. "But that was a long, *long* time ago. I was scarcely out of my salad days at the time. Now, it would seem, she has regretted her decision and for some reason was hoping to find comfort in my arms."

Constance looked up at him and tried to place these new facts into the proper compartments in her brain, but all that she could think was that Ramsdell had loved this woman once and had been rejected. "Is that why you've never mar-ried?" she asked. "You loved her so very much?"

He seemed surprised by the question. "No," he said som-berly. "No, not at all. I mean, I loved her—or believed I did. I was very young then and too green by half. I don't think I knew what love was." His expression as he looked at her grew very soft.

Strange sensations began working in her chest, and she found she couldn't quite assimilate them all at once. She felt angry that Ramsdell had been so poorly used by the ambitious wench, yet grateful at the same time that she had jilted him. Subsequently, another thought and sensation rose—of fear, of exactly where her next thoughts might take her—to Aston, of course—and away from Lady Brook.

"We should return to the ball," she said hastily. "And have you heard that there is a new resident at the Priory?" She found suddenly that she was trembling.

"What's wrong?" he asked, drawing close to her.

"Nothing," she responded brightly. She saw that he was reaching toward her, and she quickly took a step backward. "Come, we should return to the ball. It won't do, you know, for us to be found alone in—in the conservatory."

"If you fear that *my* reputation will be harmed—" he suggested, a crooked, teasing smile touching his lips.

"No—no!" she cried. "Don't be absurd!" With that, before he could catch her or further entice her to remain, she turned quickly away and headed for the door.

She felt him on her heel, and the next moment he caught her hard by the elbow and whirled her about. He was kissing her wildly, and her heart made its usual dancing and shouting efforts, but tears were burning her eyes and her mind had become hysterical. "Don't," she breathed on a sob she didn't understand as she pushed him away.

"Constance, what is it?" he cried. "Are you upset that I was here with Lady Mercer?"

"No," she said, shaking her head. She swiped at more, fresh tears. "Good God! I've become a watering pot, and for no reason."

"I didn't mean to overset you. Only tell me, what's wrong?"

"I don't know," she responded. "Only please, let me return to the ball. I feel very confused of the moment. I so easily fall into your arms, but—oh, pray, Ramsdell, take me back to the ballroom. Perhaps we can converse later, when my senses are better ordered."

He looked at her for a long while. "Very well. As you wish."

With a feeling of great relief, Constance accepted his escort back to the ballroom.

When she arrived, with Ramsdell still holding her arm tightly, she found that the waltz had ended and most of the guests were now crowded into the ballroom. On the dais, in front of the orchestra, Lady Bramshill was speaking. "You all know my penchant for the dramatic," she said. The crowd groaned, laughed, and applauded all at the same time. "And though I know I tend to draw out the moment more than necessary"—more groans and laughter—"I think you will be pleased with what I have to impart to you this evening."

A violin squeaked suddenly behind her, an occurrence—planned, no doubt—that caused the entire ballroom to erupt into a roll of laughter.

"How very rude," the lady said, turning to catch the eye of the violinist.

The musician bowed and begged pardon, with a great flourish.

"At any rate," her ladyship continued, "I should like to make known to you our newest neighbor, who has just purchased the Priory and who intends to restore every acreage and stone to its former glory, and"—she lifted her hand in the air dramatically—"who has also promised us a ball at summer's end!"

Whispers, murmurs, and excited rumblings rose to the rafters along with all manner of speculation.

She continued. "May I present"—and here she extended her hand rather dramatically toward a darkened recess of the room, near the long windows of the ballroom that opened onto a balcony—"Sir Jaspar Vernham."

The sudden burst of applause that followed did not in any way affect the ringing sound which so quickly entered Constance's brain. Lady Bramshill's surprise had completely dumbfounded her.

Sir Jaspar Vernham! Here? In Berkshire? Owner of the Priory? And knighted!

"Jaspar," she murmured. "How very like him to steal upon me in this manner. But where is he? Ramsdell, do you see him?"

Ramsdell leaned down and queried. "Is this *your* Mr. Vernham? The one you were in love with as a child?"

"The very one," she responded, looking up at him.

Oddly, she heard him growl.

She might have been inclined to ask why he had emitted such a peculiar sound, but at that moment the first love of her life strolled through the crowd and leapt lightly onto the dais beside Lady Bramshill.

She would never have known him. She stared at him as one who was looking at a ghost.

Jaspar!

He was so devilishly handsome and wore a style of clothing almost identical to Ramsdell's except that a large ruby pin blazed in his neckcloth. His smile was charming, and something more, for it gave him a decidedly rakish air. She immediately thought of pirates and scandalous adventurers.

When the general applause began to die away, the orchestra began a simple Mozart tune as Lady Bramshill drew Sir Jaspar from the dais and began to introduce him to her guests.

Constance stood watching him, or at least the top of his head, as he mingled with the crowd.

Her father's stable boy. A wealthy Indian nabob. Her friend of so many years.

She waited for the crowds to thin a little more. She had to see him, to speak with him. Her heart was beating fiercely in her chest.

The crowds finally dwindled. She could see him fully now. A quizzing glass dangled to his waist. How animated he was. How very handsome with his dark brown eyes and dark hair and deeply bronzed complexion from having lived in India for so many years.

As though he realized she was studying him, he glanced

in her direction, and though he hesitated for only a moment, recognition sprang quickly to his features.

"Constance," he murmured softly.

She began walking toward him, with Ramsdell at her side, as one in a daze.

Lady Bramshill, still beside Sir Jaspar, glanced down the line of his gaze and promptly let out a trill of laughter. She said, "I knew it would give our dear Miss Pamberley a shock!" She laughed a little more.

When Constance was ten feet from him, she disengaged herself from Ramsdell's hold on her arm and ran to him. He opened his arms and she embraced him fully.

"Hello, brat," he said in a soft voice.

She chuckled through misty tears. "You've come home," she said, thrilled utterly and completely.

He drew back, releasing her. "Lady Bramshill made me wait to see you and your family. I didn't want to. You don't know how many times I nearly marched the path that connects our properties, just to see you again."

His voice was richly deep. He had become a man and more, and his accent had improved dramatically. She knew he had hired a tutor, but only his own intelligence and dedication could have achieved such a remarkable transformation. He was in every respect a gentleman now.

She took up his hands. "Besides my dearest friend, Mrs. Spencer, Lady Bramshill is one of the wickedest women in all of England for preventing you to come to us. But that is something we shall quickly amend. Join us for nuncheon tomorrow if you are able. Mother will want to see you. I read every one of your letters to her—to all my family."

"I will be there. Nothing would keep me away."

She heard a rumbling behind her, that odd, low growling sound again. Ramsdell drew close and cleared his throat, which prompted Lady Bramshill to introduce him.

"How do you do, Sir Jaspar?" he said.

Only then did Constance realize something was amiss.

Ramsdell's voice was remarkably cold and challenging. She glanced up at him, and a series of invasive chills snaked down her neck. His eyes were narrowed and his chin set. He stared at Jaspar, who was two inches shorter than he, as though he meant to eat him alive.

She had seen more than one of Stively's hunting dogs guard a bone in a similar manner.

Then she realized with another disturbing start, that he was guarding *her!*

Her former panic asserted itself. She began to feel like an animal caught in a cage.

"Ramsdell, is it?" Jasper queried. "I've heard a great deal about you from his royal highness. You've Prinny's ear, it would seem. He recommended I speak to you about some reform ideas I have in mind."

"You've ambitions for the Commons, then?" Some of Ramsdell's bristles began to settle against his neck.

"Yes." He smiled, but his gaze reverted to Constance. "Tonight, however, my first object must be to meet all the Pamberley ladies again, for when I left, with the exception of Constance, they were children."

Lady Bramshill, who was clearly enjoying herself hugely, cried out, "And here is Miss Katherine and Miss Celeste."

Constance watched as both her sisters stared and wondered and ogled the handsome knight. Quick reminiscences were shared of long-ago visits to the stables, especially Katherine, who had been underfoot since she was old enough to toddle from the house. After a few minutes, Marianne left what Constance could see was her usual complement of beaus and made her way to Lady Bramshill.

Was it her imagination, or did the air immediately begin to crackle as soon as the next-youngest sister extended her hand to Sir Jaspar. "I remember you," she said with a lift of her chin. "You used to pull my braids when I would come to the stables. Stively nearly turned you off without a reference a dozen times for being so mean to me."

Constance drew in a shocked breath that her sister would remark openly on Sir Jaspar's former lowly employment on the estate, but Sir Jaspar only threw his head back and laughed. "You deserved every tug—you were the most obnoxious child—I see you haven't changed a whit."

Marianne lifted an ominous brow, one that would have signaled to any of her present beaus that she was seriously displeased. "I take it unkindly of you to have said so," she responded depressively.

His lids narrowed. "Still a bit of a baggage, eh?"

"I don't know what you mean, sir," Marianne returned, her eyes blazing.

"You know precisely what I mean. I've always thought you were a fishwife—and now I know I wasn't mistaken in the least."

Marianne had never had a man speak to her in such terms, and drew in a sharp breath. "And I see that your manners are the same as they ever were."

"Silk purse and all that, then?"

"If the shoe fits," she responded curtly.

Constance felt a decided impulse to take Marianne by the ear and drag her back to Lady Brook on the instant. She was embarrassed by the exchange and wondered what on earth her sister was thinking.

Sir Jaspar, however, did not appear in the least offended. Instead, his expression grew very sly as he bowed to her and expressed his conviction that he was certain his manners would improve in her company. Marianne seemed flustered and unable to respond to such a provoking remark.

Sir Jaspar turned back to Constance. "I am so happy to have come home at last, to see you—all of you. But there is one more Pamberley sister, is there not? Where is Miss Augusta?"

Both Constance and Katherine glanced about the ballroom.

"I don't know," Constance said. "In fact, I haven't see her for the last couple of hours. Have you, Katherine?"

"No, come to think of it, I haven't. But I'll go in search of her—and Alby."

At the mention of Charles's name, Constance realized she had not seen him either, for a very long time. If a certain suspicion entered her mind, she quickly set it aside. Her younger sister had the finest sensibilities of all the inmates of Lady Brook, and whatever her sentiments toward Alby, she knew Augusta would be sensible to the last.

Jaspar was speaking. "Though I would enjoy nothing more than continuing our reminiscences, Lady Bramshill has many personages to whom she wishes to make me known. So, if you'll forgive me?"

"Of course," Constance responded. "Nuncheon tomorrow, then?"

He nodded with a smile as Lady Bramshill drew him away. She watched him go, her fondness for him rising to warm her cheeks.

"Are you in love with him, then?" she heard Ramsdell ask in a solemn voice.

She was stunned by the question as she turned to look at him. She saw the hurt in his eyes, and for the barest moment wanted to lie to him. She wanted to tell him, *Yes, I am in love with Jaspar Vernham.* That way, she would not have to worry about the next words Ramsdell would speak to her.

She paused and considered, but her natural honesty asserted itself. "Only when I was fifteen. I account him but an excellent friend now."

"Truly?" he pressed her.

Oh, no, she thought. She knew what was coming next.

"Truly," she responded.

"Then there is something I must say to you."

"Can it wait until tomorrow?" she asked, feeling quite desperate. "After all, we're at a ball, and—"

He shook his head. "No, Constance. I must have my say now, before I lose you to tomorrow and to Sir Jaspar's charm."

FIFTEEN

The air was cool on the terrace steps. Constance had listened to Ramsdell's declaration as one trapped in a nightmare. All her fears rose upon each loving word he spoke, fears that had taken shape within her eleven years earlier, the moment she had learned of her father's debts following his untimely demise.

She might have recovered her equanimity eventually had not her mother suffered a fit of the apoplexy four years later and left her with the sole management of Lady Brook as well as the care of her sisters. Something about the pairing of the two events had left her changed—forever.

Lady Brook had become her sole concern in recent years, the force that gave her stability and security. Yet Lady Brook was far better than flesh and blood—she could manage the property without the smallest skirmish, she could tear down parts of it at will and build up other parts when it suited her, and she could rest in the sure knowledge that Lady Brook would always be hers.

"Why do you hesitate, Constance? Don't you love me?" he asked.

She did not hesitate. "I cannot accept of your hand, Ramsdell. I'm sorry. I can see now that I have used you ill."

He was holding her left hand with his right. "I don't understand. I was so certain . . . Constance, you must tell me, do you not return my sentiments?"

She wanted to lie again. Why was he making this so hard for her? "What I feel for you is not at all pertinent," she responded.

He chuckled uncertainly. "Whatever do you mean? Your feelings toward me, for me, are all that matter."

"I won't leave my home," she stated flatly. "I won't. I have my sisters to care for, and my mother. I refuse to abandon them."

She stared up at him. She dared him to respond.

His lips parted and he drew in a breath. "I hadn't considered these things," he said slowly. "And I do know how very much your family depends on you. But surely there is some way we could sort out what must be done. I certainly did not offer for you with the intention of demanding you concern yourself with only my wishes, only my desires.

"Ramsdell, it's not as simple as that. I can't marry you. I can't marry anyone. I want, I prefer, to remain at Lady Brook—forever. I belong there."

He narrowed his eyes. "It was your father, then—"

"He has nothing to do with this."

He took a step toward her and slid his hand down her arm, taking a strong hold of her elbow. "He has everything to do with this, and well you know it. My God, Constance, you were left to shoulder the entire burden of your family. But your sisters are all of an age now, and your mother is regaining her facility with words and movement. You don't have to hold so tightly to Lady Brook, and . . . you're not alone anymore. I'm here."

She shook her head, disbelieving that her life could be any different. "I'm too frightened. I know you can't understand, but my answer must be no. *No,* I say."

"Just tell me this, do you love me?"

Tears began filling her eyes. "Of course I love you. I have from the first, I think, from that stupid moment when you rose up in your curricle like . . . like a *god* or something! Oh, why did you have to come to Lady Brook?"

He drew her gently into the circle of his right arm. "I was sent to you, but not just for your sake, for mine as well. I didn't know I was so alone until I met you, my darling Constance. I need you by my side, as my dearest companion and, one day, the mother of our children. I want you more than anything in the world to be my wife."

She held him tightly, struggling to keep so many forceful emotions from overwhelming her. She felt certain there was only one answer she could ever give him, yet her heart was near to breaking.

After a long while, when several tears trickled unbidden down her cheeks, she realized that they were no longer alone.

Katherine stood in the shadows near the doorway.

"My sister is here," she whispered.

He released her, but only sufficiently to be able to take her arm firmly in his in order to support her better. She found she needed to lean on him, for she was trembling mightily.

She swiped at her tears as Katherine solemnly approached. "I don't know how to tell you this, especially when I can see you are already overset, but I went in search of Augusta, and when I could find her nowhere, I—I went to the stables."

"Oh, no," Constance murmured, her heart sinking.

"Our traveling coach is gone and the head groom told me that Mr. Kidmarsh had commandeered the vehicle, saying that the lady was ill and had to be taken home at once. He said he might have been suspicious, except that the lady did indeed look poorly and nearly swooned when he assisted her into the carriage."

"Good God," Ramsdell said. "Are you telling us that Charles has eloped with Augusta?"

Katherine nodded. "So it would seem. The worst of it is, they left four hours ago by the head groom's best calculation, since he recalled clearly that night had not yet fallen when the coach pulled from the stable yard."

"Four hours ago!" Constance cried.

"Then it is too late," Ramsdell said. "Even if I saddled a

horse now and rode after them swiftly—and had every good fortune of following their precise path—I wouldn't be able to catch up with them until the morrow. And though I don't like to admit it, Charles is quite skilled at eluding me."

Constance shook her head hopelessly. "Then there is nothing to be done except to tell the others." She thought of Mrs. Kidmarsh and felt quite ill suddenly. Charles's mother would not take the news stoically.

"But is this such a bad thing?" Katherine asked earnestly. "When they are so deeply in love—and the obstacles so overwhelming?"

Ramsdell queried, "Do you believe they are in love?"

Katherine began to smile, though her expression still seemed a little sad. "Whenever they were alone or with me or Celeste or Marianne, it was as though the world ceased to exist for them. And Alby is so gentle with her, so tender, something Augusta must have in a husband if she is to know any happiness—a brutish man would be the death of her. As for an elopement, I don't wonder that she appeared nigh to swooning—Augusta will not like stealing away in such an offhand manner, not by half."

"This is my fault," Ramsdell stated solemnly. "I should have intervened with my aunt long before this and gotten rid of at least half my servants, who have so doted on Charles, one would think he had been born the infant Christ instead of my cousin."

Constance looked up at him, her sensibilities returning slowly to order. "Indeed?" she queried, a smile touching her lips. "The infant Christ?"

He looked down at her and, seeing the amusement in her eye, chuckled softly. "There," he murmured, taking her chin in hand. "That is much better. I don't like to see you so sad, you know."

Constance felt her heart soften, and fresh tears sprouted. "Will you at least count me as a friend even if I can't wed you?"

"I absolutely refuse to answer that question at present. Right now I know I must face my aunt, and I am trembling at the mere thought of it."

Constance gave a watery laugh. "Indeed!" she cried facetiously. "I can see that you are."

He chuckled again.

Katherine interjected. "I saw Mrs. Kidmarsh not five minutes past, just before I came to you, in the card room on the ground floor."

"Then let's go to her," he said. "She ought to be informed at once."

Constance was sorry for Mrs. Kidmarsh, who heard the terrible news while in the presence of the four remaining Pamberley sisters as well as her nephew and her sister. She seemed torn, however, by Katherine's recital of the history of Alby's disappearance with Augusta. Her face would grow alternately flushed with displeasure then pale with a need to swoon. She seemed caught between two powerful emotions that vied for supremacy.

In the end anger won the day. "My poor Charles!" she cried at last when her tongue found speech. "I have done everything I could to protect him. But, oh, what agony to have seen him taken in by a conniving fortune hunter, when I strove so very hard to prevent it!"

Constance barely suppressed her own shocked disapproval of Mrs. Kidmarsh's angry condemnation of Augusta and at the same time heard her sisters' sudden gasps, mutterings, and murmurings against Alby's mother. She knew what would happen next if her sisters were left unchecked—Augusta, with her sweet temperament and superior mind, would be defended to the death. Marianne in particular seemed ready to take up the gauntlet with a vengeance.

She was just about to intervene, taking a hasty step forward, when Lady Ramsdell cried out, "Eleanor Kidmarsh!

Of all the bacon-brained things I have heard you say in your five and forty years, this must be one of the worst yet! I have been in Miss Augusta's company for less than twelve hours but not without comprehending full well that a less grasping female you will never find. There is nothing of the fortune hunter about that fine young lady who seems to have won your son's heart.

"But beyond your stupid pronouncement I would only pose this question, where the deuce are your manners? Miss Pamberley is our hostess, and you have offered her so great an offense that were I in her shoes, I should turn you out of my house in the twinkling of an eye. Fortune hunter, indeed! Now, make your apologies, or I shan't share my coach with you and you may walk the distance back to Lady Brook for all I care!"

A fulsome silence followed this speech. Constance gazed upon Lady Ramsdell in amazement. How greatly she admired her at this moment!

"But you don't understand—" Eleanor began on a wail.

"But indeed I do!" the dowager continued. "We have all been at fault to permit you to carry on as you do, as though your son were . . . were—" She searched for exactly the right word.

Katherine suggested, "The infant Christ?"

Lady Ramsdell seemed stunned by her choice of symbol, but her eyes lit up. "That's it, by Jove! Eleanor, I doubt that the infant Christ received as much coddling as your son. Were it not for Ramsdell, you silly woman, Charles would have long since been wed to the Duke of Moulsford's mistress, who was, as you very well know, a frequent dancer on the Drury Lane stage!"

Mrs. Kidmarsh stared up at her tall sister and turned an ominous shade of white. "What—what do you mean?"

Lady Ramsdell narrowed her no longer long-suffering eyes at her sister. "I am as much to blame as anyone. I protected you, but from what? I shan't anymore. If you must know, Ramsdell interrupted four previous elopements of

Charles's, and each with creatures so vile as to make one's head spin. I have seen great improvement in your son since his sojourn at Lady Brook, but I have little doubt that it was your very presence that prompted this ridiculous elopement. However, I refuse to say another word. Instead"—and here she turned to the Pamberley ladies and to her son—"I suggest we retire to Lady Brook and begin making arrangements to receive the bridal couple once they return from Gretna or wherever it is they've gone."

Mrs. Kidmarsh, who was pouting severely, muttered, "And won't even be able to plan a suitable wedding breakfast, for they shall already be married."

Constance bit her lip and dared not glance at her sisters, who were just barely managing to withhold their amusement. She had never known such a ninnyhammer as Eleanor Kidmarsh and hoped she never would again.

When Charles had arrived at Lady Brook, she had thought him a child. Looking down at Mrs. Kidmarsh, she understood why—he had been raised by a child even younger than himself.

However, Charles was no longer an infant. In fact, he was well on his way to taking up a manly place in the world because of time well spent at Lady Brook. The elopement with Augusta she felt to be a setback, but nothing so severe that time and continued effort on his part might not put right.

As for Augusta, she trusted that her superior manners and mind would give a proper shape to what would in the early years of her marriage be a most tiresome relationship with her beloved's mother.

So it was that the entire party crammed themselves into the two larger coaches and began the ten-mile journey back to Lady Brook.

Both coaches disgorged the despondent revelers at the front door of Lady Brook just before midnight. Morris opened the door and Constance could see at once that something was amiss. She was greatly fatigued from the day's strange events, which began with the arrival of Lady Ramsdell and Mrs. Kidmarsh earlier that morning, continued with Lord Ramsdell's heartfelt offer of marriage at Lady Bramshill's ball, and ended with Alby's elopement with Augusta. The drive back to Lady Brook seemed to rob her of any remaining strength, and so it was that after taking a look at Morris, she whispered, "Whatever has happened, Morris, I shall tend to it in the morning. I am fagged to death and cannot possibly—"

He interrupted her with a pinched brow. "I'm 'fraid that will be impossible."

The entire party was now grouped in the entrance hall. She stared at him wonderingly. "And why is that?" she asked. "Have the stables caught on fire or the well run dry or all the servants left to join the navy?"

"Well, no," he responded uneasily. "However, Mr. Kidmarsh—"

"Mr. Kidmarsh will not be joining us this evening, nor will Miss Augusta. They've—"

"Taken sore advantage of a kind hostess and most excellent sister."

Alby's voice drew Constance's gaze flashing toward him in stunned disbelief. "Charles!" she cried, as did nearly every other person in the entry.

Mrs. Kidmarsh screamed, then rushed toward him. "My poor son! Then you have not eloped! Oh, happy day! Happy, happy, happy day!"

"There, there, Mother. No need for your tears or your ecstasies."

"M-mother?" she queried tremulously, lifting her face to him. "Oh, Charles, does this mean you know me at last?"

"Yes, Mama. I'm 'fraid I have a confession to make. I—I've been shamming it the whole time. I've always known precisely who I was, where I lived, and to whom I've been related. However, until I met Augusta, I didn't know how I was to go on at Aston Hall anymore. But now I do."

"Of course you do, my pet. Miss Augusta undoubtedly had an attack of conscience, just as she ought, and has sent you back to me. We'll return home on the morrow, and in a few days everything shall be as right as rain. After all, no harm has been done, and I'm certain in a year or two I shall forget entirely about this nasty episode of yours. Until then, however, you shan't hear a single word of reproach from me—not one." She took a single long breath and began her condemnations. "Oh, Charles, how could you have done this to me, wicked, wicked boy?"

Constance was spellbound by the sight before her, as, it would seem, was everyone else. Had Lady Ramsdell's words meant nothing to Mrs. Kidmarsh? Did she not see how much she was the cause of her son's unhappiness and erratic conduct?

Apparently not.

"Mother," Charles began strongly with a shake of his head. "You might wish to avail yourself of your vinaigrette, for I am convinced you will not like what I have next to say to you. But first, will you not, all of you, come into the drawing room, for I want everyone to be witness to what I have to say tonight."

The party moved as a flock of sheep might move under the firm direction of an experienced shepherd. So solemn was the moment, as well, that not a single murmuring could be heard from anyone, except, of course, Mrs. Kidmarsh, who was begging to know which of the ladies had a vinaigrette she could borrow.

Once within the drawing room, Augusta was found to be standing by the mantel, her eyes red and puffy, her expression indeed conscience-stricken.

Alby forced his mother with a gentle push of each hand on her shoulders, to sit on the sofa adjacent to the fireplace. Afterward he joined Augusta, sliding an arm about her waist, supporting her tenderly in what was obvious to everyone was her supreme misery at having distressed her family.

"We are to marry," he stated, his gaze fixed on his mother.

Mrs. Kidmarsh blinked several times and cried out, "My son is lost forever!" She then stuffed the vinaigrette up a nostril. The powerful vapors, however, sent her into a sneezing fit that had the happy effect of taking the solemn air entirely from the occasion.

Katherine burst into laughter first, followed quickly by Marianne and Celeste. Sir Henry was not long in following suit, then Lady Ramsdell and Constance. Afterward, Ramsdell, smiling broadly, moved forward to clap his cousin on the shoulder. "May I offer you my congratulations, Charles. You will be very happy. And to you, Augusta, my very best wishes."

Augusta's eyes began to lose their unhappiness as she murmured her thanks in response.

Mrs. Kidmarsh, however, continued to sneeze, weep, and wail for the next quarter hour, which afforded the rest of the party to offer their congratulations as well.

When Mrs. Kidmarsh's voice was again the only sound to be heard in the drawing room, Lady Ramsdell finally told her in no uncertain terms to stubble it, a curt command that brought her sister to a place of silence, followed by several hiccoughs.

Lady Ramsdell then addressed the question everyone wanted to ask. "But, Charles, what made you abort the elopement, for we were convinced you meant to take Augusta to Gretna?"

He nodded. "I had meant to. But we had not gotten very far past Lady Brook on the northern road, when I could no longer bear Augusta's unhappiness." He hugged his bride-to-be and kissed her cheek. "She never complained once from the moment I had persuaded her 'twas the only way to overcome a number of familial obstacles, but the look in her eyes broke my heart. In the end, I decided to take Miss Pamberley's sage advice and to confront the dragons that have beset me since I was a babe."

"You . . . you would refer to me as a dragon?" Mrs. Kidmarsh wailed.

"Only your good intentions for me, Mama. I know your heart is given fully to me, I've no doubt of that. But it is time that all your wishes, hopes, and dreams for my life be slain. I am a man now, and heretofore I fully intend to set my own course and raise my own sails. Augusta and I will be married, here, in a small private ceremony in a week. We shall honeymoon in Ramsdell's hunting box in Leicestershire—if that is agreeable with my cousin—" Ramsdell nodded his acquiescence. "And afterward we shall remove to Kingsholt and begin our married life together."

"I shall come with you, of course," Mrs. Kidmarsh said hastily. "Though I am not at all partial to Leicestershire and find Kingsholt a veritable ice house in the—"

He shook his head. "Not for the first twelvemonth. You will have to find someplace else to live—perhaps you may continue on at Aston Hall, or remove to London, for I know you adore our town house there. But I shan't have you underfoot for the first year of my marriage, except for a sennight at Christmas, if you wish for it."

Mrs. Kidmarsh appeared as though she had received a cannonload of grapeshot full in the chest. She collapsed against the back of the sofa and silent tears began to flow down her horrified cheeks.

Constance watched as Charles struggled for a moment within himself. She could see that he was wavering. For all his desire to become independent of his mother, the binds to her were intensely strong.

"Charles?" Mrs. Kidmarsh wept, her voice trembling dramatically. "Do but consider . . . oh, my poor, poor *Charles!*"

His name spoken in just such a manner, as though his mother were shaking a branch with her vocal cords, seemed to decide the day. Perhaps he had heard her intone his name in exactly that fashion one too many times, for his shoulders grew straighter and his eye less sympathetic. "A year, Mama, then, if you are so inclined, and only if you promise on pain of death to stay away from the housekeeper at Kingsholt, you may take up residence at the dower house."

Mrs. Kidmarsh said nothing further, but dissolved completely into a heap of tears and hysteria. Lady Ramsdell finally led her away but winked at Charles by way of encouragement just before the pair disappeared into the hallway beyond.

After her unhappy presence was gone, the Pamberley sisters descended on Charles and Augusta in a rustle of silk and satin, exclaiming a hundred times over their united belief that their marriage would be the happiest yet.

So it was that the hour advanced long past one before the party retired to sleep for the night.

Constance was so tired when she fell into bed, forgotten were her own concerns and unhappiness. Instead, she dreamed of Ramsdell in the best way, of being with him, of conversing delightfully with him as was their habit, and of embracing him.

However, a nightmarish quality soon descended on her dreams as she passed through a darkened doorway and, turning around, watched as Ramsdell grew smaller and smaller. Panic rose up within her. She knew she would never see him again and tried to race back toward the doorway. But the faster she ran, the smaller he shrank until she was shrieking after him.

A strong hand grabbed her and held her, so that she could no longer run. She began to strike at the hands, attempting to peel them off her arms, but to no avail.

Finally, she awoke with a start and found that Ramsdell was indeed holding her tightly by the arms and shaking her.

"What are you doing?" she cried, then began coughing.

"Come! The house is on fire. I'm sorry, Constance. Lady Brook is ablaze in the entire east wing."

Her bedchamber was full of smoke.

She leapt from her bed and with his arm supporting her raced toward the door.

The hallway was thick with gray, acrid billows. Her thoughts became consumed with helping her family and her guests, but she could hardly breathe. The most she could do was turn to the left and run toward the stairs. Footsteps resounded in front of her, beside her, and behind her. Ramsdell, her sisters, her guests, surely. But what of her mother?

She covered her face with her arms and raced down the stairs, stumbling and coughing, finally to emerge through the front doors and into the cool morning air. She dragged in a clean breath and doubled over to cough until she felt as though her lungs would turn inside out. Her throat burned and her eyes stung.

As soon as she could, she rose up and took stock of who had arrived out-of-doors. The servants were all accounted for, along with Charles, who held both Augusta and his mother close to him, her sisters, and Lady Ramsdell.

The dowager approached her and took her hand. The expression in her eye was one of terror, and Constance realized why—Ramsdell had not followed her out. Where was he?

Lady Ramsdell said, "I believe he is trying to save your mother."

Constance turned back and looked up at the ancient edifice, now blazing from every first and second story window. Flames leapt and smoke billowed from the roof. A roar began to consume the house as the inner wooden walls, the draperies, and furniture were eaten up in the flames. The effect was so stunning against the pink-gray dawn light that for a long while all she could do was watch in stupefaction as her home from the time she was birthed began to crumble inwardly.

A weeping began, first with Augusta, and quickly spread, like the flames now engulfing the house, through all her sisters. Lady Ramsdell, beside her, gripped her hand painfully hard and was heard to sob, but not for the house, for the son who hadn't yet emerged.

The front doorway was suddenly bursting with smoke and flames, followed by another enormous crashing sound.

"The staircase," Constance murmured. "Oh, God."

She had lost her mother as well as the man she loved in that fierce, consuming sound.

SIXTEEN

Devastation.

The word had new meaning to Constance as she watched the flames begin to settle and the bricks to fall one by one. Yet she was no longer thinking of Lady Brook but of Ramsdell and her mother. Whatever the house had meant to her, it was, after all, only red, fired clay and mortar.

Ramsdell and her mother were flesh and blood, spirit and soul, intelligence, companionship, love unequaled.

The house was wood and fabric and cotton ticking.

Ramsdell was a caress and an argued opinion. Her mother, a soft word and an eye that twinkled with merriment.

The house could be rebuilt, again and again and again.

Ramsdell could only return to the earth never to be seen, or touched, or embraced again, his spirit rejoined in heaven. Her mother could only take her place beside her father and be no more. In such a fire, their remains could not even be placed in a grave to revisit in symbolic physical reunion.

Devastation.

Awareness.

How silly her fears seemed now, about loving and marrying Ramsdell and about leaving Lady Brook. How silly and absurd and useless. If he suddenly appeared and asked her at this moment to be his wife, she would say yes, because the present thought of living the rest of her days without his company was unbearable in the extreme.

"My darling son," Lady Ramsdell whispered in agony. "Gone. Just like that."

Constance turned to her. "I loved him," she stated, her eyes misting with tears, her heart seizing into a painful knot.

"I know you did," she returned, meeting her gaze.

Constance could hold her tears back no more. Lady Ramsdell gathered her up in her arms and held her as she wept. An ocean of pain flowed through her as she sobbed. She felt as though the pain would never end. Would life ever be as sweet as when he had been with her, walking beside her, speaking with her, kissing her? Never. *Never.*

"Stay a moment, Constance." Lady Ramsdell's hushed voice intruded through her tears. "Dear God, but it can't be! They must have escaped through the back of the house somehow."

Constance felt Lady Ramsdell push her away and didn't understand until she heard the screams and cheers of her sisters and followed the direction of Lady Ramsdell's gaze.

There, attempting to push through the shrubbery and calling to everyone, was Ramsdell. "Help us!" he cried. "I can't get through. I have Mrs. Pamberley. We're all right, but I can't find a deuced break in this godforsaken hedge. Damn and blast! The devil take this ridiculous—oh, thank God!"

He broke through finally with Mrs. Pamberley cradled in his arms.

Constance began to run, as did everyone. The blaze was forgotten in a riot of joyous shouting.

Constance pushed her way to his side. She stood up on tiptoe and kissed his cheeks and his forehead and his lips. She touched her mother's face and saw that she was perfectly well, though she coughed several times.

Joy reigned at that moment, of the dead coming to life, of lives having been spared, of futures changing and becoming what they ought to be.

Katherine suddenly called out. "Carriages are coming! Look!"

Because the party had moved to the end of the front garden, they had an unobstructed view of the lane approaching Lady Brook Bend.

What Katherine had said was true! Three men could be seen, traveling at breakneck speed, two in carriages, the third on horseback. "I believe the first is Sir Jaspar," Katherine called, having run to the edge of the property. "The smoke must be visible for miles around by now. My, but he has excellent, light hands and manages his team to perfection. The second is Sir Henry. And the third, who is riding a spirited black horse, I can't make out precisely."

"Indeed?" Celeste cried, moving quickly to stand beside her younger sister. "It is just like Sir Henry to be precisely where he is needed most. But who is that third gentleman? I have never seen him before."

"Ramsdell," his mother called to him. "I think the third man is Evan!"

Constance glanced up at Ramsdell and saw that he was staring hard down the lane. "Indeed, you're right!"

"Evan said he was thinking of selling out," Lady Ramsdell cried, "but what a rascal not to have breathed a word of coming home to England so soon!"

Constance squeezed Ramsdell's arm and murmured, "How grateful I am that he is arriving to find you well and unharmed."

He glanced down at her, and though still holding Mrs. Pamberley in the cradle of his injured arm, leaned down to kiss her on the lips again. "Indeed, my precious Constance. We shall celebrate this day as long as we live. Pray, put me out of my misery and tell me you mean to marry me for, if nothing else, I can at least put a roof over your head."

She chuckled and smiled. "The insurance will restore Lady Brook, Ramsdell, so I shan't need your roof, but I think I will marry you anyway."

He smiled crookedly. "And to think it only took a consuming fire to bring your heart round at last."

Tears brimmed once more in Constance's eyes. "I would like to believe I should have come round eventually, but yes, it was the mere thought that I might never see you again that showed me the truth of my heart and what my life ought to be."

Marchand and Morris arrived at that moment. "M'lord," his valet began, "you forget your arm. Do permit us to care for Mrs. Pamberley."

Ramsdell, whose complexion was a trifle pale, carefully handed her over to the servants, but Constance insisted they remain close by for a few more minutes so that she could gaze lovingly into her mother's face. "You are safe," she murmured.

"Yes," her mother breathed. "And you . . . are to be . . . married."

Constance chuckled through more tears. "Yes, Mama."

"Oh, no!" Katherine suddenly shrieked.

Constance jerked her gaze toward the lane and saw that a wild-eyed buck was bounding across the road in front of Sir Jaspar's carriage. His horses took a quick and sudden fright and a split second later his curricle was heading pell-mell through the hapless breach in the fence. A moment more and they were trampling the petunia border as Sir Jaspar struggled to control his team, rising up as Ramsdell had done so many weeks earlier.

In like manner, the horses responded, but so abruptly that when they came to a halt, Sir Jaspar was thrown head over ears to land unconscious near the gravel drive. Constance thought she must be dreaming.

"What, again?" Morris murmured.

Everyone stood for several seconds in stunned silence, except for Marianne, who began to run toward Sir Jaspar's still form. She dropped to her knees beside him and pressed her head to his chest. "He lives!" she cried out.

"Thank God," Constance murmured.

Both Stively and Jack were immediately moving, intent

on controlling the panicky horses before they injured themselves in fleeing the burning house. Cook and three housemaids offered to help Marianne in tending to Sir Jaspar.

The fire had begun forcing a variety of panicked game from the trees and shrubbery. An entire squadron of rabbits suddenly burst into the lane in front of Sir Henry's curricle. Constance watched in complete stupefaction as his team plunged wildly in response to the unexpected creatures and followed in Sir Jaspar's wake.

"Oh, no!" Celeste cried, immediately setting her feet in the direction of Sir Henry's careening carriage. Because he had not been going as fast as Sir Jaspar, he was able to bring his team under control. However, the left wheel grazed the trunk of an elm, which ripped the wheel from the body of the carriage and sent Sir Henry tumbling on the lawn. He led with his shoulder and came up with only a slight limp, which set everyone to cheering again.

"Thank God," Constance murmured again.

Celeste arrived to offer her shoulder to him, which he took with warm gratitude. She gently began leading him away from the house, which was belching smoke though the flames had begun to die down a little. Jack moved to secure his team, since Stively had Sir Jaspar's horses under control and headed away from the house.

Evan, the last arrival, skillfully guided his black horse through what was fast becoming a maze of anxious darting rabbits and squirrels, bringing his mount through the breach in the fence to stand among the smashed petunias.

He smiled crookedly. "Hello, Mama, Hugo. I've come to help. The flames were visible for miles."

"Your arrival could not be more timely," Ramsdell said.

"The village nearby is already marching on Lady Brook," Evan added. "I should think they'll be arriving in the next half hour, so you can be assured of all the assistance you'll need, but what can I do now?"

"You may help to revive Sir Jaspar, who took a hard fall

when a deer bounded in front of his carriage." Ramsdell pointed to the place where Marianne was cradling the newly knighted nabob on her lap.

Evan immediately began guiding his horse toward the group surrounding the prone man.

Lady Ramsdell looked back over her shoulder at Constance. "How often does this happen?" she queried.

"Several times a year," Constance said, "though once the new lane is finished, hopefully never again."

Mrs. Kidmarsh looked up at Charles and said, "I am beginning to think it is the only way the Pamberley ladies can find husbands. The gentlemen must be coughed up at the doorstep of Lady Brook like the whale delivering up Jonah."

Everyone fell silent for a long while, then a general burst of laughter ensued. Even Mrs. Kidmarsh, grateful that her son had survived the blaze, smiled weakly. There was hope for her yet.

"Sir Jaspar is coming round!" Marianne cried. At these happy words, everyone moved quickly to group around him. "You took a toss from your carriage," Marianne explained to the dazed knight, who sat up quite suddenly.

"There was a deer," he murmured, rubbing his head and neck. "Good God, are my horses all right?"

"Is that all that concerns you?" Marianne asked, leaning back on her heels, her knees still sunk into the grass.

He blinked up at her, and his expression became quite sardonic. "Oh, 'tis you," he murmured. "I suppose you mean to chide me. Well, to answer your question, why wouldn't I be concerned for my horses? I paid a fortune for them at Tattersall's."

"Spoken like a nabob," she stated. "Have you no interest in knowing whether you killed anyone in your ridiculous flight?"

His lids narrowed and his smile took on a challenging edge. "I have little doubt that had I committed even the smallest infraction, nonetheless murder, you would have already informed me of it, am I right, Miss Marianne?"

She harrumphed and lifted her chin. She tried to rise graciously to her feet, but since she was still clothed in her nightdress, she stepped on the hem and tottered awkwardly before regaining her balance.

He had the audacity to laugh at her. "Never try to make an elegant exit in a mobcap, Miss Marianne. 'Twill never do, you know."

She glared at him and pushed her way from the crowd as Sir Jaspar gained his feet. He complained of a little dizziness, but otherwise seemed fairly unaffected by his accident.

The odd circumstance of two more accidents occurring on Lady Brook's lawn was suddenly overshadowed by an ominous creaking and groaning sound. Constance's attention, as well as everyone else's, was suddenly drawn to the smoking building, which collapsed in a heap. Only several partial fireplaces remained to show the original design of the structure.

Augusta summed up the sentiments of her family. "Dear, dear Lady Brook," she murmured sadly. "So many things lost, never to be recovered again."

"Indeed," Constance murmured. But in the deepest place of her heart she wondered if this was not such a very bad thing after all.

EPILOGUE

Seated in the gold and crimson drawing room at the Priory, Constance marveled again at how much a brigade of servants had accomplished in so short a time. The Priory had been abandoned for many years, and though there were numerous areas of the house that needed to be refinished and replastered, a coat of paint and fresh wall dressings had worked wonders for the dilapidated mansion. Of course, the elegant presentation of the rooms was naturally heightened by the fine furniture and draperies Sir Jaspar had brought back with him from India.

After the fire, Sir Jaspar had opened his home to the Pamberley ladies and their guests until such a time as plans for two weddings, two honeymoons, and new residences for Miss Marianne, Miss Katherine, and Miss Celeste could be arranged. Of course, Celeste's residence was soon settled on when shortly after most of the arrangements were made, she accepted of Sir Henry's hand in marriage and a third wedding was quickly in the works.

Constance did not foresee trespassing on Sir Jaspar's hospitality very long, since both Lady Bramshill and Mrs. Spencer were fully involved in making elegant plans for all three weddings.

In the several days since the fire, Constance had been to the ruins a dozen times, accompanied by Ramsdell on each occasion. The stables and adjacent living quarters had been

pared entirely, which meant that all the horses were being
ared for as well as the gardens. Even Cook made the trek
rom the Priory to Lady Brook each day, along with the un-
ermaids, to tend her extensive kitchen garden, which suf-
ered some scorching during the blaze but which was still
eplete with bushels of ripening vegetables and fruits.

Presently, a delightful evening breeze wafted through the
pen windows of the gold and crimson chamber and billowed
he muslin underdrapes so that the westerly wall looked like
a sailing ship in full mast. Many candles blew out as a result
f the breeze, which sent two servants running to find glass
himneys and oil lamps as well as rags to wipe up dripping
ools of wax.

To the soft scurrying of the servants, Augusta and Charles
sang a duet, a popular ballad entitled "The Mansion of Peace."

And so the Priory was, mostly, a quite peaceful place except for the rather incessant brangling between Sir Jaspar
and Marianne. Even now, seated as Constance was next to
her sister and Sir Jaspar, she could hear their whispers.

"You are spoiled by being so pretty," he was saying to her
n hushed accents. "You argue only because you are used to
having every beau sitting in your pocket, contriving ridicu-
ous sonnets in your honor and making sheep's eyes at you
until dawn. You are mad because I will not follow suit."

"How ridiculously obtuse you are!" Marianne snapped in
a whisper. "And my beaus do not sit in my pocket and they
do not contrive ridiculous sonnets—"

"You forget Mr. Hampton's, 'Her Eyes Are Like Heavenly
Orbs.' "

Marianne grunted her displeasure. "He is a budding poet
and cannot possibly be grouped with the remainder of my . . .
my *gentlemen* friends."

"Oh, now you will not even call them beaus?"

"How can I when you have given the word such a tawdry
meaning in our conversations. We might as well be speaking
of turkeys as beaus."

Sir Jaspar nearly burst out laughing as Charles and Augusta reached the beautiful climax of the song. "How apt," he murmured in choked accents. "For they are all turkeys, if you must know."

"Hush," Marianne retorted angrily.

"I shan't."

"You are such a brute."

And so it went. Constance would have adjured her sister to attend to Augusta's performance, but she was far too intrigued by the typical exchange. What would the end of this badinage be, she wondered, for she had never seen Marianne so at sixes and sevens before.

The ballad ended and Ramsdell crossed the room from his mother's side to beg her to take a turn about the gardens with him. She did not in the least demur and before long found herself alone with her betrothed.

"You will love Aston," he murmured, taking her fully in both arms. He still wore his sling for the most part but had recently left off the cumbersome article at such moments he deemed absolutely necessary—as now. "But you mustn't permit my servants to dote on our children as they have on Charles."

She slid her arms about his neck. "If they become far too incorrigible—your servants, *not* our children—we can always bring them back to Lady Brook for an extended holiday."

"What? You want to bring my servants to Lady Brook?"

"No, *stupid,*" she murmured fondly. "Our children."

"Our children will love Lady Brook and we shall tell them the story of my accident every night—"

"Until they are so bored of hearing it, they will groan and grumble at the very sound of the words, 'Did I ever tell you how I met your mama?' "

"Oh, now," he breathed deeply, "I do so like the sound of that and I don't give a fig if they grumble or not. Fate brought us together in the most marvelous manner, and I would wish such a chance encounter for each of them."

"I too," she whispered.

His lips found hers in a deep kiss that went on forever. A breeze teased the skirts of her silk gown and cooled her ankles. The smell of freshly cut hay was in the air, and the summer was on the wane once more.

He released her only when Marianne's voice cut through the warm mistiness of his embrace.

"You say the most absurd things, Sir Jaspar, and I am all out of patience with you!" she cried. "And I haven't the faintest notion why I let you talk me into coming outside with you."

"Don't you?" he murmured provocatively.

The pair stood on the walk at the bottom of the terrace steps, hidden from view from the drawing room where Evan and Katherine, Augusta and Charles, and Sir Henry and Celeste could be seen going down a country dance. The sound of the pianoforte, and Mrs. Spencer's lively playing style, could be heard in the distance.

Sir Jaspar continued. "Because you are sick to death of the beetle-witted halflings who trail after you at every ball, soiree, and assembly." He then took her roughly in his arms, much to Constance's shock, and kissed her soundly.

"Good God!" Ramsdell breathed. He then spoke face-tiously, "Ought I to do something? Defend her honor? Demand satisfaction? What is the procedure in such a case?"

"Hush," Constance responded, repressing a laugh. She then watched as Marianne drew back, a look of stunned surprise on her face. She promptly slapped Sir Jaspar lightly across the face. The nabob, however, did not seem in the least daunted and merely kissed her again, this time with his arms wrapped so fully about her that even Constance was slightly scandalized by it. Since she was reminded, however, of the first kiss she had shared with Ramsdell, in the center of the yew maze, she found herself entirely unwilling to interrupt the wholly inappropriate embrace.

The kiss finally ended, but not without Marianne's arms

snaking about Sir Jaspar's neck. When he drew back, she blinked several times as one who had been mesmerized, then slowly disengaged her arms from about his neck. She blinked a little more while he seemed unsure of what to do next.

When Marianne finally came to her senses, however, she gasped and pressed her hand to her mouth. "What a beast you are! Oooh, I shall never, *never* speak to you again as long as I live!"

His throaty chuckles followed her as she brushed past him and immediately ascended the terrace steps. He was not long in following, and once again the night air was quiet and serene.

"What do you make of that?" Ramsdell queried, brushing his lips against her cheek.

She smiled and leaned into him. "The birth pangs of love, I expect."

"I wanted to kiss you the first moment I awoke from my illness and saw you lying in that most awkward position in my bedchamber."

"I was not long in following suit," she confessed.

"And you said nothing to me?" he queried teasingly.

"Don't be such a goosecap," she said, feathering his hair lightly with the tips of her gloved fingers. "I could no more have said something of that nature to you than I could have tied my garter in public, as very well you know it."

"Certainly not," he murmured in response. "Kiss me again, Constance, that I might know I'm not dreaming, for I do love you to the point of madness and can hardly wait to make you my wife."

Constance obliged him, not once but several more times until Katherine sought them out and begged them to come back to the drawing room. "For Marianne and Jaspar are quarreling again and she refuses to dance."

Ramsdell returned his arm to his sling and offered his right arm to Constance.

Another breeze whipped at her skirts, swirling about her shoulders and making a promise of the future. She glanced up at Ramsdell and thought how odd that what had begun as a simple country flirtation had become a betrothal and would soon be a marriage.

"I love you, Hugo," she murmured.

He caught up her fingers to his lips and kissed them in response. "And I you, my darling Constance."

ABOUT THE AUTHOR

Valerie King lives with her family in Glendale, Arizona. She is the author of twenty Zebra Regency romances, including *A Poet's Touch* and *Bewitching Hearts,* and two historical Regency romances—*Vanquished* and *Vignette.* Valerie is currently working on her next Regency romance, *My Lady Mischief,* to be published in May 1999. She loves hearing from her readers, and you may write to her c/o Zebra Books. Please include a self-addressed stamped envelope if you wish a response.

BOOK YOUR PLACE ON OUR WEBSITE AND MAKE THE READING CONNECTION!

We've created a customized website just for our very special readers, where you can get the inside scoop on everything that's going on with Zebra, Pinnacle and Kensington books.

When you come online, you'll have the exciting opportunity to:

- View covers of upcoming books
- Read sample chapters
- Learn about our future publishing schedule (listed by publication month *and author*)
- Find out when your favorite authors will be visiting a city near you
- Search for and order backlist books from our online catalog
- Check out author bios and background information
- Send e-mail to your favorite authors
- Meet the Kensington staff online
- Join us in weekly chats with authors, readers and other guests
- Get writing guidelines
- AND MUCH MORE!

**Visit our website at
http://www.zebrabooks.com**

YOU WON'T WANT TO READ
JUST ONE—KATHERINE STONE